Catch and Release

a novel by

J. T. Twerell

CATCH AND RELEASE
TWERELL

Catch and Release
Published by arrangement with James Terry Twerell
ISBN-13:978-0615556857 (Living Word Publications, Inc)
ISBN-10:061555685X

This is a work of fiction. Names, characters, places, and incidents either are the product of the author's imagination or are used fictitiously, and any resemblance to actual persons, living or dead, business establishments, events, or locales is entirely coincidental. The publisher does not have any control over and does not assume any responsibility for author or third-party Web sites or their content.

CATCH AND RELEASE
TWERELL

This is dedicated to the original " J", who inspires me and fills my life with love and adventure. Thanks for being my wife.

CATCH AND RELEASE
TWERELL

PROLOGUE

"Usted bastard salir."

Jenny woke to the noise of her mother screaming at Julio, followed by the familiar sound of breaking glass. Glancing at the clock, she noticed it was just past two in the morning. She quietly whispered, "Happy birthday to me."

"Don't you throw things at me, you bitch. I'll knock the shit out of you."

In an attempt to drown out the all too predictable shouting match, Jenny pulled the pillow over her head. The chaos would go on for at least another half hour until, in the end, Julio would either pass out on the couch or in her mother's bed. For the millionth time, Jenny wondered why her mother stayed in any kind of relationship with a loser like Julio. When Dad was alive, the house was a place of order and calm, but since his death, her mother seemed to be picking men out of some slime pit. The last six years had been hell. Jenny desperately wanted to run away and never come back, but her mother would be in even worse shape if she left. Staying was the only option.

Julio was the latest slime to crawl out of the pit and he'd lasted, on and off, over a year. Every time he looked at her, she felt his eyes all over her body. Jenny made sure she avoided him whenever possible. Too many times, he'd "accidently" come into the bathroom when she was showering. But her mother never seemed to do anything about it, and Jenny decided she was on her own when it came to protecting herself from Julio. She'd learned through experience with some of her mothers' boyfriends that most men could not be trusted. Fighting off their hands and unwanted hugs, she'd paid some painful prices. The only person in the world she trusted was Uncle Bob, a close childhood friend of her father. Uncle Bob had taken care of her and Mamá after Dad died, but in recent months, he'd been more withdrawn. Jenny was sure Uncle Bob and her mother had fought over something.

The sounds of conflict in the other room grew louder by the minute, and Jenny found it difficult to block the noise with her pillow. Suddenly, her mother screamed in a way that signaled something was very wrong. Throwing off the covers, Jenny ran to the door and listened. The house was unaccountably quiet. Opening the door, she slowly entered a room littered with broken glass and overturned furniture. It looked more like a war zone than a living room. She could see no sign of her mother or Julio. Carefully stepping over the broken glass, Jenny made her way to the kitchen, where she spied Julio standing over something on the floor. Moving closer, Jenny saw her mother covered in blood, clutching her stomach.

"Mamá, qué usted?!"

Julio turned at the sound of Jenny's cry and grabbed her by her arm, "Your mother fell and is hurt. Go back to bed."

But when she saw the large blood-covered knife lying on the floor, Jenny knew her mother hadn't fallen. Pulling away from Julio, she reached over to her mother. "Mamá, what'd he do to you?

Grabbing Jenny's hair, Julio pulled her back and snarled, "I did nothing to her, understand? It was her fault."

Trying to get free, Jenny reached for Julio's hair, grabbed a handful and yanked, but he only pulled her tighter, grabbing her pajama top with his other hand. As she tried to spin away the buttons ripped off her top, but she was in too much pain to notice.

He pushed Jenny against the wall and pinned her hands over her head. Leaning close to her, he leered at her naked breast. "Como madre, como hija," he whispered as he pressed her against the wall. "Now you'll know what a real man can do." Jenny tried to duck away, but he grabbed her throat and began to squeeze hard. Gasping for air, she felt his free hand slide down into her pajama bottoms. Struggling to breathe, she desperately tried to push him away as his pressure tightened on her throat. Attempting to grab his hand as he slid his finger between her legs, she suddenly felt his grip loosen and sensed him move away from her body. He was

8

frantically try to reach for something, he was turning around. Then Jenny saw the large knife wedged deeply in Julio's back. Behind him stood her mother, covered in blood, leaning on the kitchen table.

As if in slow motion, Jenny watched both Julio and her mother fall against the kitchen table and slide to the floor, neither speaking, neither moving. Jenny ran to her mother, slipped on the blood-drenched floor, and finally tumbled next to her mother's face. Mamá reached out, touched her, and then quietly whispered, "I am so sorry, Juanita. I am so sorry."

In a trance, Jenny watched her mother's hand slide away and splash onto the bloody floor. Jenny took off her torn pajama top, folded it, and slipped it under her mother's head. She knew her mother was gone, but she quietly sat next to her for a long time before finally reaching for the phone on the counter. She saw a cake that read, "Happy 13th Birthday Juanita." A voice answered the phone, and Jenny quietly said, "Uncle Bob? I need you to come over fast. Mamá is dead."

CATCH AND RELEASE
TWERELL

CHAPTER 1

20 years later

Watching the blue and red lights flash on the dance floor, Jennifer Blade sensed the stirring of anxiety. She was in serious trouble and she knew it. The lights played off her long dark hair and turned her body into a kaleidoscope of colors matching the décor of the crowded club. The tightness grew deep inside. This was her assigned place in case "the Boss," as his lackeys referred to him, needed her. However, the Boss hadn't been anywhere near her in three days and she was tired of showing up, sitting, waiting. It was unusual for him to be out of contact for so long. She worried about her future.

The mirror across the bar reflected a 33-year-old woman whose lifestyle was quickly aging her otherwise beautiful features.

Men still played to the beat of her energy, providing any attention necessary to keep her happy. But it was all an old game, and she was tired of playing by the rules. Continuing to observe her reflection, she wondered if the woman who used to live in her body had died. Smiling, she realized she didn't even remember who that woman was.

Above the blare of the music, she shouted to the bartender, "Tommy, I'm gonna wrap things up. What time is it anyhow?"

"Hey J, it's just past 3:30," he hollered. "You're taking off early tonight."

She smiled to herself. Even her nickname was a step away from who she'd once been. So much had changed — and yet so much continued to be the same.

Nearing the bar, she shook her head at Tommy. "No offence, lover, but this place just isn't cutting it and I need to get some rest. Catch you tomorrow."

About to turn away, she sensed someone next to her. Johnny. The night would be longer than she wanted.

"Boss wants to see ya, baby," he said as his body caught the rhythm of the music. Johnny could never stand still when music played. Having him in her space really got on her nerves. Standing about five and a half feet tall and a good thirty pounds overweight, Johnny believed he was the Latino gift to women. Somehow, he seemed to have the ladies fooled, but J was not now, nor ever would be, a convert to his thinking.

Turning away from his swaying presence, she laughed, "Hard to believe the Boss wants to see me since the Boss is out of town, God only knows where."

12

"Hey, maybe he's back, maybe he ain't. You don't have a say in this, just follow orders." He reached for her arm and she pulled back, putting a hand on his chest. Facing him, she went taut as she saw a level of confidence he'd never shown around her. Something was very wrong, and she was at the center of the problem.

"Listen, Johnny, don't touch me unless I say so and believe me, in your case, I'll never say so."

He smiled as he continued to sway to the beat of the music, "Hey baby, you better do what you're told, I don't think your ratings too high up the chart right now. So just stand up, go to the elevator, and don't give me any shit. ¿Usted comprender, J baby?"

She looked him in the eye. As a flunky, he'd never be bold enough to cross her. Unless he knew something she didn't. This stuff about her ratings not being high confirmed something was wrong, and this meeting wasn't one she wanted to attend. Glancing over Johnny's shoulder, she looked around the crowded club. She needed room to operate.

When Johnny showed up to escort somebody, it was usually on a one-way trip with slim chance of coming back. She sensed a problem for the last few weeks, but was now certain this meeting would put a bullet in her brain. Johnny continued to watch her. She decided to play along, but with caution, until she determined how to make an escape. When her gut felt trouble, she followed her gut.

She turned toward the back of the building and headed through the door toward the private elevator, feeling Johnny's eyes examine her short dress, nothing under its flimsy cover. As she pushed the call button on the elevator and watched it descend to the main floor, an alarm system went off in her mind. She knew if she didn't make her move now, there might never be a second chance.

The empty hallway.

She watched the elevator door open, also vacant. Stepping in, Johnny close behind, J set her feet and pulled her long hair away from the back of her neck, "Is the top of my dress hooked? It feels loose."

As his fingers touched her dress and the heat of his breath drifted near, she tensed, spun quickly, lifted her elbow, connecting with the side of Johnny's head. As he fell from the force of the blow, she drove her knee into his sternum and struck the back of his head with her elbow, sending Johnny to the floor, out cold. J pushed the button for the top three floors, stepped out of the elevator as the door closed and, without hesitation, headed down the hall and out the back door. She might have a 5-minute head start, but that would narrow quickly when Johnny's friends found his bruised body in the elevator.

Rounding the corner, she pressed the remote for her car and heard it start as she ran to the door. Jumping in, she pulled the 45 out of her purse, set it on the console, jammed the car into gear and exited the alley. Turning left, she floored it and sped toward the Belt Parkway going west. Once on the Belt, she eased a little.

Obviously, things had turned to shit, which really wasn't surprising. With her friends, you sensed when they no longer needed your loving company. There was no way of knowing where things had fallen apart or who had caused the problem. Realizing she needed to get somewhere far from her current location, J turned onto the ramp for the Verrazano Bridge and headed to the only safe

14

place she knew. Before arriving there, she needed a lot of travel time to make sure she was alone.

CHAPTER 2

"He was always a bastard. Selfish, cheap, untrustworthy."

She stopped midway through her dissertation and looked toward me as I meditated on how much I truly disliked being with this woman. I enjoyed most of my clients, but Laura was the exception to the rule. Glancing at the clock I discovered, to my dismay, we still had fifteen minutes before the session ended. Returning my gaze to the woman sitting stiffly in her chair, I suddenly had great compassion for the man Laura emphatically referred to as "the Bastard." For thirty-five minutes she had complained, blamed, vilified, and deeply demeaned the character of her husband. In short, she'd spent a magnificent thirty-five minutes playing out the well-rehearsed role of "the Victim" and, in all honesty, it was one of Laura's better performances. She

16

rehearsed her lines for years and perfected their delivery on any stage she might find available.

Today her stage was my office and I, her faithful psychologist, was an audience of one. Now the performer waited for me to sympathize with her and provide reassurance that her status as "the Victim" was secure and well deserved. I only had to survive thirteen more minutes, then I could leave this story far behind. However, to allow her performance to pass without offering any special comment was more than I could resist. Looking into her clear blue eyes, I smiled at Laura's frowning face and said:

"Do you ever have anything nice to say about him? In twenty years of marriage, you have three children with him, a comfortable life in the city, and seem to enjoy the financial success he provides. If he's such a bastard, so selfish, cheap, and untrustworthy, why did you stay with him for twenty years? It seems if he were that bad, you'd have left him long ago. However, no, you prefer to stay with the predictable bastard. So, who's the problem, you or him?"

I smiled at her and saw the volcano preparing to erupt. This was our tenth session and, predictably, it would end the same as the previous nine. Laura, the simmering Mt. Saint Helens seated before me, was a "borderline personality." As a psychologist, I held a belief that the God of the universe provided certain people with borderline personality simply to humble people in my profession. Laura was my humbler every week. Sometime during the session, I would disagree with her victim approach to life and she'd proceed to inform me that I was a complete asshole who needed to come before the bar and be beheaded. Laura hadn't figured out that

17

lawyers were brought before the bar and not psychologists, but far be it for me to correct her in the midst of a tirade.

Don't get me wrong; what I do for a living brings me great enjoyment. The vast majority of my clients are good people who do a lot of work to move through their troubles and who truly want to take responsibility for their own problem making. Not Laura, however. She is a predictably difficult person who blames everyone and anyone for her problems. That day, watching her take in my words, I could tell she was nearing the point of no return. I braced for the impact.

"You're such an asshole doctor," she began as the red level of her face approached crimson. "You tell me I'm crazy and you don't even listen to what I say. You're simply another fucked-up male who bleeds hurting women for all they're worth and casts us aside. You asshole, I should take you before the bar and have you beheaded."

The bar thing. As usual, I let it go. Her words stopped echoing in my ears as I noted her color was returning to normal. She had a cathartic moment and felt relieved. For Laura, there was nothing better than letting off some steam to improve the old personality.

"Laura, I'm sorry you feel that way, but we're trying to bring you into a place of healing. You have no control over your husband; you can only control your own emotions. I know you can do this and I'll willingly help you toward healing. Nevertheless, if you expressly desire to find another therapist, I'll help you with referrals."

That always got to Laura. Along with her borderline personality, she had severe abandonment issues. She would come

18

back again. With a lot of patience on my part and a thick skin, she might even get better.

"No," she said quietly, "you're an asshole, but at least you're a quiet asshole. I'll be back next week, but you better think about what I said. I'm not a victim here; I'm simply the person who sacrificed everything to keep this bastard happy."

"I can't see you next week, I'll be on vacation." I'd informed her of this for several weeks, but could tell by the rising color in her face that she'd forgotten and was about to explode at my lack of caring for her. To head this off I offered the following, "Tell you what, I'll give you my e-mail address and you may e-mail me while I'm gone. I'll reply if I genuinely believe you need insight, but I think you'll do well by simply sending me your feelings. We'll discuss your e-mails when I return."

The color returned to normal and I knew I moved an orange threat situation to a yellow one.

"Oh, I'll e-mail you and let you know in detail what that bastard is doing to me."

Standing, I led her to the door and said, "Ask Shirley for my e-mail address when you set up the next appointment. Have a good day, Laura, and remember you are a strong person."

She smiled, an unusual happening for Laura, and exited from my space. Normally, I felt drained after her session, but not that day. She was the last patient before I set out to the mountains for a week of fishing far away from everyone.

I packed up my laptop, a few journals I intended to read, and went out to the waiting room a few of us shared. Shirley was our highly organized, unflappable receptionist. She had the uncanny ability to comfort the infirm and still stand up to the Laura types as needed.

"Okay, doc," she smiled at me as I passed by. "Go out there and forget civilization for a week."

I laughed and said, "Dr. Steve Sanders has left the arena. If the fish are hitting, I may not be back at all." Good joke, very funny, and unfortunately, very prophetic.

CHAPTER 3

The drive calmed her nerves as J retreated from the city and all the pain it held. The early morning sun bathed the mountains in a glow of spring. Rounding the high mountain roads, she reviewed the events of the past few days. There was nobody to trust.

"Jennifer Blade, how the hell did you get so far out and not remember to leave a net under you?"

However, doing a tightrope walk often precluded building a safety net. The last friends she had trusted were from grade school. They wandered off as she chose a different path. In her neighborhood a person either grew streetwise or got lost in the struggle. Her father, a cop, died on the job, leaving a bitterness that set her course into the troubled waters she now traveled. Uncle Bob was as close to a surrogate father as she had ever found, but his lifestyle digressed far from the straight path of her NYPD dad.

21

Drawing on the life lessons provided by Bob, she was determined to even the score in the game that had taken her father. Every day she walked the tightrope, alone in the world with no net to protect her fall.

J found the entrance to the small lot she used over the past years. It was empty as expected. Most people didn't come this far up the mountain until late spring. The nights were still cold up here and the water was fifteen degrees cooler than in the foothills. After backing the car into a space at the far end of the lot, she turned off the motor and listened to the soft pinging of the cooling engine.

From this corner, it was easy to see if anyone entered. "Always watching my back; what a fucked-up way to live." She looked over the lot and watched the sway of the tall trees on the far side. "In my next life I want to be a tree. They just stay in one place, fulfill their purpose, never have to fight."

Sitting there for about twenty minutes, she reviewed her hasty exit from the city, knowing she covered a lot of territory in the attempt to lose anyone on her trail. Years of running and hiding had taught J how to accomplish the "hide-and-seek" game of life and her experiences had refined this skill. The people looking for her were also good at their trade, but they weren't accustomed to the mountains and that was her key advantage.

As she opened the car door, the coolness of the shade refreshed her emotionally drained body and she stretched her legs allowing the blood to flow into places that had been cramped for the last five hours. The wind pulled at her long hair, and she felt a sense of peace as freedom began to overtake the weariness. The trip normally took less than three hours on a straight drive, but this time she backtracked to make sure she wasn't followed.

Pulling a backpack, fly rod case, and tent pack out of the trunk, she returned to the front seat and removed the 45 from its holder in the consol. Flipping off the safety, she stuck the gun in the side of the backpack, hoping she wouldn't stumble and set the damn thing off. She didn't like to have the safety off, but didn't want to take chances on anything slowing down quick action if she did find trouble. She shouldered the backpack and stopped to listen one more time before heading up the hill. The wind whispered through the tops of the trees, the only sound in the silence around. She reflected on how different the quiet was from the crushing sounds of the city and the blasting music her "friends" listened to with a passion.

J breathed the fresh air and felt it cleansing her soul. She couldn't wait to reach her campsite, set up for the night, strip off her clothes, and swim in the cold mountain waters. Her body felt soiled by her lifestyle, but she knew no amount of soap and water could wash it away. Nevertheless, she felt the cold mountain waters might penetrate the filth of her life and make her feel like a whole person once again. She laughed at that thought, doubting it, but knew the water could restore some of the life the world had so ruthlessly taken from her. Picking up the fly rod, she entered the trees and disappeared into their sheltering arms, leaving behind the brokenness of her chosen journey.

She found her favorite spot just as she left it last, finding it hard to believe it was only a month since she had been there; it felt more like years. She saw the large, carefully placed tree limbs still covering the trail to the clearing, her spot. Long ago, J had stopped feeling guilty about covering the path, as she considered the campsite her own private hiding place. If others found it while she was gone, that was okay, but she wasn't going to make it easy for them.

She set up her tent and cleared a space for the evening fire; however, the sound of the rippling water compelled her need to be free. Walking to the edge of the stream, she pulled off her t-shirt and shorts and stepped down to the riverbank. Practice taught her that slowly entering the water was a bad decision, as the chill could drive one away. Holding her breath against the predictable shock of the cold, she dove into the deep pool and felt the chilled mountain waters penetrating the depths of her soul.

Swimming rapidly out to the middle of the deep, clear waters, she was finally able to breathe without gasping. She floated for a few minutes until the depth of the water gave way to the shallows of the rocks and small rapids of the stream. A large rock, drenched in the warmth of the sun provided a place to sit and recover from the chilling swim.

She ran her hands over her body and rubbed life back into the places where the blood had retreated, then laying back on the warm rock, she watched the trees dance overhead as the clouds rolled by in their lazy but determined pattern. There was always a strange excitement in lying naked in the middle of the water. With no protection and no place to hide, others could observe her and she'd never know it. The excitement quickly gave way to the realization that she was here to hide; so if anyone was lurking on the sidelines it wasn't a welcome thought. Nevertheless, this temporary moment of peace was worth the risk.

As the sun warmed her body, she heard the splash of a fish jumping farther upstream and rolled onto her stomach to see if the sound had any other friends doing the same. The quiet waters began to show small ripples as the fish started a feeding frenzy on the hatch of small flies now sitting on the surface. "Okay guys, let's start the competition," she whispered sliding off the rock and making her way back to the shore. "Today I fish naked, just to give you a thrill before I catch you." J laughed at the stupidity of her thought, but decided it fit into the current fantasy and besides; who else was around to tell her that a naked woman wasn't a turn-on for a fish.

CHAPTER 4

"Dr. Steve Sanders has arrived!"

This announcement was an unnecessary ritual, but one I performed every time the beauty of the river before me exploded into my senses. The stream was a perfect resting place for the truly big rainbow and brown trout inhabiting such a God-provided haven. The trout was a predictable and yet tremendously stubborn creature; its instinct for survival protecting it more than its pencil-point-sized brain. Guessing which instinct may be operating was the joy of fishing for the great trout in these high mountain streams.

I came to this place of challenge and rest, prepared to be both elated by success and humbled by my inability to think as a fish. As I settled into this tranquil place, memories of my youth came flooding back, when my Dad and I would work these waters. Now that he was gone, I found I really missed those days. The fond recall brought with it the pain of things lost that I may never have again; therefore, I simply enjoyed the present moment.

The only interruption to the quiet around me was the distant sound of rolling water emanating from the nearby stream. My now free soul nudged my body away from the mountainside and toward a clearing by the stream, which would become my monastic hideaway for the next few days.

Setting up camp was an exhilarating time in the adventure; even so, it was also a mystery, as I literally felt driven to perform the entire task in record time. I believed this frenzy was the last-ditch effort of my high-control mind to retake my soul; nevertheless, it would be an intense and yet futile battle, for ultimately my soul would win. This internal competition was a place of unrest in my private world; an arena where I fought a gladiator battle with my ego in "winner-takes-all" matches.

The ego was an interesting development in mankind's evolution; a place of great creativity and even greater destruction. Our ego had a core belief it was going to die. Though it was correct, given the obvious limitation of the human flesh, the ego assumed we were in peril every moment of our life and therefore must expand or die. The expansion, unfortunately, took each of us into a constant quest for more things to call our own. The need to turn a car into my car was an ego expansion. A home became my home, a spouse became my spouse, a thought became my thought, money became my money, and God help anyone who got in the way of my quest.

The real joke of life, however, was that we couldn't keep anything because we left it all behind when we died. The sadness

27

of the ego was how we literally destroyed everything that interfered with our ego's quest for expansion. Examples of the futile struggle ranged from simple road rage to the World Wars, all because someone wouldn't let us keep what we thought we owned. But in the mountains, I owned nothing, sought nothing, and lived only in the energy of gratitude for all I had in life; not because I so deserved, rather because I was a human living on this earth.

By the time I had set up my tent and cleared the area for a campfire, the afternoon breeze was cooling the air reminding me that the night was going to bring in a taste of late winter rather than early spring. The growing shadow of the pines threw a blanket across the stream and formed large pockets of dark still water. I heard the breaking of trout feeding on surface hatch and could no longer wait to see what the mysteries of fishdom had in mind for my joy and frustration.

Taking the fly rod from the travel pouch, I assembled it threading the line up the rod and attaching it to a tapered leader with a small nymph. The nymph was a small fly that sank to the bottom of the stream when the fly line fed out on the water. I knew the younger fish had been feeding on the surface, but the older, larger rested in the deep shadows along the sides of the stream.

The cold stung my legs as I entered the waters and I wondered about my decision not to bring waders. I soon adjusted to the chill and began to move slowly upstream toward a bend in the river, which provided a deep, natural pool on the shaded side of the bank. I fed out the line in a long, slow motion until it was above the pool. Letting it drop quietly in the water, I tugged the line enough to sink the nymph and then slowly retrieved it as it floated with the

28

current. There was nothing more peaceful than being on a stream watching the water with anticipation of a sudden movement and strike.

Settling it into the current, I continued to retrieve the slack in the line until suddenly, I felt the moment when all life was truly ecstasy. The tug at the line and the slight move of the rod tip showed a strike. Pulling with a quick light touch, I felt the resistance and knew the game had begun. I released some of the slack line with my left hand and kept the rod tip bent slightly. Too many trout attained their release by being given too much freedom, and this one would not fool me.

The line pulled hard and I released more and more until all the slack was now gone and it was up to the reel-and-drag to determine what came next. The trout began to make a move upstream and the drag on the reel let him run. He was moving into the weed and rock of the shore and I needed to take charge before he caught the line and snapped the leader. Pulling him back toward the middle, I felt him follow with resistance and then it happened.

Generally, trout I caught didn't break water when hooked, but this one was really angry and he broke straight up from the water making a missile shot into the air above. Trying to free himself, he shook his body and smashed hard into the stream. What a sight! The majesty of this wild, free creature that fought for his life using all his tricks and instinct to rid the obstacle that snared him.

He ran for the rocks again, but now he had weakened and I slowly moved him toward me. As he came closer, he began to move in a frantic side-to-side motion until at last I had him. I lifted the line and grabbed his lower jaw with my thumb and forefinger.

29

He was a good 14" long with speckled brown skin that glistened in the water. My rule for the first fish was to use "catch and release." If I released the fish, he then told others what a kind person I was and I could catch more fish. I hadn't shared that thought with many people, for obvious reasons.

"Today, Dr. Steve Sanders is king of the river!"

I decided I really had to stop making announcements about my minute-to-minute accomplishments or I would be the one who needed the psychologist. Looking up, I saw the sun rapidly moving across the mountain as night prepared its descent. Deciding I'd done my damage to the fish world for the day, I wandered back to the campsite and prepared to dine in the pleasure of the wilds.

Night came quickly as the sun moved across the mountainside and disappeared into the valley. I pulled enough dry wood to keep the fire going for some time and cleaned up the remainder of my gourmet meal. Packing all my food supplies in my backpack, I secured it to my tent to keep it away from wandering raccoons.

A night in the woods was an indescribable experience. The silence of the day gave way to a chorus of sounds making my fireside a natural cathedral of new melodies. Whittling away at a pine branch, I heard the cracking of twigs caused by the multitude of small animals who became my neighbors. Sometimes I saw the fire reflected in their eyes, but only the raccoons venture into the shadows around the camp. There was little danger in these woods, but bears wandered around periodically, though I had never seen any. Mostly, it was simply small chipmunks, squirrels, raccoons, and other scavengers finding prey and settling for the night.

Sleep came early and quick in the dark night and as I moved toward my tent, I was aware of another bright light about a mile upstream. It was contained and not a forest or brushfire, which led me to believe another camper must be up there settling in for the night. It was unusual to have others this far up in the early spring. I didn't know who it was, but I went to bed hoping they were as happy that night as I was. My soul was free, the trout was free, and all was well with the world.

CHAPTER 5

J turned as the sound of laughter erupted from the river behind her. She was startled to see two people, a man and a woman, swimming and splashing a few feet from the shore. The woman in the water waved to J and beckoned her to come closer. Approaching, J stopped suddenly when she recognized the woman. "Mi Madre," she shouted. "What are you doing here?"

Her mother laughed and shouted back, "My Juanita, I am having so much fun in the water. Come in with us and play; it is such a good feeling."

J froze in the spot, watching as her mother splashed water on the man next to her and then dove into the river. Looking over to the man, she felt her breath stop. The man was her father.

"Daddy, is that you?"

"Hello my little trouper," he called as he smiled back at her. No one had called her "little trouper" since her father died, and she began to cry as she watched him stand in the river. "Daddy, where did you come from? How did you get here?"

"Honey, I'm always in the water. It's such a fun place to be; come on in and join us."

Still frozen in her place on the shore, J watched as her mother surfaced in the stream, laughing and splashing. J always loved her mother's robust laugh, something she hadn't heard often after her father died. She watched as her mother and father chased each other in the river, looking more like schoolchildren than adults. They both appeared so young and alive. How could this be?

Her mother waved at her and once again dove under the water, the sound of her laughter echoing around the campsite. Her father smiled, "Come in the river with us, Juanita, or you will have to stay with him."

"Stay with who, Daddy?"

Her father pointed toward the campsite behind her and as she turned she spotted Juan standing next to the campfire. Startled, J felt herself tense, then looking closer at Juan, she discovered he was standing naked with a gun in his hand.

"Juan, why are you naked?" she asked as though in a trance.

"I came to say goodbye to you, J. I came to say adios." He lifted the gun and pointed it at her. She knew she should move, but felt trapped in the place she stood. As she watched, the gun exploded and she felt the bullet rip into her chest. Stunned, she realized she was lying on the ground, caught in something that

33

wouldn't allow her to move. She sat up and grabbed her chest, only to realize she was in her sleeping bag inside her tent.

Breathing hard, she unzipped the bag allowing the cool night air to refresh her sweaty body. "My God, what a terrible dream," she whispered to herself as she felt her heartbeat return to normal. "Where the hell did I come up with that series of events?"

Climbing out of her sleeping bag, she slipped on her jeans and stepped through the entrance of her tent. The first light of dawn was just starting to break through the horizon as J stirred the warm coals of her campfire. Still too keyed up by her dream to sleep, she added wood to the fire and placed the coffee pot on the grill.

She looked at the river; half expecting to see her parents still playing near the shore. The memory of her father brought a deep pain, one she'd long ago tried to bury. He was such a loving and kind man who always thought the best about everyone he met.

An Irish cop with a Puerto Rican wife was a crazy combination, but her father and mother always enjoyed every moment of their time together. One night, while working on a drug bust, things went very wrong when her father received a fatal gunshot, an event that changed J's life forever. Her mother never recovered from his death, spending her remaining years in a haze of alcohol and deadbeat men, which lead to her murder when J was just thirteen years old.

When her mother died, J stopped being Juanita forever and became Jennifer, a woman who was hard, tough, and would take no shit from anyone. J hadn't really counted the cost of those years until she dreamt of her Mom and Dad in the river. J realized she lost the ability to have fun and her life was one of constant tension and strife.

Looking toward the river, a large part of J wanted to simply jump in and never come to the surface. Maybe if she drowned she would find her Mom and Dad and they could laugh together. A tear formed in the corner of her eye causing J to shake her head and return to the coffee pot and fire.

Pouring a cup, she returned to the dream and thought about Juan shooting her. The shooting was not a surprise given their present unfriendly status, however, she thought for a moment and finally said aloud; "Why in the hell would he be naked?" Juan was a very prideful individual who took great care in always being properly dressed. Maybe she just wanted to see him vulnerable before she died, or maybe she was just losing her mind.

She had spent two years of her life trying to gain his trust, a period of time that cost her more than she could ever recover. She worked in one of his Miami clubs for a few months before she finally hooked up with Juan, and for the last two years, she lived in his shadow, watching him destroy everything only to replace it with his own filthy stain. He used her, but in the end, she had used him just as much, so in some ways they were both sick and deserved each other. J tried to keep emotionally detached from her life, but after two years with Juan, she found it hard to respect herself and truly wondered how low she would go to survive. Now it was all crashing down around her and she would probably end up with nothing to show for all her efforts.

Standing, she threw the remains of the coffee into the fire and declared through clinched teeth, "I will survive and I will win."

Taking a deep breath, she relaxed a little as she decided the dream, much like her life, was too real and too crazy to ponder any further. Looking at the river, she decided to focus on fishing and leave the dream and her thoughts about drowning to another day. Turning, she shook off the self-evaluation and declared, "Fuck Juan and all my shit life. For now I need to go fishing; tomorrow I'll deal with reality."

CHAPTER 6

As quickly as night appeared in the mountains, morning followed the same pattern with the sun rushing across the valley penetrating the dark with swords of light and life. In the tent, my watch reported it was 5:00 am and I felt a rush that came from waking in the midst of God's creation and having nothing to do but fish.

My fire, but a warm reminder of the night before, held enough heat to rekindle it and start anew. Normally I ate a light breakfast; however, I learned the hard way that a trout stream didn't have any place for snack and coffee in the wilds. While the water for coffee boiled, I opened my fly book and began to seek the perfect lure for the day. I wanted to work the surface for some time and next try wet fly on the stream rapids. This was every angler's ritual, and each would probably decide on the perfect fly for the morning.

Normally, that thought changed at least a dozen times as you worked your way up a stream; but nonetheless, it was a practice followed as a strict ritual each time.

After breakfast, I assembled my rod once again and braced myself for the early morning chill of the water. Fortunately, the air was cool enough for the water to feel dramatically different and, as the sun warmed the air, the stream would offer a welcome relief. A light fog covered some of the river as I moved into the current and headed upstream.

I'd fished for about two hours when I heard the sound of another person walking in the river. It was faint and expert enough to demonstrate that they knew how to walk a stream. Nevertheless, out here sound carried well, no matter how soft it was. Rounding the bend, I spotted my unknown neighbor. Dressed in an army shirt and baseball cap, this angler was good at moving the rod and line. The stream was deeper where he was fishing and the water was almost to his hips.

With his back toward me, I approached unnoticed and, trying not to frighten the person, I coughed gently when I was still about 100 yards away. The angler lurched around toward me and cried out, "You scared the shit out of me!" The angler was not the only one surprised. I was somewhat taken back to find the voice and face of my neighbor was not of a man, but of a woman.

"I am sorry. I tried to warn you, but you were really intense and I didn't want to surprise you."

Her shock turned to a beautiful smile and she laughed from the bottom of her belly. "You seem a bit surprised to find a woman out here." She waded down the river and extended her hand. "My name is Jennifer, but people call me J," she said, "I do get lost in thought and it wasn't your fault I dropped ten years just now."

I introduced myself as Steve Sanders and asked her how the fishing was going.

"This pool is great. I got three browns and just landed a nice rainbow. How you been doing?"

I showed her my catch and smiling she said, "We almost have a good meal between us. I'm camped over there if you want to join me." I really hadn't been thinking of eating yet, but I said sure, I'd love to join her.

She smiled and said, "Let's go another hour and meet back here with the results. You clean and I'll cook, or the other way around if you prefer; makes no difference to me." With that, she smiled and headed farther down river as I headed upriver. Somehow, I felt my free soul slipping away as the confines of another person now intruded into my world.

By nature, I was a private person and being with people always drained my energy. This was somewhat a handicap for a psychologist who worked with people all the time, but I trained myself to retreat into privacy when I felt overly drained by human interaction.

This trip was one of those "retreats from the human species" occasions and I thought about begging off from the get-together with J. But then decided to simply have lunch and move on to my own camp as soon as we finished. I'd come to fish, not make small talk.

The river was good and I snagged three more of which I kept one. I knew I had the king of the river once, but he snapped my leader and got away. When that happened, you declared they were any size you wanted to make up, making sure you blamed their size for the leader breaking and not your poor fishing technique.

In about an hour I turned back down the river and found the warm sun provided a siesta time for the fish, indicating it was wise to move to the bank and head to J's campsite. She'd set up in a location I missed in my other excursions into the woods and I discovered it was nestled on the edge of a turn in the stream, very close to a beautiful open view of the mountains and valleys. In all honesty, she had a better spot than mine and I wondered if she lucked out or if this was from previous experience.

The fire was going, but other than her fly rod leaning against the side of her tent, I saw no signs of J. Next to the rod, I found her fish bag and a note saying, "Only added one more – clean away will be right back, J."

In her sack, I found four nice browns and the beautiful rainbow. I walked to the stream, took out all our catch, and started the process of preparation. The fish were well fed and provided good meaty remains. Turning back, I spotted J as she came through the woods and entered camp. She waved as I headed up the bank toward the fire.

"Found some fresh raspberry bushes in the upper field and thought they'd be good with lunch." She said as she set down a small container with fresh red raspberries. "How are the fish doing?"

"They're ready to become a full meal. I should go back to camp and bring something for lunch. I feel I'm a guest without a gift."

"I have plenty." She said as she stirred the fire into a compact set of hot coals. "A nice bottle of white wine would be good, but I didn't plan on entertaining, therefore we're going to have to settle for powdered Gator-aide. You did the cleaning now I'll do the cooking."

She set about fixing the lunch as someone who was no novice to camping and cooking outdoors. "Do you come here often?" I asked.

Squatting near the campfire, she looked up and waited a moment to reply, "I've been here before; I enjoy the peace and quiet away from the pressure of life. Do you like lemon with the trout? I have some fresh that I usually use."

"Lemon would be great. Tell me where they are and I'll get them and cut them up." Assuming the lemons were in her backpack, I started toward it when she jumped up and cut me off.

"That's okay," she said quickly. "I have everything packed in certain order and I know right where they are."

Glancing over at her backpack, I saw a clear indication of the butt end of a 45 automatic sticking out of the side pocket. This was very unusual tackle for a trout fisher, but I let it go as it was none of my business. "No problem. It's your party and I'm prepared to help in any way you want."

Returning with the lemons in hand, she tossed them to me. "You can cut up about a dozen slices. What brings you here at this time of year? You'll say fishing, but what's the real reason?"

"I guess it's for the quiet. It really has an effect on me, which is hard to describe. I guess it's similar to a large dose of Prozac. What about you?"

Focusing on her cooking, she replied, "The same; I had to get away from civilization in order to regain my sanity. It's been a tough time at work and I needed a break."

Handing her the cut lemons, I asked, "What do you do for work?"

Again, she hesitated and then replied, "I'm self-employed doing this and that. What about you?"

Realizing she was not going to give much information about her work, I also pulled back from too much self-disclosure. "I write."

"A writer and a fisherman," she laughed. "Must be a Papa Hemmingway incarnation."

"I only wish I could do either as well as he did. This is a great spot for a campsite. I usually don't come this far up the river. How'd you find it?"

"If you wander far enough and long enough, you find what you're looking for in just the place you want. I love the mountain views and the sound of the stream. A tributary feeds this about three miles higher. It has a great view and a damn nice waterfall. Ever been there?"

I remembered the spot and knew it was similar to a lost paradise. "Been there, but it's not good for fishing. I forgot about it until you mentioned it. I think I'd enjoy going there again. It was beautiful when I saw it before. Are you up for a hike after lunch?" I heard the words come out of my mouth and wondered why I'd spoken them. I liked J and she was easy to be with, but I was still not looking for a hike. I came to fish.

She sat quiet for a minute working on the cooking fish and finally said with a smile. "I think I'd love that. I must warn you though; there's a magical touch in that place which really gets to me."

"A magical touch? Now that's intriguing. Do you turn into a vampire or something?" I asked laughing.

"No, the atmosphere simply warms me up inside. Let's eat. The fish are ready."

So my "let's make everyone happy" side had once again opened its mouth, and now I was stuck. As we sat and ate, I found J was good company and definitely a beautiful woman, so I decided to take the hike. After all, what difference could a few hours make, I had all week to fish.

Little did I know!

CHAPTER 7

J sat and made small talk as they enjoyed their meal, but her mind was analyzing every move Steve made. While it wasn't unusual to find another person fishing up here, it was strange for her to be this open and inviting to someone she didn't know. She found his almost boyish simplicity to be refreshing after living with the low-life she called her "friends"; but that didn't really explain her reactions to this stranger. She tried to remember when she'd spent this much time with a "normal" person, and decided it had been more years than she cared to consider.

The only uncomfortable time was when he went toward her backpack to get the lemons. She didn't know if he saw the gun in her pack, but if he had, he chose not to remark about it and she guessed it was a good sign. In many ways, Steve was like the only man she had ever loved and the pain of that relationship hardened her to the possibility of ever being vulnerable again.

Thinking about those days, she was flooded with memories long ago forgotten. She'd met Jason in law school and he was so innocent and bright eyed she first thought he was putting on an act. Thrown together for a casework assignment, she'd been her normal hard-ass self for the first few days. She still remembered how he finally had enough and, slowly closing his book, stood and confronted her.

"Jennifer, I don't know what you're trying to prove, but it isn't working. You try to be such a bitch and frankly, you do a great job in the impersonation. However, I really believe that under your well-rehearsed facade there lives a very beautiful and gentle woman. Frankly, until you decide to let her come to the surface I don't think I want to continue being with you."

J remembered watching him walk out of the library and for the first time in her life, she was speechless. She did mutter a profound, "Well, fuck you Jason," but he was out the door and missed her little speech. It took her a long and sleepless night before she finally broke down in tears and allowed the pains of the past to overtake her. Years of being strong and independent were her only protection in a world gone mad. What would she be like if she ever let down her defenses? How would she be able to survive if she approached life with trust?

Around 6:00 am, she finally called Jason and told his rather sleepy voice she wanted to meet him right away. By 7:00 am, they met and never parted from each other after that moment. For the first time in her life, she really felt safe and watched his gentle and simple outlook work its way deep into her troubled soul, providing a breath of fresh air in a dark and empty room.

They graduated law school together and she took one direction while Jason took another at about three times the money her choice was paying. They spent the next year trying to sandwich a relationship into a schedule that was slowly killing both of them. The trip to France was their agreed-upon escape from the realities of life and they marked off the days until the much-needed break was finally tangible.

Jason left her apartment that night filled with exuberance about the upcoming journey to Paris and assured her he would pick her up for the trip to the airport at 8:00 am sharp. The last minute packing and details of leaving so distracted her she never even kissed him goodbye, a sorrow she carried in her heart forever. At midnight, a call came from the local precinct and informed her that Jason was injured and they found an emergency notification card in his wallet with her name and phone number.

J arrived at the hospital to find the situation with Jason was more than a simple injury. A street gang near his home had brutally beat and robbed him. Before J could ever get to him, Jason died. She spent the weeks subsequent to that night living in a trance, with each day simply following the last. In time, she recovered enough to pour her life and love into her work, but she withdrew from the soft and gentle woman Jason had discovered to the bitch he so despised. Too often, she had loved only to have that love taken from her by violence. J was alone in an unfriendly world, and it was her plan to keep it that way forever.

Nevertheless, here she was, making friendly conversation with Steve and feeling the woman deep inside trying to launch a desperate attempt to come to the surface. She looked at Steve as he ate his meal and talked about his different experiences on the river. Obviously, he loved fishing and was very detailed about all the great trout he'd both caught and lost over the years. He was a handsome man, with thick dark hair and blue eyes that appeared filled with electricity. He said he was a writer and she could see how it would be something he would love, except he also seemed to be empty inside, not out of what he was saying, but from something she could just sense. When he smiled, she could see that little boy side of him just as she saw in Jason and it touched something deep inside her.

Picking up the remains of their lunch, she ventured the question, "Not seeing any signs of a ring, I am to assume you are single?"

"I was married, but my wife and I decided to remain friends rather than kill each other. So we got divorced. It's been a few years now, so I guess I'm officially single. How about you?"

J sat down next to him, "Never been married, never been engaged, but I've been loved and that's important."

Steve leaned back against the nearby tree and said, "It seems love is a rather mercurial state of being. I have grabbed at it, but it continues to slip through my fingers and only leaves me with memories. I think that's why I like being up here alone. The trees and water never go away and always seem glad to see me again."

J laughed, "Do the trees and water tell you they miss you when they see you?"

He was quiet for a minute and finally replied, "You know, in all honesty, they do. When I'm up here, it's as though they are always talking to me and telling me deep truths about life. The human mind is capable of many deceptions, but I think I like talking to the water and trees. So I'll just claim insanity and let it go at that."

J looked out across the river and tried to remember when her life was so uncomplicated that she could sense nature communicating with her. The feeling inside started again and she was afraid the woman Jason loved was going to finally make her way to the surface. She stood and with effort pushed the sensation back into the dungeon. It was a beautiful day, Steve was a handsome man, and she needed some real fun. Looking at him, she smiled, "Let's take our hike to the falls, I think they're calling me."

CHAPTER 8

The meal was a true angler's delight. The taste of fresh caught trout cooked over a campfire was more of a gourmet meal than anything Manhattan ever produced. Our conversation was easy and she became more relaxed as we shared our meal. J was in her early thirties and had a trim athletic figure that moved with grace and agility in everything she did. She pulled her long, dark hair back in a ponytail making her look somewhat adolescent, but her eyes told of intelligence and insight acquired only through time and experience.

I lost my concern about sharing time with another person, as J also knew what it meant to seek the healing power of silence. We cleaned the camp and she changed into a pair of shorts for the walk up the mountain. The sun was hot and I wished I had cooler clothes for this time of the day. I thought about going back to my camp, but the time loss would have been too long and we would have missed the best part of the day for the trip.

As we walked through the woods, she led with a confidence that spoke of one who knew her direction. We cut away from the river and straight up the mountain toward the other stream flowing from the falls. It was about a 45-minute trip straight up, and we were both sweating and out of breath when we finally heard the gentle rush of distant water. The falls were only about twelve feet high, but dropped rapidly into a large pool below amplifying the sound of the water.

As we continued up, the land started to even out and finally slope downward. When we approached the falls, their beauty and power once again overwhelmed me. The water poured out of the forest above and over a solid wall of granite rock. Over time, the water worked itself into the rock-face to create several small ledges. The falls hit these plateaus on the way down creating several smaller falls and a light spray that filled the air around the base of the water. The pool at the bottom was also solid rock and about ten to fifteen feet deep. The spring snowmelt was over in the mountains, but the water was still strong and powerful as it ran from the pool and down the mountain to meet with our own stream. We walked to the edge and felt the mist on our faces, which was welcome refreshment after the long hike up the mountainside.

"God I love this place," she murmured. "It's a piece of another planet someone left behind as a thank-you gift. The mist has magical power you know."

"There's that magic talk again. What's that all about?"

She turned her back to me and began to talk as someone telling an ancient fable. "The waters come from a place of total freedom and they journey to the land below to open hearts that are bound tightly by social and cultural restraint. The waters weaken as they travel and don't have enough power to cause great change in the hearts found in the cities far below. But here, they are strong and those who walk in their magic mist are freed from cultural and social moderation." She turned and smiled, "How is that for an enchanted vision?"

I laughed as I sat down and enjoyed the cool mist blowing through the air, "I feel like it's story time in the Land of Oz. What 'cultural and social moderation' are we being freed from as we sit here in the mystical mist?"

She sat next to me and was quiet for a few minutes, "I don't know; I decided to head down a path and for some reason I changed direction. The plan was to strip to my underwear and challenge you to jump into the water with me. But I had this feeling it was a bad idea, so I changed my mind."

Somewhat puzzled by her explanation I looked at her and asked, "Two questions obviously come to mind; why were you going to do that and why did you stop?"

Crossing her legs, she leaned forward and rested her arms on her knees, "Behind the falls is a beautiful place which brings me a great peace. I guess I could say, wanting you to see it was why I thought about leading you into the waters. But in all honesty, my real reason was to control this situation."

I waited for further explanation, which I truly needed at this point, but she seemed to have once again shut down the conversation. Deciding I would continue walking into the rather confusing space I hesitantly asked, "What the hell does that mean?"

Continuing to look out at the water she replied, "I don't like to feel vulnerable around people, especially men, so I use power plays to maintain control. Obviously, I know how to use my body as a place to gain this control. I don't have to be a rocket scientist to figure out that one."

Turning away from the water she looked over at me, "I don't know you at all Steve, other than one lunch and some small talk. However, I found I was getting very relaxed with you and becoming somewhat open. I decided back at the campsite I would play with you, probably use my sexuality to draw you in, maybe have sex with you but definitely regain my sense of power. Then we got here and I didn't want to play the game anymore. I just wanted to spend time with you and enjoy all the beauty around us."

She turned away and looked back at the water, "I'm sorry, Steve. I guess I'm just a little screwed up at this point in my life and very used to manipulating the situation to fit my needs. You'd be wise to head back down the mountain and just let this day pass into history. Thanks for the time together, and for the fish. Maybe I'll see you on the river tomorrow."

I looked at her for a minute and then laughed, "You're definitely a handful for anyone but at least you're an honest handful. I suppose I should be offended you thought you could manipulate me, but in all honesty, you probably would have and I'd never have seen it coming. I'm a sucker for a beautiful woman who is honest, but I'm curious why you feel vulnerable."

"See how the water runs down the mountain," she said pointing to the stream before us. "Even if it hits an obstacle, it finds a path to follow because it will complete its journey down the mountain. I try to run my life like the water, never allowing any obstacle to interfere with my destination; always pressing forward and finding a path of least resistance. For some reason, these last few hours I stopped trying to force myself down the mountain. I just enjoyed being where I was and then I realized I couldn't take a chance on getting stuck. So I needed to continue down the mountain like the water. Does that make sense?"

I decided J liked to talk in allegorical statements, as they often entered into her explanations. I looked at her and realized that under her confident exterior there was a very wounded woman. "Our journey is the only thing we can really control, J. Therefore, your picture of the mountain stream makes perfect sense, although it does cause me to wonder what you expect to find at the bottom of the mountain. In my experience, we all seem to be on a quest to find some purpose to our journey, be it accumulation of things or people. The sad part is, after we accumulate the 'things,' we find they don't really bring us a sense of satisfaction. So we go seeking even more things. What's at the bottom of your mountain?"

J leaned back on her elbows and looked into the clear blue sky. "I used to think it was justice. I've had a lot of pain in my past and I really wanted to even out some of the rocky places that interrupted my life. But at this point, I'm not positive that goal is what I really want. Maybe that quest is just another spot in my journey demanding a change in course. I know I'm vague, but it isn't something I talk about easily."

I stood and walked to the edge of the pool at the bottom of the falls. Picking up a smooth stone, I skipped it across the water until it disappeared from sight and then said, "I'm not sure what justice you're seeking, but I do know the feeling of getting to a place where you thought you would find satisfaction or purpose, only to discover it wasn't what you thought it would be. I've worked hard to achieve my goals and do the right thing, but I'm not sure I'm happy with the results. One of my reasons for being up here is to try to sort out the question, 'What next'?"

J got up and stood next to me as I chucked another stone across the water, which skipped a magnificent twelve times before sinking. Smiling she said, "No manipulation, no control, no power plays; do you want to see the spot behind the falls?"

"I assume that means a journey into this rather cold water," I skeptically replied.

"Yep, but it's great once you get used to it. You game?"

I sighed, "Well, as long as I already know I'm being manipulated. What the hell, why not?"

She turned and laughed, "I promise this is not manipulation and I'm not going to take advantage of you." She walked away from the water and unbuttoned her shirt, "However, I do have to bring you back to the mystical understanding so we can truly experience this part of the journey. We'll walk in this mist of freedom and discover its power is real. However, it forbids us to ignore its voice; such action will cause us severe consequences. I need to be in the healing powers of the water."

Having said that, she slipped off her shirt and stood before me in a very tight-fitting sports bra. Smiling at me, she continued,

54

"Freedom of the water is a blessing that must be honored or it will become a curse for those who disobey. Having touched a human body, it demands total sacrifice."

She bent down and slipped off her hiking boots and socks. "I will not be disobedient to its demand, but only you may decide for yourself. Don't take too long to decide, or you will turn to stone." She laughed and slid down her shorts and kicked them off. Standing there in her bra and rather brief panties, I could see her body was magnificent and she was right, part of me was definitely turning to stone. With a smile, she turned away and plunged rapidly into the cool deep pool.

Not wanting to have the curse on my life, I quickly stripped to my shorts and jumped into the pool. Whatever part of me had turned to stone suddenly lost all its strength as the cold water hit my body with a Mike Tyson punch and I went into shock. I could feel ice particles forming in my blood stream as the water drove the heat out of my body. "Keep moving," she shouted. "You'll get used to it."

I swam down into the heart of the pool and pushed toward the bottom. The water was even colder as I touched the bottom and quickly rushed toward the surface. J was right — as I came to the surface, I felt the warm air and the pain subsided in my feet and hands. I looked for J and saw her heading toward the falls. Swimming after, I watched her dive as she approached the bottom of the falling water. I waited for a minute, treading water to keep in one place and when she didn't come back up, I began to worry she was in trouble until I finally heard a shout, "Come under and behind the falls."

CATCH AND RELEASE
TWERELL

Diving under the water, I felt its power hitting above me as I
swam through the turbulence. Noticing the water beginning to
calm, I pushed up to the surface and found myself in a small cave
area behind the falls. The sun was shining through the shimmering
water as a lamp through a waving curtain. The sound was
tremendous and yet calming at the same time. Moving toward the
ledge of the cave, I pulled myself out of the pool and saw J sitting
near the cave wall pulling water out of her long dark hair. Her body
was a rose color from the water's chill, and yet I found the cave
was mysteriously warm.

She said something to me, but her voice was lost in the sound
of the falls. She waved me to come closer and I obediently
followed her call. Sitting beside her, she leaned toward me to say,
"Well done, human. The waters of freedom are pleased you
allowed them to work their magic." As she laughingly smiled and
shouted in my ear, her body brushed my arm and I could feel her
heat literally pouring out on my flesh.

"Why's it warm in here?" I shouted.

She smiled again and leaned against me. "It's warmed by the
exchange of body heat from those who yield to the magic of the
waters. It is the gift that those who are empowered with new
freedom give back to the magic cave." With that, she turned toward
me and kissed me with such softness that I was lost in her embrace
without the ability to move or think.

She smiled and ran her fingers through my hair as her warmth
and softness continued to invigorate my senses. "Steve, we're
strangers who have fallen into each other's presence with no cares
or concerns for tomorrow. Thank you for putting up with my

56

craziness, but you must admit this is a magnificent place to hide away."

In all honesty, I was so entranced with J's presence I forgot to look around me. The space in the cave was about a 20'sq ledge that protruded out from the cliff wall. The power and beauty of the falls defied description as it passed before us like liquid glass and then crashed into the water below. Mesmerized by the falling waters, I asked her, "Why do you really think it's warm in here?"

"I think the water acts like a magnifying glass during the day and pulls the sunlight into the cave. I've been here after sunset and it does cool down."

Turning to face her, I brushed the wet hair from her face and looked into her eyes, "Thanks for allowing me to come into your sanctuary and for being honest with me."

J pulled close and we kissed once more, while the pounding of the water played in the background. "Thank you for allowing me to just be who I am, Steve. I haven't felt this free in years and I want to capture every feeling." She grasped the bottom of her bra and pulled it over her head. Pulling close, J closed her eyes and buried her face in my neck as I continued to hold her, feeling the excited beat of her heart on my chest. Rolling to our side, I looked into her beautiful green eyes and lightly caressed the last remnants of the cooling waters that ran as small streams down her flesh. Somehow, in that moment it all made perfect sense, and even if it didn't, I'd lost the ability to rationally process the events around me. We kissed and in the roar of the waterfall, far from the confines of the world we knew, we lost our problems and concerns

57

as we gave into the passion of the moment permission to rule our every thought.

***

Following our time of ecstasy, I became aware of the sound of the falls and the abundance of warm mist now clinging to our bodies. Breathing deeply, I rolled to my back still holding her in my arms. Throwing her arm heavily over my chest, she whispered in a weak deep voice, "The cave is very happy." I didn't know about the cave, but I knew I was very happy and not at all disappointed that I'd missed an afternoon of fishing. As we lay there on the cave floor, with the roar of the falls all around us, I wondered who this woman was that had so mysteriously transformed my world. Little did I know how often I would repeat that question in the next few days.

CHAPTER 9

I don't know how long we rested there; it was a time of complete freedom of spirit and body. Dozing off for a few minutes, I woke to find J sitting on the edge of the pool behind the fall. Sliding up beside her, I slipped an arm around her waist as she leaned her head on my shoulder and shouted over the sound of the water, "Let's go back to the other side. It'll be quieter." She kissed me, jumped into the water, and disappeared from sight.

The water was cold as before, but somehow it didn't bother me this time. Swimming through the turbulence, I surfaced to find her walking out of the water and on to the shore. I was once again intrigued at her beauty and well-formed body. While only around 5'4" tall, she gave off an energy that brought an illusion of being much taller. Her body was tight and hard, but offset by the softness of her femininity and allure of her sexuality. I didn't know how we ended up as we did, but I wasn't going to ask questions or try to figure things out; I was simply happy for what we had together.

As I came toward her, she opened her arms and held me tight. Her breast and warm body pressed into mine and she simply said, "Thanks."

I didn't know what to say but simply held her tight and kissed her lips and neck. She pulled back saying, "Let's get back to camp before it gets too late. I don't know about you, but I strongly believe I have a great place for two people to spend the night. The rent is cheap if you want to join me and will only cost you the price of a good dinner with whatever you may find in your backpack."

Smiling the irresistible bright smile, she dressed and started down the path toward camp. Walking with her, I felt a sense of peace and happiness that had long escaped me. Who was this woman who had directed my life these last few hours? I was normally a very independent individual, content to spend most of the time alone and unattached. Since my divorce, a relationship was the last thing I wanted; nevertheless, here was a wonderful woman who I'd followed up a mountain and into passion. While it all seemed rather strange, I knew I had to follow this story to its conclusion.

As we neared her camp, I separated and headed toward my place so I could pack and move back to J's. As much as my habitat was a location of peace and tranquility, it felt empty without her presence. It wasn't only the sex; she was a person who had such a free spirit it forced mine to become alive. That feeling gave me hope that I may be able to escape from the mundane aspects of a life, which were draining my very existence.

The daily routine I lived was good, but I felt life slipping away and needed a change. Unwilling to let my ego blindly rush into another accumulation quest, I was spending more time in a quiet inner focus, which provided me with renewed strength. My thoughts were the manifestation of my opportunistic ego and unless I could quiet the thoughts and feel my inner being, I would continue to find more empty results, which provided nothing but unfulfilled expectations. I didn't know where this interaction with J might lead, but I was in for the trip, short term or long term, because it was an adventure and a promise of newness I couldn't bypass. As I checked my camp and headed back to J's to see what the future would hold, I sensed the woods were alive with the sights and sounds of nature, growing and thriving so they may bring comfort and hope to a mere mortal.

I took the high path near the crest of the mountain and proceeded into the camp area above J's. In the clearing above her camp, I came to a halt as I listened to the voices below me. I thought she had found a new neighbor or some other friend had joined her in my absence. However, my disappointment changed as I realized the new voice, which was clearly male, was also loud and threatening.

Instinctively, I shed my equipment, dropped to my knees, and crept toward the rear of her tent in the back of the campsite. Whoever was with her was not a happy person, and I needed to see what was going on below me. As I crept beyond the side of the tent, my first look past the edge provided a view of a man who obviously was not a close friend. He was forcefully holding J from

61

behind. The visible tension in her body showed she was in serious trouble.

The unwelcome visitor snarled as he applied pressure to J's arm, "So little trouble maker, you've really fucked us all this time. I told Juan not to trust you, but oh no; "the woman was to be trusted, she was good." Shit, if you're good, then cow shit must be gold." His anger rose as he pulled her close and further jammed her arm behind her.

Through clinched teeth J hissed, "You're a shit above all shits Carlos, but that came from the womb long before I ever knew you."

"Bitch!" He pushed her with his left hand and spun her to the ground as he pulled a 38 caliber from his belt and held it to her head. "You'll pay for being a snitch and a fucking slut." He picked up a rope, threw her face down on the ground, and put a knee into her back. Pulling her hands over her head, he tied her wrists together and yanked her to her feet.

Menacingly he pushed the gun into her face and growled at her, "Juan knows you talked and he sent me to find you and get some information from you, no matter what or how. I want to know who you talked to, how much you told, and where you put the numbers. Juan thinks you being dead will stop the problem, but I think you're the start. So tell me Juanita, what happened with you and the Feds?"

"Carlos, you're still as dumb as the day I met you. If I talked to anyone, would I be here camping by myself? You and Juan are looking for someone to hang for your stupidity, and he decided I would be a good one to use. But you know better than that."

Carlos grabbed her and snarled, "It seems you don't remember your fun time with Johnny in the elevator. I don't think you're out here in these fuck'n woods for your health, I think you're on the run. You forget I never liked you. Your clever words won't work on me, but you'll work for me before I kill you and you'll tell me all that happened. You treated me like I was some scum you couldn't stand, but now you'll talk to me and you'll remember me as you die."

J was relaxed and still in command of her emotions. I was amazed at her strength in the face of such terrifying circumstances. I knew I had to do something, but the 38 in Carlos' hand greatly limited my choices. As I considered my options, J pressed closer to Carlos and snapped, "The only way you'll ever fuck me is if you rape me. You're such a piece of shit, no one would go near you willingly."

His fist dove deep into her midsection and she exhaled loudly. Taking a knife from his pocket, he cut her shirt open from top to bottom, "How much you tell the Feds?"

"Up yours, asshole."

He backed up and held the gun to her head. "See this, shit face. Its next resting place is between your legs and your love making will be quick and painful. I've had enough of your shit, I'm going to use you and lose you."

I'd worked my way to the front of her tent and was able to see her 45 still in the side of her backpack. Taking a deep breath, I lurched toward the pack. Unfortunately, my shoulder hit the tent upright and I felt the canvas collapse around me. Grabbing the gun with my left hand, I quickly switched to my right, praying that the safety was off. The tent had collapsed and was blocking my view as I heard his gun go off and felt the bullet pass over my left shoulder and through the tent canvas. I rolled to my right clearing the tent. As I came around I saw him aim again and fire. Squeezing the trigger, I watched him fall back to the ground, Suddenly I was aware of a sharp pain in my right leg accompanied by a feeling of frozen ice going down my calf. I looked down, saw the blood flowing from my pant's leg, rolled again, and aimed once more at the downed man who'd shot me — but he was on the ground and not moving. J was watching both of us with total astonishment in her eyes. "Quick, cut me loose," she shouted.

I jumped up only to immediately fall to the ground as the pain in my leg became overwhelming. Regaining my balance, I moved over to J and found Carlos' knife. After I cut the rope between her hands, she reached down, grabbed the gun out of my belt and turned it on the fallen felon. She walked over to Carlos and, as she still had on her hiking boots, kicked him hard in his ribs. When he gave no response, she bent down and turned him on his back.

"Damn," she sighed. "You got him in the head."

"I was aiming for his shoulder and must have missed. Is he dead?" She reached down and checked his pulse, "Like yesterday's sunset."

"J, what the hell's going on here? I came for a fishing trip, ended up in a cave making love to a beautiful woman, killed a man, and got shot in the process. I need explanations."

"First we need to see your leg. After that, I'll try to fill you in as best I can. Take off your pants and let me see the damage."

I obediently followed her instructions and then stretched out on the ground. J pressed on my leg and said, "The bullet entered and exited in the calf of your leg." She wiped away the blood with her torn shirt. "No major damage, but it'll hurt like hell for a couple days. I have a first aid kit in my pack. Let me clean and wrap it to keep the blood loss to a minimum. Here, drink a lot of water while I fix this."

She poured something into the wound and I genuinely thought I would die on the spot. As she wrapped the leg, the pain started to subside to a dull roar and I felt the strength return to my leg. She slapped me on my ass and said, "You'll live."

"Now explain," I said as I pulled up my bloody slacks. She went to my backpack and grabbed another pair of pants. "Put these on," she ordered. "You have to get the hell out of here and you don't need bloody pants to draw attention." As I changed, she went to her own pack and pulled out another shirt.

Gathering my things and her torn shirt, she sat down with me and said, "Here's the quick version. I'll explain more later on, but we need to move fast. I'm a Federal Agent with Narcotics and I've been undercover for two years working with this gang of idiots on a Colombian connection. Their leader is Juan Cardova and I worked my way into being his girlfriend. My cover started to leak about two weeks ago and I split while the agency tried to clean things up. Carlos here was a number three man to Juan and, while Carlos didn't know it, I suspect Juan took off and left him holding the bag. I guess they figured out my connection and sent Carlos, who hated me because I'd never given him the time of day and that had really pissed him off. I thought the agency would catch up with

65

him before he found me, but no such luck. Now that Carlos is dead, Juan's going to be looking for me and I need to distance soon."

"What about him?" I asked pointing to our lifeless associate.

"I'll call in, but I believe our best bet is to get you the hell out of here ASAP. I can cover and not bring you into this. I'll tell the Agency I shot him and they'll clean up the mess. Juan is the problem. We don't know where he is or what his plans are at this point. Some big people will want answers from him about the problems he's causing and he'll want to show he's still in charge. I'm surprised that El Stupido here came alone, but Carlos always was a Mr. Macho and figured I'd be easy to take down. Hey, by the way, I owe you big time. You saved my life!"

She leaned forward and kissed me deeply. The experience had taken place so fast that I felt myself relax in her arms and finally started to deal with reality.

"I just killed a man and that fact is finally catching up with me."

"Carlos was an accident that was going to happen sometime. It was killing him or him killing us. Let it go as a thing that happened."

"That'll be easier said than done. What happens now? What do we do with him?"

She got up and went to her pack. As she slid the 45 into the side, she pulled a small telephone and said, "Motherload, this is Plaything, over." She waited a minute and said, "Problem up here. Carlos found me and he's now departed. Need a cover and sweep ASAP." She waited again and said, "You got leaks in your boat and I'm going low. Nobody but you and associates knew my location. Fix the leaks and I'll surface. I'll contact." With that, she threw the phone in the backpack and turned to me, "Can you walk?"

I got up and felt a knifelike pain shoot up and down my leg. It was difficult, but I took a few steps and found I was mobile. "I'm okay," I murmured as I picked up my pack and rod case.

"I'm so sorry for all this, Steve. I wish I could make it up to you, but we have to separate quickly. The office crew will be here in a few minutes and you have to be long gone. Where's your car?"

"Down the mountain by the lake," I answered.

"Head toward it and I'll meet you later."

"Where will we meet?"

She wrote on a card and handed it to me, "This is a Doctor in Monticello, New York, who works for us. You can't go to a hospital with a gunshot wound because they will have too many questions. I'll call him, tell him you're coming, and give him a number for you to find me. Go quick; I have a lot to do and not much time."

She pulled me to her and kissed me deeply. "Thanks again, I really owe you big. Don't worry, I'll find you. I really will, I promise."

After painfully making my way down the mountain, I got the hell out of the area. Monticello was about an hour trip south and gave me some quiet time to reflect on the last few hours. Every time I thought about killing Carlos, I had the great urge to pull over to the side of the road and throw up.

I considered myself a nonviolent, peace-loving man who still struggled with killing spiders in my apartment. I even had some qualms about killing the fish I caught; nevertheless, I buried that struggle when it interfered with my fishing fun. Now I was a killer of a fellow human being and had terminated a life. Granted, Carlos may have been less than friendly in my brief acquaintance with him, but there had to be another way to deal with the problem other than killing him.

I tried not to feel guilty about killing Carlos, as he was the one who had started shooting. I knew guilt was a futile emotion, which only confused my personal worth with my actions. I may have killed him, but I was not a killer in my heart. But I was disappointed I'd acted like God and brought rather swift judgment on him, one from which he would never recover. Other than the reoccurring thought telling me I was also going to die, I found my ego to be rather silent at this point — seemingly overwhelmed by the turn of events it had just experienced.

The other thing bothering me was the coldness and emotional detachment demonstrated by J. It appeared she was as concerned about killing Carlos as she would be about burning toast. What kind of life had she lived that made her so callous and cold? I know I saw a depth in her that spoke of a warm, loving person, but she was able to bury that side like yesterday's garbage when she needed to be in control. As I neared Monticello, I decided I needed to deal with the killing as something I regretted, but not terrible or horrible. The downside of that decision was the concern that if killing someone wasn't terrible or horrible, then what else was I capable of doing?

By the time I made it into Monticello my leg felt like it had a hot piece of steel stuck in it. J's doctor was located above the old theater and his office looked like it was a leftover from a bad movie. The office had no receptionist or no waiting room — it was just an open area with a table and a refrigerator. As I entered, he got off a folding chair and locked the door behind me. Obviously, he did not have a large practice but I was sure the Feds paid him well for his service. I wondered if they needed a shrink who had recently killed a man. The leg pain stopped me from further thought as he told me to drop my pants and lie on my stomach. The table had a cloth cover, which appeared clean, but in this office, I was somewhat concerned about who had used the table last. The good doctor never asked my name and never told me his. I felt him give me a shot in the calf and suddenly the pain washed away, and I was again a whole person.

"Clean shot, not deep. I'll close it up and give you antibiotics. You'll have some pain, so I'll give you pain killers. But don't drive and use them."

This was all too much. I had a doctor telling me not to drive with painkillers in my system and two hours before I had shot a man to death up in the mountains. I wasn't a person who spent his days walking around shooting people and having them shoot me in return. It took all of my self-control not to simply jump up and scream at the mechanical medical man. But I knew he would simply finish his task and promptly forget he ever saw me. He was a professional, "don't ask, don't tell," government doctor.

It took about another fifteen minutes to wrap things up before he handed me my meds and smiled. I smiled back and looked at him. Finally, he said, "Is there something else I can do for you?"

"I don't know where to go. J said she'd tell you where I should meet her."

The doctor again smiled and said, "I don't know a J. I get calls from unknown people and they tell me to fix up whatever is wrong. I do it and we all part company. Beyond that, I can't assist you."

Suddenly I knew I was on my own and didn't have a clue how to proceed. I thanked the doctor who promptly pointed me to the door and turned his back. Guess the Feds didn't pay for bedside manners, but I didn't really care as I was in no mood for small talk anyhow.

Limping out to my car, I sat for a minute with the engine running as I gathered my thoughts. I noticed the streets were unusually busy for early evening and I tried to remember what day it was. To my amazement, I discovered it was only Saturday evening. I had only walked out of my office a little over 24 hours ago. My God, if I'd done this amount of damage in 24 hours, what was the rest of the week going to look like?

Sitting there, I knew I was in no condition to drive back to the city, and I sure as hell didn't want to go back to the mountain. When the pain started to act up again I decided to go over to a motel by the racetrack area and take a room. A few painkillers and some sleep would clear out my garbled mind. I was a little angry that J hadn't followed through on her part of the deal, but considering she was left with a dead body and people looking to kill her, I guessed I could cut her some slack.

I pulled out onto the main street and headed to the Holliday Inn down the road. The Monticello Racetrack was a horse track that was empty until June, so I knew the motel would have plenty of vacancy. Pulling away, I noticed a black SUV making a U-turn on the main street and following me. Well, I didn't know if it was following me, but it was behind me. Pulling into the motel lot, I watched the SUV as it drove past and continued down the road. My imagination was running amuck, and I needed to get away from everything. I assumed the motel would allow me that place of escape; little did I know it was the first of the many stops along the way.

CHAPTER 10

Heading down the mountain road, J finally collected her thoughts and wondered how in the hell she'd been so stupid to believe she could run away from these people. Obviously, Juan was pissed beyond reasoning and wasn't going to rest until he caught her and inflicted his wrath. Carlos was as dumb as the night was dark and she knew he'd never have found her unless someone helped him, which again meant there were others trying to get to her and she just didn't know who they were.

Letting her concern slip away for a minute she thought about poor Steve. Knowing how Juan worked, she was going to have to make sure she took care of him or he would also become an unwilling accomplice to her death. If they captured him, they had tactics designed to force him into disclosing information. Nevertheless, in reality, what did Steve know about her that would ever be useful? They'd shared some thoughts, had fantastic sex, and that was about all they'd done together.

She smiled as she remembered their conversation at the falls. While her original goal was to have sex with him behind the falls, she still found it curious that she'd been unable to follow through with her plan, and even more puzzled about the level of vulnerability she expressed with him. Her smile turned to laughter as she remembered his scream when he jumped into the water and felt how cold it was. Her laughter turned back to smiles as she recalled their time together and decided the afternoon had been worthwhile, even if it turned to shit rapidly after they got back to camp.

At the end of the mountain road, she turned on the highway and began the trip back to New York. She had to find out where Juan was and settle this thing permanently, or her life would continue to be a living hell. Experience had taught her that to permanently solve the problem one of them had to die. She was rather surprised to find herself concerned she might be the one to die, as death had never been a concern in her life. She often took chances and risks that looked death in the eye, simply because death was not a fear, it was an escape. But now the realization that she wasn't ready to die confused her.

The thoughts began to clarify as she turned onto the expressway and headed south. She didn't want to die, because she wanted to see Steve again. What the hell was that all about? She didn't even know this guy and yet something deep in her wanted desperately to see him again and hold him in her arms. Maybe she felt guilt about getting him involved in her life and then getting him shot protecting her. Maybe she actually wanted to live because she finally found someone she could trust, but then she didn't know Steve well enough to make that decision. If she started to fear anything, she would lose her edge and this was no time to get weak.

She slammed her hand down on the steering wheel and screamed into the void around her, "No fucking way." Steve was just another guy and she didn't need the complications of someone who was so innocent and naive about life, especially her kind of life. He was just a passing fancy that she needed to use for her pleasure and that was all he was to her.

As the road continued to stretch out before her, the tears began to run down her face and fall on her body. Since she could remember, she'd always been a person who faced fear and never let it get the best of her. Now here she was — 33 years old, very alone, and finally facing the fact that she was afraid to live an empty life.

She set her own course, but other than loving Jason, she'd never allowed herself to be open to anyone. Since her early teens, no man had ever touched her unless she decided she needed his touch and after she got what she wanted, she easily walked away. The years with Juan were pure hell as she had pretended to please him by doing whatever he wanted. But no matter what he demanded, she knew she gave it to him only to fulfill her quest. Now she had met someone who she wanted to be with, just because she enjoyed being together.

She remembered the dream and how her father told her to come have fun in the river or she would have to stay with Juan. She

74

knew Juan would definitely shoot her if he saw her, so maybe she needed to see what was going on in the river.

Finally, she picked up her cell phone and made a call as the sun set in the mountains behind her. "This is J. I need the cell phone number of a Steve Sanders in New York City. And I need it right now." She waited for the reply and quietly said to the darkness that began to surround her, "Oh Jason, I don't think I can keep the woman inside me locked up anymore. I miss you so much, but I think I have to be what you always told me to be."

CHAPTER 11

I fell asleep as soon as I lay down and only came to consciousness about five hours later. My watch indicated it was a little after midnight and I was hungry. My feet hit the floor and I was quickly educated about the power of pain. Dr. Mechanical Man said there would be some pain, but according to my current status, he greatly underestimated the word "some."

I hobbled to the bathroom, did my thing, and then paced back and forth until the pain went from the "I want to die" level to "I think I might die." I needed a shower and decided to keep one leg outside the tub as I cleaned the remainder of my body. A good trick, but if nothing else, I am adaptable. I pulled out my remaining pair of jeans, a clean shirt, and headed out into the wild nightlife of Monticello, New York. In the summer, it was somewhat hectic, but winter and spring were off-season for the horse track and, other than fishing and hunting, the area was dead. After midnight only a few places even looked open; however, I found a diner up by the highway and had a solid meal and a cold beer. I took another painkiller and washed it down with the beer. After what I'd been through today, alcohol and painkillers were my least concern. I brought my laptop along to see if I could get some internet connection, but in Monticello, even the wireless phone call was spotty.

Heading back to the car, I now had to face the question of where I went from here. As I walked up to my car I felt my bootlace was undone and I definitely didn't want to trip and fall on this bum leg. Bending over to tie the lace, I heard an explosion and felt glass shatter all around me.

Instinctively dropping to the ground, I sensed the pain go through my leg, but it was only the stitches and not the flying glass. Two more explosions, quickly followed by the sound of more breaking glass, kept me in my ground-clinging position. Peering between parked cars, I saw a black SUV speed out of the parking lot and head off to route 17. It looked like the one I spotted earlier, but as I stood and saw my jeep with three shattered windows, I became totally convinced it was the same one.

People were coming out of the diner and cautiously looking at me as I heard a siren in the distance indicating someone had called the cops. All I needed was the local constable trying to find out why someone had shot at me. I made a quick decision, jumped into the jeep, and took off in the opposite direction from the siren. Unfortunately, my direction took me away from my motel.

The more I thought about the situation, the more convinced I became that the motel I checked into was not a safe place. If it was the same SUV, and I would bet my money it was, the driver knew I was at the motel and would try to follow up on his kill. I was consumed with the confusing thought that I was a target and didn't know who the shooter was, what I had done, or what I was supposed to do now. Somewhere deep inside me I had a strange desire to simply go back to my office and spend the rest of my life with Laura and her borderline personality. Compared to where I found myself, she sounded heavenly safe.

My cell phone interrupted the blissful thoughts about my lunatic patient. I looked at the number and didn't recognize it, but figured I would take a chance. Having been on the wrong end of a gun twice in 24 hours, what the hell — how could it get worse?

"Dr. Sanders," I said to the phone and the phone said, "I didn't know you were a fucking doctor. I thought you said you were a writer." At first, I couldn't recognize the voice, but finally it all came together.

"J, where the hell are you? I have people shooting at me."

"Damn, damn, damn!" she replied.

"Uh, J, that response isn't building the level of confidence I need right now. Do you have any idea who these people are? Is it Juan?"

"Stop!" she said tersely. "Do not say another word and when we finish this talk, turn off your phone until you get to JFK."

"JFK? As in the airport?"

"Yes. Drive there now and go to the international terminal. When you park, turn on your phone, listen to the message, and then turn it off. I'll let you know what to do."

"Wait a fucking minute, J. I'm not going to JFK or anyplace else until I know what's going on here." That strong demand went no place, as I found she had already hung up.

JFK, why would I go to JFK? I could stay here and let these people kill me. I could go back to New York and let them kill me there. Hell, I could go to Afghanistan and let them kill me there. Alternatively, I could go to JFK and see what I do next. For some reason, that sounded like a good idea and with that conclusion I caught the back roads to route 17 and started the three-hour run to John F. Kennedy International Airport. I wondered if the trout were jumping in the stream, but the pain in my leg quickly took the thought away.

At that hour of the night, traffic back to the city was less and I was able to get there in good time. Nevertheless, once caught in New York's web, things slowed greatly. I was always amazed that no matter what the hour in New York, there were still thousands of people traveling somewhere. I heard there were over 10,000,000 people in a 25-mile radius of the Empire state building. Sometimes I thought each of them had two cars.

The drive provided me time to collect my thoughts and try to put things into perspective. I was really counting on J for a plan, and I didn't even have a clue as to her real identity. I'd known her for about six hours, had great sex behind a falls, and then I ended up killing a man who wounded me. This was not a strong foundation for a long-term relationship and a definite problem for short-term trust. I had strong visions of Carlos lying on the ground with the bullet wound in his head. Even if Carlos was some kind of terrible person, I still didn't feel great about being his executioner.

The ride in the jeep was interesting with three windows shot out. Fortunately, they shot out only the side windows and not the back and front, so at least I didn't have wind in my face. I'd pushed out the broken remains so the highway patrol wouldn't become suspicious. A part of me really wanted to go to the police, tell them what happened, and ask for help. But I just didn't know how to explain all I'd been through without making my situation worse. My only choice was to trust J and see what the future held.

Now trust was not one of my strong suits as I valued the independence of my own decision making process. In addition, my friendly ego constantly reminded me of all the people who had betrayed me and told me I should trust no one. I then went into a process of asking my ego just who "all the people" were who had betrayed me and after some time we usually came up with Sammy Carridine in fifth grade and Brenda Sommerwald in my sophomore year of college.

My ego loved to make global assessments (everybody hates you; nobody is as dumb as you; everybody is watching you). My job was to ask the ego for clarification, which usually pointed to Sammy and Brenda — who really were not bad people, just not my best memories.

In reality, my trust issues came from being an only child and having to make decisions on my own, without siblings to talk too. At least that was what I believed and I'd read a couple of articles that also said the same thing. For me to trust J, was an unusual happening in my life, but in all honesty, it wasn't a threatening thought. Hell, Carlos threatened me and he ended up dead! How could trusting J be any worse? I decided not to answer that question.

It was 4:00 am when I finally cleared the city and caught the Van Wyk to JFK. This day had started on the trout stream at 6:00 am and provided me more than my share of adventure since. The sex by itself was enough to wear me out, but the other things, such as bullets and blood, definitely had taken their toll. Two days into my vacation, in worse shape than when it started, I headed to the international terminal at JFK with no idea what would happen next. I only hoped I would finally get some rest. Unfortunately, much to my surprise, that was not to be part of the plans for the future.

CHAPTER 12

The sun was showing signs of a new day as I wound around the ramp of the international parking garage and finally found an empty slot. I reminisced about the early morning on the river and wondered how my life could have changed this much in such a short time. Processing my current life during the long ride to the airport had been helpful, and I came to one solid conclusion: my fate, similar to the trout, was on the hook and could not get away. The line was tight in my mouth and I found myself pulled slowly toward my destination. My only hope was the possibility of an angler at the other end who believed in "catch and release," and not "catch and kill."

I turned off the engine and flipped on my cell phone. The screen flashed one new voice message and I called to retrieve the information. When the connection was established, I heard J's voice.

"Steve, go to the Air France desk and tell them you have come to retrieve the package you left on flight 5427. It's under your name and you can use your identity. Do not use credit cards or give your identity to any other person. All you'll need is in the package. I'm sorry you're caught in all this, but I'll fix it shortly. You should be ahead of the game at this point, but keep moving as the instructions indicate; your window will not be open that long. Catch you later."

My window would not be open long — what the hell did that mean? I might have ventured a guess, but decided not to do so. I had three windows open in my car from gunshots and they were the only open windows on which I could focus. At this point the trout doesn't think, it reacts out of instinct in an effort to survive. My instinct was to follow her instructions before someone shot out my personal windows.

With my backpack still in Monticello, my luggage now consisted of one laptop and a small briefcase. I decided I wouldn't need the camping equipment for this part of the journey and with a deep sigh walked away from my open windowed car bidding my equipment a fond farewell. Some thief was going to think he was in heaven.

Heading to the Air France information booth, I found the terminal dead at this hour and hoped someone was still on duty. I saw an Air France station open and proceeded to it, trying to remember my rather sketchy French. A young man, busy reading some magazine, was rather startled to have me suddenly appear at his station.

"Bonjour, j'ai laisse un pauet sur le vol 5427," I smiled at him hoping I'd asked for a package on flight 5427 and not told him I was going to blow up flight 5427.

"May I have your name please?" he asked in English, which greatly relieved my stress.

"Dr. Steve Sanders and here is my driver's license."

He looked at the license and said, "Je verifierai, esatisfaire l'attente," which I think was something like hang on while I check. He returned shortly with a box about the size of a 5"x7" picture.

"Please sign here, Dr. Sanders," he said as he handed me a form and the box. I signed my name and he gave me a copy back.

I smiled at him, "Merci."

"Aucun probleme," he replied. "Thank you for flying Air France."

Having retrieved the package without someone shooting me was a major accomplishment, considering all that had taken place in the last few hours. Finding a seat in the lounge area, I opened it and was pleasantly surprised to find several bundles of $100 bills. In addition, I discovered a passport, driver's license, and credit cards that all had the name Robert Klingman and looked quite real. I saw a note under the passport addressed to "Dr. Sanders." I opened it and found the following:

Steve,

Enclosed is your new temporary identity and $5000 in cash. Use the new credit cards only if you must, pay cash for everything else. DO NOT USE YOUR PERSONAL CREDIT CARD OR ID.

This is only for a few days, at which point, I promise things will be okay. Go to Terminal 6 and take Jet Blue Flight 2 to Ft. Lauderdale. Remember you are Robert Klingman from now until I tell you differently. When you get to Lauderdale, go to Hertz and pick up the car I reserved for you. The Hertz Gold Card in the package will be all you need in order to complete the transactions. You are going to 2337 South Ocean Drive in Hollywood, Florida. Park in slot #180 and go to apartment 1803 (18th floor). I will let you know what to do after that. I know it's hard, but trust me; fish where I suggest. The tippet is very light tackle; play the fish slowly so you don't lose it.

    J

    PS: Make sure you destroy this letter.

"Ft. Lauderdale — what is this, spring break?" I quickly looked around me and realized I'd spoken aloud. Fortunately, no one was around. I read the letter again, tore it into small pieces, pocketed the cash, and replaced my identification with the new Robert Klingman ID. I threw my own identification in my briefcase and hoped the security check would not find them and wonder why I was carrying two sets.

I packed up my small possessions and headed to the tram that would take me to Terminal 6. Jet Blue was starting to fill with Sunday morning travelers, but I was able to purchase the ticket easily. Using cash and my phony identification, I was now the proud owner of a ticket on Flight 2 to Ft. Lauderdale, Florida. The flight was two hours away, so I wandered into the rest room and tried to improve my rather haggard face. Deciding it was beyond help, I left it in ruins and headed for the gate.

Finding Starbucks open, I had a venti black coffee with a large overpriced muffin. A newsstand was also open so I picked up a paper, headed to the gate, and settled in for the wait. As I thumbed through the paper, I almost spilled my coffee all over myself. On page 3, I saw a picture of a face I would never forget. The headline read, "Local Agent Slain by Drug Ring." The picture next to the headline was J. The caption read, "Jennifer Blade, killed by Columbian Cartel."

I sat and looked at J, lost in a thousand thoughts. The article said they had found her body in a rural area and she appeared to be the victim of a violent shootout between the FBI and the drug gangs. The article also stated a Carlos Rodriquez of Bronx NY, reported to be one of the top people in the local drug rings, also died in the gunfire exchange. Looking back at J's picture, I tried to sort out my thoughts. How could she have died and still provided me the information on how to leave town? Did she set things in motion and then die while I was driving down to JFK? She said she was worried about a snitch in the Feds. Did they sell her out? What the hell was I going to do now? If they got to her and they knew of me, I was a marked man. Shit, the only thing I wanted to do was go fishing. *"Fish where I suggest. The tippet is very light tackle; play the fish slowly so you don't lose it."*

What did she mean by putting that in the letter? "Fish where I suggest," could mean a thousand things, but in this case the only suggestion I could think of was the trip to Ft. Lauderdale. It was her suggestion and I either trusted what she told me or ... or what? There was no plan B.

The tippet was the fine line between the regular fishing line and the lure itself. It was thin and supposedly invisible to the fish. Because it was thin, it didn't make a splash or sound when you cast the line. Nevertheless, it could break easily if you pulled too hard or too fast. *"The tippet is very light tackle; play the fish slowly so you don't lose it."* If I was hearing her correctly, she was saying not to do anything drastic or panic. Just slowly keep pulling in the line until you land the fish. Panic was definitely part of my thinking and I knew I needed to calm down. She'd given me a plan, a course of action, and I needed to play it out slowly until I was ready to catch the fish. The question echoing around my mind was — who's the fish? Alternatively, maybe I was the fish?

CHAPTER 13

I sat quietly during the flight and dozed off several times. At one point, I had a dream about Carlos shooting at me and jumped in my seat knocking over my glass of coke. The person next to me pretended they weren't sitting one seat away from a crazy man, and I simply muttered an apology as I cleaned up my mess. I was two days without a shave, wrinkled beyond comprehension, and walking with a decided limp. Hell, I would have been scared sitting next to me.

The flight landed without incident, which I considered a gift from God. The palm trees of Florida waved a greeting and I realized I had nothing to wear in the tropics. For that matter, I had nothing to wear anywhere as my clothes were scattered all over New York State. A clothing shop open in the airport provided me an opportunity to spend my newfound cash on some shorts, shirts, and a new pair of jeans. I only paid five times what they were worth, but I figured it was the taxpayer's money and they'd all be happy they had provided for me. Outside the terminal, the warm fresh smell of Florida asked me why I lived in New York. My reply was I would be happy to live anywhere that provided hope of keeping me alive.

As J indicated, the Hertz gold card worked wonders for Robert Klingman as I received the keys for a new Chevy Impala and a map of the greater Ft. Lauderdale/ Hollywood Florida area. Everything worked as the letter indicated and my only concern was for J. If she was dead — and part of me was in the early stages of denial about that fact — then what was my next move? From all I could tell, she had things under control when I left her and while her short conversation on the phone was not reassuring, she seemed to be free from trouble. Nevertheless, I'd learned in the last 48 hours, things could go to hell in a very short period.

I followed the signs to Hollywood and went further east until I crossed over to the beach area. The road, which was the old A1A highway, ran through a series of motels and restaurants that appeared to be right out of the fifties. It reminded me of the old days in Miami when my folks would bring me here for family vacations. I remembered how I could see the water from the highway without 40-story condominiums blocking the view. About five miles along the beach things began to change as the high-rise condominiums and hotels started to overtake the view of the water.

I found 2337 South Ocean Beach and pulled in spot #180 as instructed. The building was about 25 stories with a great view of the ocean and the obligatory pool for those who hated sand in their swimsuit. Watching the ocean, I considered my next move. It was Sunday morning, three days into my vacation, and I was in Florida with two shopping bags of clothes, a gunshot wound in the leg and no clue what the hell to do next. Part of me desperately wanted to simply wake up and find this was a bad dream, but remembering the coke all over my lap on the airplane, I decided I was definitely awake.

The thought bothering me most was how they had found out about me in the first place. I assumed "they" was Juan and all his friends, but in reality, I could have been a target of the Feds. Shit, this all might be a setup by J and I wouldn't even know it. I had a thought about going to the police, but somehow I didn't feel quite secure reporting that I had killed a man in New York and was now following instructions from a federal agent. I had worked with delusional people and that story qualified me for a person needing psychiatric help.

Moreover, if the Feds had set me up, a local police force would be of little or no help. On the other hand, if Juan was after me in South Florida, the cops could all be working for him. I decided I had to stop watching Miami CSI; my ego was struggling to decipher reality from fiction — a job it struggled with even in the best of times. I'd experienced enough life to know that success in all my endeavors depended not on my shallow, ego-driven thoughts; success would come only through listening to my inner sense. Trusting in my instincts was the key to survival that had never failed me before and hopefully would not fail me now. The bottom line was this, I was on the hook, and as the line pulled me into shore, I had to trust that the angler was a nice person who believed in catch and release. I gave a short prayer ending with, "Shit God, give me protection," and exited the car.

Entering the lobby of the condominium, I smiled at the concierge who smiled back but looked at me with a curious eye. I didn't blame him for his suspicion, given the way I looked, but I was in no mood to explain my situation to him. Frankly, I couldn't even explain my situation to myself, so screw him.

The elevator opened on 18 and the sign said 1801-1815 to the right. I dug in my pocket and pulled out the key J had provided me in the package. Standing before the door, I felt a deep dread about opening it. I had a vision of a loud explosion and the sense of a hard impact on my chest. I saw myself fall to the ground and start to die. Not exactly a happy welcome, but entirely possible given the direction of my new life.

As I unlocked the door and pushed it open, I waited in the hall for the explosion, but none came. Tenants came out of the apartment down the hall and I decided I couldn't stand looking into an empty room without drawing some attention. Closing the door, I found myself in a beautiful living room with a view of the tropical blue ocean. I threw my meager packages on the couch, opened the glass door, and stepped out on the balcony. If a person had to die, this was a great place to do it.

Back inside, I surveyed my new temporary home. The refrigerator was empty, but I found a bottle of Johnny Walker Red in the cupboard and ice in the freezer. My last meal had been in Monticello and I had been fortunate to keep it down after the gunfight. I never finished my overpriced muffin after reading about

J's death, so I knew Johnny Walker and I had to be careful friends until I got some food.

There were two bedrooms furnished with casual but expensive Florida décor. The large bedroom had a walk-in shower with water gushing from seven different directions. As dirty and grubby as I felt, I knew I would need all of them from every direction. There was a new razor, shaving cream, and other products designed more for male needs than female. Either someone expected me here or someone else had left them behind. Either way, I stripped down and removed the bandage from my leg wound; then Johnny and I entered the shower.

In the next twenty minutes, a major transformation changed me from a grubby killer on the run to a person who was actually somewhat decent. I finished Johnny and left the bathroom looking to pour some more of his friendship. I never made it. Standing in the bedroom holding a very large and very scary gun was another person. I automatically raised my hands, but realized I was stark naked and immediately went to cover my manhood. The figure lowered the gun and moved out of the sunlight enabling me to see a face. It was a woman with blond hair and familiar-looking facial features.

"Hey doc, welcome to sunny Florida."

Even though I didn't recognize her looks, I knew the voice.

"Damn J, you scared the shit out of me. I thought you were dead. What's with the hair?"

She set the gun on the desk, came over and held me close. She pulled off the blond wig and shook out her long dark hair. Smiling, she kissed me in a way that made all the craziness of the last few days seem normal.

Pulling away, I looked into her beautiful green eyes and said, "The reports of your death have been greatly exaggerated."

She laughed and ran her hand down my chest, "I had to appear dead to try to slow down Juan. I don't think he bought the story, but it gave us some time to work things out. I only hoped you'd stick with the plan I sent you and not strike out in some other direction. I'm sorry for the 'death' thing, but I had to make a lot of quick decisions and that was the quickest plan I could come up with that provided cover."

"When you say, 'it gave us some time'," I asked, "who's included in that?"

She smiled and threw herself across the bed. "Unfortunately, you're now included. Apparently, Carlos didn't come alone and one of his friends stationed up the mountain saw our little going-away party. He followed you when you left and I guess his boss told him to put you away to even the score. My people found that Juan's people discovered your car at JFK, but think you left on an international flight and haven't figured out you came down here. I don't know how long that cover will last, but we need to find Juan before he regroups and finds us."

"Is anyone else involved with us? In case you forgot, I'm not trained in the cop-and-robber routine."

She laughed and said, "Tell Carlos that. I think he's convinced you were a good shot."

"Damn J, that's not funny. I've never even gone hunting; I went to a range occasionally to remind myself where the trigger

93

was, but with no real love for guns. Besides, I was trying to hit him in the shoulder and missed."

"Sweetheart," she said softly. "In this game you don't go for the shoulder, you go for the head. In my book, you're qualified to stand by my side and work with me. I just want you around and not involved in the day-to-day operation. You saved my life and I won't easily forget that. Now go put on some clothes and let's get something to eat." She then stood, put her arms around me and said, "After that we can come back, relax, and start where we left off in the mountains."

I was hungry for food and for her. Nevertheless, my friend Johnny Walker had worked his way into a small headache indicating food would win out for now.

As I dressed, she piled her hair into the blond wig and I was amazed how the look transformed her instantly. However, I was somewhat curious about the wig, "If we're safe in Florida, why wear the wig?"

She picked up the gun on the desk, locked the safety, and stuck it in the waist of her jeans. "Baby," she said as she left the room, "the tippet is pulled tight, and we have to play it carefully. This trout is smart and we can't afford to let it get away."

I looked at her as she walked out and knew I was crazy for this woman. Then the thought crossed my mind that maybe I was simply crazy. That was not a comforting thought for a psychologist.

J was driving a beautiful red Mustang Shelby and I obediently moved to the passenger seat, settling my limpy leg in slowly. She exited and headed north much faster than I'd driven south, finally pulling into a place called "The Tub," which, on the outside, appeared condemned by the board of health. Most of the tables were along the Intercostal Waterway and provided a view that soon changed my original opinion as I found the Tub a rustic and charming place.

We sat outside by the water and watched the yachts move up and down the Intercostal. At $6.00 a gallon for fuel, these boat owners were not living off social security. For a dumpy-looking place on the outside, the food was great and I found Johnny Walker had cousins who provided close friendship.

Looking at J, I felt relaxed and safe. I supposed, in a normal relationship, a woman usually felt this way when with a man; nevertheless, I was damn glad I was with her and safe. However, if I had never been with her, I would be in a hell of a lot less trouble. "Tell me beautiful federal agent, how'd you get yourself into this line of work?"

She hesitated for a while and looked out at the boats on the water. "My Dad was a cop in New York and I always looked up to him. He had the bad luck to stumble into a drug setup and the scum he ran into killed him. I vowed to get even and do something about the problem. I received my law degree and planned to use it as a tool against the drug lords, but the FBI made an offer I couldn't refuse. About two years into the job, we made a taskforce with the Drug Enforcement Agency and I went undercover. I've worked the boys from below the border until I hooked up with Juan. We were about to really close him down when the leak came and I jumped ship. That's where you came in and became my newest partner. That's my life in thirty seconds."

My beautiful woman was a cop, lawyer, federal agent, and girlfriend of a drug dealer. What a combo! Finally, I asked her, "Back at the falls you said you always believed 'justice' was at the bottom of your mountain, but now you weren't so sure. Was the justice for your Dad or just justice in general?"

The waiter brought another beer for J and a Johnny for me. When he left, she leaned back and sighed, "I don't know, Steve. I always thought it was for my Dad, but I began to see that it was also a hiding place for me. After my Dad died, my Mom was never the same and her life exposed me to things that left some deep scars. I was seven when he died and for the next six years, I lived in a chaotic environment with a mother who was rapidly heading toward alcoholism. By the time I was ten, several of my Mom's 'boyfriends' had sexually assaulted me although I quickly learned how to defend myself in most of the incidents. At thirteen, one of my Mom's boyfriends stabbed her and she died, leaving me in a journey with relatives and other people until I was 18. I went to college, law school, and finally joined the Feds without ever having anyone close to me I could trust. Therefore, I think my journey for justice really came out of my own anger and self-pity. I just wanted to get even with life for all the shit I'd experienced. Now I'm not sure the journey was really worth all I went through to get where I am."

I digested her story for a few minutes as I tried to figure out the best response. As a therapist, I heard more horrible stories than I cared to remember, but J wasn't here as a patient and I didn't want to be clinical. Finally, I said, "The wounds of our childhood are buried so deep it's hard to know they even drive us. I know

96

how much our pain forces us to even the score, but in the end, it never really evens out by our actions. Either we settle things inside ourselves and enjoy our journey, or we try to settle things outside and become victims."

J looked out at the water and quietly said, "Victim — God I hate that word. My drive has always been to be a victor and not a victim."

"And what happens if you're not always victorious?" I asked, unconsciously slipping into my therapist mode.

She laughed, "I'll let you know if it ever happens."

I leaned forward and took her hand, "Seriously J, is your entire life victorious? What happens when things don't turn out the way you planned?"

She entwined her fingers with mine and sighed deeply, "A few days ago I would have told you I would just try another direction until I was victorious, but then I had a weird dream that changed my perspective. It was about my Mom and Dad. At the end of the dream, Juan shot me."

Always interested in dreams, I asked, "Where were you in your dream?"

"I was near the river at the campsite," she replied. "Mom and Dad were in the river playing and they kept telling me to come in with them and have fun. They were so happy and alive, but I couldn't move from the spot I was standing. I wanted to join them and have fun yet couldn't move forward. My Dad told me I had to join them or spend my time with Juan, who was standing behind me."

97

I thought about her dream as I filtered it through my experience as a therapist. "Whenever we find water in our dreams, it is usually a thought from our deep unconscious. Your Mom and Dad are generally figures who define a primary understanding about your self-identity. The fact they are having fun and enjoying life shows that you have a very free, fun-loving part to yourself that you may be denying. What happened next?"

She smiled, "You can take the psychologist out of his office, but you can't take the office out of the psychologist. I've never had a therapy session in a bar; maybe you should open a new practice."

I leaned back and laughed, "My ex-wife constantly reminded me that I was not her therapist — I was her husband. I'm sorry. I didn't mean to start digging into your dream. It's just second nature to me."

"I'm sure you'll bill me," she laughed. "So I might as well get my money's worth while I'm at it. When I turned to see Juan standing behind me, I noticed he had a gun and that he was naked. I asked him why he was naked and he only told me he was there to say goodbye. Then he shot me and I woke up."

"What does a naked Juan mean to you when you think about it?"

"I thought about that," she replied, "and decided I was seeing him as vulnerable. What does that mean?"

"Your dream isn't about your Mom and Dad, nor is it about Juan. Mom and Dad represent the fun-loving, free side of who you are; however, Juan is the place of fear."

She looked at me with intensity, "I don't fear Juan or anyone else."

Knowing we had hit a sensitive place, I gently said, "No, but you fear being vulnerable and are afraid that may kill you."

She looked at me and I could sense the inner turmoil warring in her mind as she quietly muttered, "Fuck."

She looked away from me and I saw the tears welling up in her eyes. It was now time for me to shut up and wait; where this went was strictly up to her.

J released my hand and took a sip of her beer. "Since I was a little girl, I taught myself to be strong and never be vulnerable. I made one exception and when he died, I completely shut down any emotion. I didn't let down my guard until the day you and I went up to the falls together. But as much as I enjoyed those moments, they frightened me."

She leaned back and continued to look out at the water for some time before finally speaking, "I want to go into the water and never come out."

"You mean the water in your dream?"

"Yes. I want to find the girl who used to enjoy life. I want to drown in the water and never come out, but I'm frozen into this person I created and I don't know how to get out. I'm afraid Steve; not afraid of Juan, but afraid of who I am and how I'll never be anyone different." She looked at me and then smiled, "Guess I'm just stuck with me."

I smiled back, "J, just by being aware of wanting something different, you've started a journey in a new direction. I know below your tough exterior there's a loving and wonderful woman. She is you, not a stranger, and you can bring her back if you want. Just stay aware of what you're thinking and doing, and don't slip into

99

an unconscious acceptance of being stuck. We are never stuck if we decide to make choices to be unstuck. If we don't make a choice to change, then we end up the victim."

J looked at me, stood up, moved to the seat next to me, then kissed me long and passionately. "Thanks, Dr. Sanders. I feel like a light came on and I promise I'll think about all we talked about tonight. For now, I think I want Steve back and let Dr. Sanders take a rest. You have no idea how much you both mean to me, but now I'm ready for Steve."

I kissed her and said, "Dr. Sanders has left the arena. So what happens now?"

She finished off her beer and stood to leave. She took my hand as we walked out and said, "Now, my straight shooting partner, I go find Juan and bring him in."

"What am I supposed to do as you go hunting for Juan?" I asked her.

She hesitated and finally said, "I think you need to lay low and stay out of the problem."

I thought about this for a minute and at last made a fateful decision. "No, I'm in this and I need to be involved. I trust your instincts and I'm a good follower, but I don't want to sit around while you go out and clean up this problem. I know you'll argue with me and tell me it's crazy, and I'll argue with you and tell you I won't change my mind. So let's skip all that. Let's simply pretend you have a new partner and I'll work with you until it's over."

"I know it's crazy," she said. "But I would like to have you with me. I really can't trust the people in my office, because there's a leak. I'm alone out here; therefore, I accept your offer to be with me. So, my partner, let's go get Juan, dead or alive."

Somehow, I had the feeling that Juan had similar thoughts about us. Moreover, the "alive" part was not one of his options.

CHAPTER 14

J drove out to Route 95 and we rapidly sped toward Miami. She explained that the majority of Juan's business ran through Miami and she was sure he'd come here to lay low. She had some friends in the area who would sell their mother for a right price. She was going to talk to them and see what they knew about Juan.

We turned off 95 and were suddenly in a world unlike anything I knew. Spanish was the common language on every billboard and the sounds of loud music filled the air with rhythmic beats. We pulled up before a not-so-charming nightclub advertising cheap drinks and cheap dancers. At least I thought that's what it said, as my Spanish was even worse than my French.

Entering the dark bar, I was somewhat startled to see a completely naked dancer on stage. I was no prude and had been to some clubs in New York, but total nudity was a unique attraction that I'd not experienced. J went to the bar and ordered two drinks that ended up being beers. Leaning over the bar, she handed the female bartender $50 and said, "Necesito ver a Joven."

The barmaid slipped the money in her jeans, which was the only place she could put it, as she was topless. She looked at J for a second, left the bar, and headed through a side door.

"Who's Junior?" I asked.

"I see you speak some Spanish," she said. "Junior's a dealer working for a man who has a dislike for Juan. I've used Junior before, and he knows I'm undercover. I keep him well paid and he's never let me down."

The semi-naked bartender came out the door and nodded for us to follow her. Frankly, I would've been happy to stay, watch the dancer, and let J have the meeting, except I was a partner and partners must sacrifice.

Behind the door, we entered a big room resembling something from a Tony Soprano show. Instead of Pauly and the gumbas, we found a 300-pound Latino dressed in a shirt that was so gaudy it defied description.

He raised his head and said, "Quien la cogida es usted?"

Roughly translated this meant, "Who the fuck are you?"

J pulled off the wig and Junior's eyes went large. He jumped to his feet and moved across the room faster than a man half his size. Grabbing J, he literally began to cry. He held her away from him, looked at her, and with tears running down his face said, "Bendiga a dios, ne angel no es muerto."

Again, I understood this as, "Bless God, my Angel is not dead."

103

He held her close and cried some more as J hugged him tight and said, "Junior, you know I would never leave you. You're the special man in my life."

Junior laughed and then appeared to see me for the first time. "This is another special man in your life? I only want you to myself; I guess I will kill him now."

I was really getting tired of people making snap decisions if I should live or die.

"This is my partner," J said, "and I don't ever want anything to happen to him that you may control. Usted entiende mi amor?"

Translated J said, "Do you understand me, my love?" — but the chill in her tone stated her meaning.

"I read you my angel," Junior said as he extended his hand to me. "Anyone J says is okay is definitely good with me."

I would have given him my name, but frankly, I wasn't too sure who I was supposed to be. Based on this lack of knowledge, I decided to be the silent partner.

Junior motioned for us to sit on a couch as he reclined in a chair, which protested loudly as he lowered his girth. The topless bartender came through the door and put a bottle of Don Julio on the table. J poured three shots and we all made a silent toast to whatever people toast when they don't talk.

As the tequila burned its way down my throat, Junior looked at J and asked, "My angel, what the fuck went wrong? One minute I hear you are living the high life with Juan, the next minute I hear you and Carlos had a shootout and that you are both dead. I was happy Carlos was gone, the prick, but my angel, I cried when I heard the news. And now you are here with me, and my life is good again."

J leaned over and touched Junior's face, "Thank you my friend for your tears. I see a lot of shit in many places and it's good to see some people are still good friends." She leaned back and continued to speak to him, "Juan and I were in New York and he started to act strange. Little things like making phone calls in the other room to be sure I couldn't hear him, yelling at me for nothing, and more anger than normal. I suspected my ship had sprung a leak, and I jumped quickly. My sources verified that someone was giving Juan information about my other life; therefore, I set a test to see if it was in or out of the office. Unfortunately, it was in the office and Carlos found me. My partner here shot Carlos before I found out anything else." She quickly looked at me and said, "But I'm damn glad you did, so don't read that the wrong way."

I smiled but said nothing. I was the silent partner. My training as a therapist helped me see when people play roles and pretend to be someone other than who they really are. In this case, I was playing the silent partner role very eloquently, since I no longer had any idea who I really was supposed to be.

J continued, "I pulled enough stuff on Juan to take him and a whole lot of people down, but I decided to take him down myself. The office gave me a week to find him. After that, they'll be taking action based on evidence. If I know Juan, he'll drop south as soon as he smells anything, and I want to get him before he jumps."

Junior repositioned his frame and the chair screamed in agony. "What makes you think he's still in Miami?"

105

J laughed, "Unlike you, I'm sure he thinks I'm still alive and wants to be sure I'm dead before he goes. However, I want to find him before he finds me."

Junior sighed deeply, "My angel, why not let this go away. If Juan wants you dead, you'll be dead. I have cried for you once and do not want to do it again. In addition, if Juan knows your quiet friend here killed Carlos, neither one of you are long for this world. Go away from here and let your white color flunkies do their legal things. You are too precious for me to lose again."

We all sat quietly for a while and finally Junior leaned forward and poured three more shots. He handed them to us and said, "I know I talk to the wind, for you'll not stop until you finish with him. He treated you badly these years and I've wanted him dead for what he did to you. Now, I will do all I can to help put your mind at rest." Raising his glass, he said "Fuck Juan."

We both replied "Fuck Juan" and downed our shot. As the burning once again set my throat afire, I pondered the fact that I wouldn't know Juan if he walked in the room. He was pissed and he wanted me dead, yet I might have passed him on the street and never known him. I wonder if the trout ever think, as the line tightens and they are pulled from the safety of the water, "Hey wait, I don't even know this guy, and what's he got against me." I doubt it; they only have a brain the size of a pencil point.

J stood and gave Junior a big hug. We shook hands and he smiled at me. "Take care of her gringo; she is the best person you will ever meet. If something happens to her and you are still alive, I will hold you personally responsible."

We both smiled at his comment, but inside I understood he wasn't kidding. Such lovely people I was meeting on my vacation. I couldn't wait to put a scrapbook together when, and if, I got home.

We left the office and I was once again an instant admirer of the dancer. She was talented, healthy, and wonderfully naked. I felt a tug on my arm as J said, "Come on playboy, she would eat you alive and not know she had dinner. I have better plans for you."

Night had fallen on Miami as we headed east toward the beach. The neighborhood changed as we progressed and it became younger and more active. The old days of Miami being the home for retirees was long past as the majority of the people on the street were closer to twenty than seventy. As we worked our way out of Miami and drove back toward Hollywood, we came to a less-populated stretch marked Haulover Beach Park where J pulled the car off the road and into the parking lot.

"Come on baby, we need some beach air," she said as she grabbed my hand and led me toward the water. I was about to tell her that the beach air on the condo's balcony was great, but decided J never did anything unless she had a plan in mind. We walked through a tunnel going under the highway and found a beautiful stretch of white sand. The half moon glistened on the water and sand as we walked hand in hand down to the water's edge and sat quietly.

"What'd you think of Junior?" She asked.

"He appears devoted to you."

She laughed and said, "He is, but will sell me out without thinking if it works for his good. I trust him more than a lot of the others, but he's only out for Junior and no one else. That's the law of this business. Trust no one, especially those you trust."

"What makes you think he won't sell you out this time?" I asked.

"Because he hates Juan as much as I do," she said with bitterness in her voice.

Sitting in the moonlight, I saw a very wounded and complex woman. "What did Juan do to you J? This seems almost a personal vendetta."

"Oh Steve," she replied, "I've lost track of all he did to me. It was my job and I didn't expect to be treated well. Your heart becomes a piece of marble when you're with these people. They laugh and joke and you have all the money and shit you need. However, in their hearts they're pure evil. Life means nothing to them."

I felt the anger in her words and knew there were deep scars left by all she had experienced. Part of my philosophy on life encompassed the thought that all humankind was good; nevertheless, we often made choices that were contrary to that goodness. Some choices come out of learned behavior, some out of stupidity. Listening to J, I decided she would disagree with my philosophy. She had seen the dark side of humanity and knew how evil it could be. My experience and knowledge came from textbooks, hers came from real life. I decided to keep my philosophy to myself.

"We're too serious," she shouted as she jumped to her feet. "We need to chill out."

With that, she pulled off her jeans and top, then headed to the water. As I had anticipated, through much contemplation, she wore nothing under her clothes. The moon shone down on her and the silhouette was stunning as she ran into the waves and dove deeply. I took off my shorts and shirt and ran to join her. I too had nothing underneath, but mine was because the airport didn't sell underwear and I made a mental note to go shopping tomorrow.

The water was warm and felt refreshing to my body. I was somewhat concerned about my stitches until J waded up and threw her arm around my neck. "My partner, we meet naked in the water one more time. Let's see if we remember what we learned last time." As she kissed me, I decided my leg was just fine.

Spreading her legs, her hand guided me into her warmth as she pressed down and held me tight with her legs. Holding her close as the waves gently washed over us, I kissed her deeply tasting salt water, tequila, and passion.

"Oh God, Steve," she whispered faintly. "If we live through all this, I may never let you go."

With that, we both rode the next wave of passion into the oblivion awaiting us. As the waves of the ocean rolled over our flesh, our souls combined into one. For some reason I remembered Dicken's quote, "It was the best of times, it was the worst of times, it was a time to try men's souls." I decided that thought was bullshit. It was simply the best of times.

We languished in the water for a while and finally headed back to our clothes. She took my hand and said, "Let's walk the beach for a while."

I was putting on my shorts, when she grabbed my hand and started walking down the beach. "Haulover's a nude beach, thus no worry about clothes," she said as we walked along. "They sometimes frown on late-night swimmers, but it's no big deal."

The moon gave some light from above, and the beach did have other people on it in various stages of undress. Another couple passed us walking hand in hand, but they were both men and I concluded there was also a gay population here. Looking at her as we walked, her beauty continued to mesmerize me. She may have lived a very different life than I had, but she definitely made this adventure worthwhile.

"What are you thinking about?" She asked.

"You're educated, beautiful, and could do anything you wanted. Is this really revenge for your Dad's death, or is it in your blood?"

"Probably a little of both," she replied. "I'm the daughter of a cop and I guess the apple doesn't fall far from the tree. Dad never complained about my being a girl and not a boy, but I guess I tried to be as tough as he was so he would be proud. The people he and mom hung out with were all streetwise and I learned to handle life from that type of perspective. I guess this life is part of who I am."

"Do you have any family?" I asked.

"I have an uncle — well he's not really an uncle, simply a good friend of my parents; however, he was in a business that was on the wrong side of the law. After Dad died, he became a surrogate father and I think Mom worried I would get involved with his lifestyle. He and Mom had a romantic fling after Dad's death, but she wouldn't stay with him because of his line of work. I

110

spent a lot of time with him over the years and got to know the people in his trade; most of them were little boys who never grew up. They were part of a club and that was their identity."

She turned and looked out at the ocean then continued, "The Columbians are different. They are cruel, cold, and life means nothing to them. We were partying one night and Juan told me to have sex with a friend of his. He and Juan had been together since childhood and this guy wasn't as bad as the others, so I complied. Later, when Juan asked me about it, I told him his friend was very good in bed. Somehow, that pissed Juan off and the next day the guy was dead. You never know what these people will do next."

I thought long about the story she told and realized she'd seen more life in her thirty-some years than the majority of people would see in two lifetimes. "How did you ever get together with Juan?"

She hesitated for a minute and finally replied, "I'm giving you too much information. I think you're a pretty clean-cut guy, and you may not like to hang out with someone who's done all I have."

I looked at her and said, "I have to admit, I'm often spun by the life you seem to have adapted to so easily, but it also brings me a certain feeling of freedom." We stopped and looked at each other as I continued, "You're a beautiful woman, and it's a real thrill to be with you. Nevertheless, I also feel there's another woman inside you—a loving and gentle person. When we were at the falls the other day, there was a sense of being in the presence of someone I knew before. It was strange because I never knew anyone close to being you, but I felt it all the same. I don't connect with many people and I've lived a rather quiet, solitary life, but with you, I felt

I was finally living the life I was destined to have. I'm sure that makes no sense, but all I'm really saying is I don't care what you did or what you do. I'm just really happy I found you."

She reached up, touched my face, and kissed me lightly. "My White Knight, I know exactly what you mean but couldn't put it into words. You said everything I've been feeling and more. I'm also happy that I found you."

We turned and headed back to our clothes. The moon had lowered in the sky and the beach was dark with magnificent stars above us. Overall, other than people trying to kill me, this was a really good vacation.

CHAPTER 15

I awoke to an empty bed. On the nightstand was a note from J saying we had nothing to eat or drink in the apartment so she was going shopping and would meet me at the pool. Throwing on a pair of shorts, I headed outside to the pool area. It was empty at this early hour and the clear water in the pool was inviting, so I dove in and did a few laps to get the kinks out of my body.

Returning to a lounge chair, I stretched out and soaked in the life-giving warmth of the Florida sun. I found my calf no longer swollen and it felt a lot better, so I guessed the warm Florida sun and great sex were cures for everything.

We returned to the apartment after our beach romp and both of us fell into a deep sleep. I remembered her holding me sometime during the night making me think that though I hardly knew this woman, her touch gave me a feeling of comfort I'd seldom

113

obtained from anyone. I'd been married some time ago but it was a mess from the start. We both grew apart about three days into the marriage and after another year agreed it would be best to separate before we truly didn't like each other. I still saw her occasionally and we were mutually supportive but it was a marriage to the wrong person at the wrong time.

Since the divorce, I had several relationships, but never anything to write home about or good enough to pursue. What was different about J? Maybe being under the threat of death since I met her had something to do with it. That does bring some level of excitement to an otherwise ordinary life, but on the other hand, maybe she was the spark I'd been looking to light my journey. Both ways, this woman fascinated me and I hoped we would get through this shit and have time to build on our rather sketchy foundation.

A waiter came by and I ordered a Bloody Mary and a black coffee. As long as I was on vacation, I may as well enjoy my life, while I had a life. I opened my laptop and powered up a Wi-Fi connection; I had twelve emails from Laura. I read three and deleted the remainder knowing if you read one, you'd read them all. The bastard was doing his normal thing and the victim was doing her normal thing. How beautiful it was when two people made each other ecstatically happy.

Thinking about the bastard, I wondered why he stayed with Laura and concluded he was probably the product of a strong-willed, non-nurturing mother. Thus, Laura would be a continuation of the drama he'd come to love and hate equally. Applying that thought to J, I wondered about her mother. J obviously idolized

Dad and tried to be a reflection of him. Maybe he was distant, non-nurturing, and she was a performer now trying to win love and affection. What the hell, I was on vacation, no more psychobabble.

I looked over the top of my laptop and saw this goddess enter the pool area wearing a bikini whose material barely covered her beautiful body. Her long dark hair silhouetted her in the sunshine and I thought how wonderful it would be to know her; then I laughed, because I already did know her. J came over, handed me a paper, kissed me deeply, and jumped in the pool. I watched her swim several laps effortlessly until she came to my side of the pool and exited the water like a mermaid vision.

Throwing her a towel I asked, "My beautiful mermaid, what's the plan now?"

She stretched out on the chaise next to me and replied, "I'm waiting for Junior to get back to me. If he knows anything, we'll follow his information. If we don't hear soon, it's back to Miami and try another one of my contacts. I checked with my office and they're sure Juan is in Miami, but word has it he's planning to exit the scene soon. I imagine he'll take off when he's finished with us. It's my plan to be finished with him before he leaves."

I leaned back considering what she said, "I feel I'm a child playing in adult games. It all sounds workable, but I don't understand the purpose. If Juan's in Miami, and you have the information to really damage his organization, why not let this thing go and use what you have to close his shop?"

She sighed and said, "Last night you said this sounded personal, and you were right. I spent two years watching this man work, and he was pure evil. I crossed him and he'll never forget that fact. If he got away, both of us would spend the remainder of our days looking over our shoulder. You have no idea how powerful Juan's connections are. He has politicians, cops, thugs, and even a few national leaders in his pocket and we're going to be outgunned at every turn. Therefore, we only have one choice— close Juan down permanently. You're much more than a child in an adult game and if I could have sent you away and known you would be safe, I'd have done it. But I believe you're up to the challenge, and I also know I don't want to face all this without you."

She reached over and took my hand in hers, "I'm a loner, Steve. It's part of how I live. Somehow, in the five days since we've crossed paths in the trout stream, I've lost some of my desire for independence. Oh, I'll always be a handful," she laughed as she rolled from her lounge chair onto my stomach. "But I sure do enjoy my life with you. I hope you feel the same or I'll have to kill you."

I wrapped my arms around her and said, "In the last five days, I've had more people threaten to kill me than I have in the proceeding 35 years of life. However, your threat doesn't worry me at all, because I feel the same about you and am relieved to know we share that common emotion. And yes, my beautiful undercover cop, you are definitely a handful, but I love it when my hands are full of you."

We looked at each other for a minute and as we kissed with gentleness, lying there in the early morning Florida sun, I realized how much I was enjoying my vacation. In fact, I was finally enjoying my life. I only hoped I would live long enough to enjoy it a lot more.

"If we stay in this position," J whispered quietly. "We'll probably draw a crowd. Some people in the complex are too old for this excitement, why not take it inside and I'll fix you breakfast."

"You're the senior partner, I follow your lead. However, I'll fix you breakfast. It's the only meal I cook and I want you to remain impressed."

We went inside and I'm sure some of the balcony sitters were disappointed we took away their show. J showered while I fixed some eggs and bacon from the multitude of supplies she had purchased. She came out to eat with a towel wrapped around her head and nothing around her body.

"Ummm. . . smells good," she said as she sat at the table.

"Damn, you look . . . . ," I stammered.

"Go ahead, say it and then sit down."

I sat down and said, "You look good enough to eat."

She pulled the towel off her head and said, "Eat your breakfast and we'll see what develops."

We small talked through breakfast, which was not easy when sitting across from a beautiful naked woman, but my cooking was superb so we focused on the food. As we were cleaning up, J's phone rang and I had the sinking feeling there would be no dessert after breakfast.

She answered, listened for a while, frowned and said, "I don't understand why." She listened intently then replied, "Don't fuck with me Junior; I have too much riding on this to be stupid. I'll do what you ask, but if you cross me, it will be a drastic end to a beautiful friendship." She listened for a minute more, closed her phone and sat on the couch.

117

"What did he say?" I asked as I sat next to her.

"He has information, but wants to meet to talk."

"Is that a problem?" I asked.

She stood, walked to the window, and looked out at the ocean. Finally, she turned and said, "It doesn't make sense to meet when he could tell me over the phone. He said it was important, and he didn't trust the phones. He's right about that, but we've used them before. He also said to come alone, as he didn't want you involved."

"What do we do?"

"We go, but set it up our way." She went to her backpack and pulled out a map. Opening it, she found the place she was seeking and pointed it out. "He wants to meet in a parking lot near the Everglades Park. I'll be where he wants, but you'll follow me and wait up here on a side road that overlooks the lot. I've used it for surveillance before and it's hidden from the main lot, but still provides access for viewing."

Looking at the map, it made sense, but I was still confused as to my purpose. "What if there's a problem? How can I help from there?"

She reached in her backpack again and handed me a cell phone. "If you see a problem push #1 and it will automatically alert my office I'm in trouble. The GPS will give tracking and they'll close in and help."

"I don't like it," I said. "If there's a problem, that plan might take too long to work."

"Junior and I will meet in a wide open parking lot that is only used for weekend overflow. I'll be able to see anything that looks

118

suspicious and be able to act accordingly. If things go bad, hit the button and head for the parking lot fast. You'll provide the distraction I need so I can take any action necessary." Saying this she lifted her gun from the table and smiled. I concluded that when a naked woman stands with a gun in her hand, simply go along with her plan.

We dressed and headed to our separate cars. J was back in her wig and wore slacks and a shirt covering her gun. I thought about asking for a gun, but after Carlos, I really wasn't into shooting anyone, no matter what the provocation. Exiting the complex, J was out of the parking lot and down the road before I cleared my parking space. Moving rap[idly, I finally got close enough to see her about a dozen cars ahead of me.

We took the Florida Turnpike south to the Everglades Park and she motioned for me to pass her so I could settle into my lookout above the parking lot. I found the exit with the service road she had indicated and slowly drove up the hill above the lot. As promised, the spot she picked was ideal for cover, so I pulled into a small clearing and faced the car toward the lot.

The density of the trees covered my location, but I still saw the lot below through the branches. J's was the only car in the lot and the park entrance was easy to spot from my location. I watched as she got out of her car and opened the trunk. As she rummaged around in the trunk, a large black Escalade approached the entrance and came across the lot toward J. I was not surprised to see the side windows darkened so no one could see inside; that seemed to be a norm for the cars and trucks these boys owned.

J closed the trunk and faced the Escalade as Junior emerged from the driver's side. It appeared he was alone once he finally got his girth out the door and walked over to J. I noted there were no fond embraces at this meeting; if anything, he kept looking over his shoulder as if he was extremely nervous. I settled into my viewing space and watched, not knowing the next five minutes would be some of the longest I had ever experienced.

CHAPTER 16

Watching Junior walk toward her, J sensed he was in an extreme state of anxiety. He stopped short and once again glanced around the parking lot as if he expected people to come out of the ground.

"Why are you acting nervous Junior?" J asked. "You expecting company?"

"Shit, my angel troublemaker—being with you is a problem," he said quietly as he stopped short of her. "I want to talk quick and get out before anyone even thinks I am here."

"So talk," J said as she quietly loosened her shirt over her gun. "What's so fucking important that we have to meet out here in the middle of nowhere?"

Once again looking around he quietly said, "You, my angel, have not given me straight talk. That is not a good way to treat a friend."

She sensed from his tone that something was definitely wrong, "What are you talking about, Junior; I didn't tell you anything false."

"That is the problem my angel, you didn't tell me anything at all. I am told that Juan is looking for you not because he loves you or because you are a snitch. He is looking for you because you took his money."

J laughed and stepped toward Junior, "You're kidding me. Do you think I'd come looking for him if I took his cash? Damn, Junior, what kind of jerk do you take me for anyway? I didn't take his fucking money, although I wish I had for all the shit he pulled on me. Why would you even believe such crap?"

"I trust the people who told me this. They would not make it up, my angel; they would rather die than lie. Now prove me wrong and open that trunk you were playing with when I drove up. It will be a good place to start to rebuild our friendship."

J took her car keys, tossed them to Junior, and said, "Here, open it yourself and have a look."

As he reached to grab the keys, J pulled her gun and aimed it at Junior. Too late, he realized her subterfuge, but he lifted his hands slowly, still clutching her car keys. "It is true what they tell me," he said with a sound of sadness.

She raised the gun and took another step toward Junior, "No, it is still a lie, but now I have control and I want you to give me answers. When you finish talking, you can open the trunk and steal the spare tire for all I care. What did you find out and why did you want to meet me here?"

Still holding his hands in the air, he answered, "I checked around after you left the other day. I heard things before you showed up, but figuring you were dead, I didn't pay attention. When you showed up at my place, I began to remember the small talk of my friends. I checked and found you've been skimming from Juan for a while and I have no problem with that, because he is a piece of shit and deserves it. However, I hear you walked off with ten big ones. That my angel was the beginning of your downfall."

J looked at him and held her gun steady, "You think I took $10,000,000 from Juan? What were you going to do today—help me spend it? Or were you going to kill me and take it all for yourself?"

"My angel, I will help you," he replied. "Juan is in the harbor and I know where. If he is gone, we split the money and not worry about him finding out." He smiled and started to lower his hands.

"Don't move a fucking inch," J said. "Where is he in the harbor?"

"Oh baby, you don't think I am going to let you know and then watch as you keep the money and run."

"Junior, I don't have his money, but I'm going to get him with you or without. Now be a good boy, tell me where he is and after that, get into your fancy car, drive away nicely, and we'll continue our friendship talk another day."

Junior smiled again and said quietly, "I don't think that's going to happen. What do you think we should do to get out of this

123

problem?" His eyes suddenly darted up and looked behind J. She was tempted to look behind, but held her vision tight on Junior. "Shit," was all he said as he spun away from her running to his car. J heard the sound of another car and finally turned to look. A large black limo was streaking across the lot, heading directly for her.

She ran toward Junior's car and ducked behind as she heard the first shots from the limo. She dove to the ground, rolled behind the Escalade as she felt the bullets impact into the car's frame. The limo slid to a stop and someone jumped out of the passenger seat firing several rounds from the automatic he held. She heard glass explode and as she looked under the car, she saw Junior slide to the ground. He looked directly at her, but he didn't see a thing. A red dot in the middle of his forehead guaranteed that Junior was no longer in the fight.

***

I watched as J talked to Junior and was very surprised to see J draw a gun on him. She'd thrown something to him and as he caught it, she took advantage of his distraction. The more I watched them, the less I liked it. Deciding I had to do something, I started the car and was about to back out when I saw a black limo race into the parking lot and head for J and Junior.

Junior ran to his car, but was unable to enter the driver's side before the limo slid to a stop as the person in the passenger seat jumped out and shot him. Junior fell to the ground and the gunman released another volley into the Escalade.

124

Without thinking, I floored my car and started down the hill, through the trees and toward the parking lot. The sound of breaking glass and crunching metal indicated Hertz was not going to be happy with my driving.

The car hit the parking lot as the gunman looked my way allowing J to stand behind the Escalade and shoot. The shot hit him in the head throwing him back from the limo where he disappeared from view.

I was heading toward the limo on the driver's side when the driver suddenly opened his door as I collided with him and the door at the same moment. The look in his eyes expressed the realization of his mistake before our pathways crossed. The impact caused him to bounce off my hood and over the car. The limo's driver side door gave way on impact and flew out into the lot. I swung around the front of the limo and slammed on the brakes. J ran to my car and jumped in screaming, "Go, go go!"

I stomped on the gas and fishtailed toward the exit. In the mirror, I saw another man get out of the limo and take aim at us. His shots rang out, but nothing touched us as we left the parking lot and headed for the highway.

"Turn left," J shouted as we sped out of the park.

"Left! That will take us up the hill where I was before," I shouted back at her.

"Just fucking do it."

I never argue with a woman with a gun. Even if she wasn't naked anymore, I did what she said and moved back up to the road overlooking the parking lot until she signaled to stop and turn off the engine. J jumped out of the car and, having no clues what else

125

to do, I followed her. We came to a space in the trees in time to see the Escalade drive off toward the highway.

"Is that Juan?" I asked her as we watched the car head out the exit and go past the road we had taken.

"Bigger than life and twice as mean," she said. She turned and put her arms around me and held me tight. "Thanks baby, that's twice you saved my life. I really owe you big time."

Holding her close, I tried to sort out what had happened. Looking down at the parking lot, J's car and the limo sat where we left them along with both the driver and the shooter from the limo lying on the parking lot. In the spot the Escalade occupied was Junior's body. All three appeared quite dead. Four days into the vacation and I already killed two men. I needed a vacation from my vacation. As J pulled back, I looked at her and asked, "What the hell was that all about?"

Turning, she headed back to the car and said, "I don't know if Junior sold me out or Juan was cleaver enough to find us. Either way it didn't work out well for Junior."

"Why did you pull a gun on Junior?" I asked her.

"He was being too cute and nervous so I took precaution. He never did get around to telling what he wanted to say. It was a useless waste of time."

Looking back at the parking lot and seeing the bodies lying around, I asked, "What now?" The reality of what had taken place began to sink into my mind and as I looked at my Impala, I knew Hertz was really going to be pissed. I took consolation knowing I rented it with a false identification and it wouldn't be on my record. Then I remembered I killed two men in four days, been shot

126

at four times, and hit once. I decided my car insurance record was the least of my problems.

"Juan is long gone and we need to get out of here fast," she said. "I'm going down the hill on foot to get my car. Turn yours around and meet on the exit road. There's a mall one exit down and you need to dump the car in the back of the lot. Leave the keys, call a cab, and go back to the condominium. I'll meet you there."

I must admit I was somewhat relieved to think I wouldn't have to face Hertz. "Where are you going?" I asked her.

She started down the hill and simply said, "Meet me on the exit road and we'll talk."

I returned to the Impala, turned it around, and drove to the exit road. I arrived as she pulled up and jumped out of her car. She had a briefcase in her hand and handed it to me through the window. "Take this back to the condo and keep it safe, it has very important papers about Juan. I have to go find some information and I'll catch up with you later. When you get back, do not go outside the condo until you hear from me."

"What about the bodies back there?" I asked. "Should I hit #1 on the phone?"

She looked quizzically as I produced the phone she'd given me. I could tell by her look that the phone wasn't what she indicated. "You lied to me about the phone," I said. "Why?"

"It made you feel safer," she said. "Keep it on and I'll call you but don't use it or any phone to call out. Now, go, we have to be out of here fast. I'm sure someone, someplace heard the shots and will come to see what happened." She walked to her car, stopped and returned. Lowering her head into the window, she kissed me,

"I'm sorry I got you into all this mess, but I'm really happy you're here." She kissed me again, ran back to her car, and made a fast exit from the park.

I sat there for a few minutes and finally caught my breath. I knew I had to get going, but needed to sit for a second and compose myself. I'd become much too casual with people dying and knew I was simply in denial of reality. My hands were shaking and my stomach was very close to making an exit through my mouth.

I was definitely in trouble for all I had done, but, in all honesty, I didn't know who I was in trouble with or what to do to make it better. J lied about the phone and I had a feeling she was not telling me the whole truth about all the events going on around us. Junior told her something—they talked too long for there to be nothing said. In addition, what was with the briefcase she gave me? I placed my hand on it as if it would explode, but nothing happened. Taking a deep breath, I put the car in gear and pulled out of the park. At least I was able to leave alive, which was more than I could say for Junior and his associates behind me.

As I hit the highway, it became obvious the last several miles had been very difficult on my rental car. The front end was shaking all around when I got over 50 mph. It was fortunate the exit to the mall appeared down the road and I limped into the back of the parking lot. The inside of the car was in good shape, but the outside had the appearance of a loser in a demolition derby.

The obvious plan for the parking lot was for someone to steal the car thus distancing my connection with the damages—but I really doubted anyone would even want to steal it. That part of the plan was not my problem; therefore, I grabbed the briefcase, left the key in the ignition, and walked into the mall. At least I would be able to buy some underwear—I was getting tired of going commando and wanted the security of my boxers. I was amazed that I hadn't wet my shorts after the last episode in the parking lot, but fortunately, my bladder kept its part of the bargain and didn't malfunction.

The sparsely filled mall provided cool relief after the hot Florida sun. I bought a dozen boxers and shirts with the taxpayer's money and decided a new pair of sneakers would also be a good idea as I was still walking around in my hunting boots and Bermuda shorts. I slipped on my boxers and sneakers in the men's room and then glanced at my reflection in the mirror. Somehow, I expected to look different. I assumed that a criminal murderer on the run from the mob would look either very cool or very haggard—but I looked the same as I did last week. "Looks are deceiving," I muttered to myself and went into the mall to see if I might find an open bar. I desperately needed a drink and water was not my first request.

I found the Caribbean Bar and Restaurant open and felt relieved that I was the only person at the bar. I ordered a Corona and tequila from an attractive barmaid with a low-cut sweater whose nametag on her left breast said "KIM." I thought about asking her the name of the other one, but fortunately, for both of us, I drank my shot, followed with a slug of Corona, and kept my sick humor to myself. Pondering my life, I felt a great kinship with the lime in my bottle of Corona. It innocently sat in the top of the bottle and now, through no request of its own, found itself down the neck floating in beer from which it had no escape. I thought about the floating lime a long time, which was a frightening indication of my mental state.

My hands stopped shaking and my stomach loved the burn of tequila, but my emotional system was on overload. Somewhere, about 1,800 miles away, a trout stream existed with my name on it. It was Monday and I had fully planned to wake this morning and catch a big rainbow. Instead, I was sitting in the outskirts of Miami, at a Caribbean Bar, with three dead bodies down the road.

Kim came by and as I ordered another round, I had a great desire to jump over the bar, hold her, and cry. Definitely manifesting some posttraumatic stress disorder symptoms, I nursed my second beer, ordered a hamburger, and finally worked up enough strength to find a cab back to the condominium.

Leaving Kim and her unnamed breast a large tip from the taxpayer's money, I walked out into the Florida sunshine. A couple of older Florida residents were slowly disengaging themselves from a cab and I patiently waited while they completed the task. I gave the driver directions and asked him to go back on the turnpike instead of heading toward the beach. As we passed the exit to the park, I tried to see if any police activity was taking place, but saw nothing through the trees.

Silently watching the park go by I thought about Junior lying in the lot. He would have no more big meals with big deals. I wondered if he liked his life or was it something he simply grew into over the years. The guy I hit with the car was an unknown, and while I was still shaken I'd killed him, it was Junior I thought about most. Two beers and two tequilas on an empty stomach seemed to

130

provide me deep insight on life. At that moment, my deepest insight was that I missed my trout stream a hell of a lot.

***

J left the parking lot, swiftly got off the main highway, and headed into a residential neighborhood. Finding a place to park, she pulled her phone and speed dialed a number. It rang a few times and then answered by, "Nuevo Auto."

"Tommy, this is J."

A long silence followed by, "I'll call you back."

She waited for a few minutes and when her cell phone rang and she heard a voice say, "I'm at a pay phone. Do you know what deep shit you are in right now?"

"Tommy, I don't need a lecture, I need a car."

"What do you want?" He asked cautiously. "I only got a few that are currently clean."

"You have something that is low profile and has a good engine? I'll give you the Shelby in trade. You know it runs great."

"The Shelby plus $20,000 and you got a deal," he said with more confidence in his voice.

"The Shelby, $10,000, and I don't turn over my notes on you to the feds," she said. "Now stop fucking with me and get things ready. Clean tags and just off the street."

"I'm waiting for you at the shop," he said. "Don't plan to stop here. Just get the car and go; I don't need you hanging around anyplace close to me. You are way too hot and people are going down for knowing you. I don't know you, understand?"

"I understand Tommy. Leave me some travel information in the car when I pick it up."

131

"What travel information, J? I don't know you nor where you want to go, so I can't give you information, can I?"

"I want to know what harbor Juan is staying in. As an exchange I won't send your wife those pictures we had taken last year."

The line went dead, but J was sure he would give her some information, however pissed he may be. Tommy was always a good party guy and ran a good chop shop. He could take a car fresh off the street, change its looks, numbers, tags, color, and have it ready in six hours. While she hated to lose the Shelby, she knew she was a sitting duck for Juan as long as she was in it.

Heading to Tommy's, she ran over the conversation with Junior and tried to piece it all together. Somehow, Juan had found out about Junior meeting her. Too much bad blood existed between Junior and Juan for Junior to work for him. In the end, Junior's greed had killed him. He saw $10,000,000 and decided some of it belonged to him. All he got was a bullet worth about $.50.

Nevertheless, it also showed J that Juan was definitely onto the money she had taken, and was not going to stop until he got it back. He now had many problems as he tried to convince people their accounts were safe and secure, especially after J managed to pull out $15,000,000 and send it to various places he would never find. Juan was in deep trouble and needed her to give him the account numbers to keep people from killing him. The thought of him being worried brought great joy to her; the thought of him dead brought even greater joy.

J found Tommy outside his shop, standing by a black Mercedes. She got out of her car and Tommy threw her keys to the Mercedes.

"Don't stay and talk J," he said as he stood on the curb and looked at her. "Put the money on the seat of the Shelby and then leave."

"Same old charming Tommy," J responded as she threw the cash into the car. "I hope you put all the information I need in the Mercedes, or I'll have to come and have a long talk with you."

"I hate to say it, J, but I really don't think you'll be alive long enough to use what I left you. But what the hell—it's been fun knowing you." He walked by her and got in the Mustang, backed it up, and drove off without another word.

J got in the Mercedes and found an envelope on the seat. Knowing Tommy was nervous for a reason, she started up the car and turned toward south Miami. At a stoplight, she opened the envelope and saw that Tommy had left an address on a sheet of paper.

Bayside Marina by the arena. You know the boat.

J knew the marina and she was sure she knew the boat. The boat was actually a 47' yacht, which served as one of Juan's toys, and she had spent a lot of time aboard it. The yacht was a floating party covering many of the deals Juan made with his people. If Juan was there, he'd be leaving soon, as he didn't stay in one place too long and a lot of people knew the yacht by sight.

What should she do with Steve? This showdown with Juan was going to be sticky, but she had other problems that complicated the situation. Steve knew most of the story about Juan

133

and he'd be able to go with the flow as she needed. However, he didn't know the other levels she was running simultaneously and they were impossible to explain to him. Whatever the case, she needed to close down all her activities and locations in Miami. After dealing with Juan, if she survived, she would never be able come to Miami again.

She came to a small housing complex in south Miami and pulled into the driveway of a pink stucco house, which was in dire need of a paint job. She sat and looked at the place for a minute remembering all the times she fled here when life with Juan just got too much to handle. How many black eyes and bruised ribs had she nursed back to health in the confines of this rundown escape?

She exited the car and went into the house by the side door. This was the only place she ever felt secure when she lived in Miami. The neighbors never interacted and it was in a part of town people didn't come visit. It was a dump, but she loved it because it provided her an escape from all the crap she lived with on a daily basis.

Throwing off her clothes, she jumped into a shower and washed away the dirt and memories of the day. Poor Junior, he could've left well enough alone, but had to push things until he ended up dead. These guys were never satisfied with what they had, they always needed to go up one more notch and then, bang, it all would fall apart. That was why she wanted out now. She'd pushed things to the limit and if she didn't stop soon, she'd join the losers six feet under the Miami sand.

Leaving the shower, she grabbed a cold beer and went to the bedroom. Entering a walk-in closet, J moved her clothes aside and bent down to the floor where she lifted a board and set it aside. Pulling out the metal box, she carried it to the bed and flipped through the combination lock. She removed three full packs of identification from inside; they were first-class passes to any place she wanted to go in the world. They'd cost a bundle, but what the hell; it was all Juan's money. She pulled out two packs of cash containing a total of $100,000 and below that, she removed a package and set it on the bed.

She touched the package and realized that it contained over two years of her life. Two years of living hell that provided her enough information to ruin Juan forever—for the package contained all the original transactions showing the new accounts that held Juan's money. One envelope had all the names and accounts for $10,000,000 and the other had names and accounts for $5,000,000. They both had mailing addresses on them and J would stop at a local Fed Ex office to make sure they went to the right locations.

After throwing a few items of clothes and the $100,000 cash into a suitcase, she pulled back the covers and slipped into the comfort of the bed. She was going to need all the rest she could get before meeting Juan. The problem with Steve still hadn't resolved itself, but as she drifted off to sleep, she was sure she wanted to keep him near her, for a very long time.

CATCH AND RELEASE
TWERELL

CHAPTER 17

I got back to the condo around 4:00 and went for a swim to loosen up my tired body. The warm water in the ocean and the light surf were perfectly in tune and brought harmony to my soul. The ocean always amazed me whenever I spent time looking out on it. There was so much life in the water that we couldn't even comprehend the abundance. Yet, from a distance, it appeared to be a vast emptiness. I couldn't imagine the early explorers heading out on the ocean and expecting the world to end. I've been on ships when you can't see land on any side and it's a rather scary situation. To be on the ocean, think you may come to the end of the world, and see nothing but water all around you—that was an overwhelming thought. The Viking explorers rocked!!

Back in the room, I showered, opened a beer, and sat on the balcony to watch the evening shadows descend. My view was the wrong direction to see the sunset, but it was still peaceful. Expecting J to be home soon, I didn't bother to fix anything to eat, instead I laid in the lounge chair, watched the ocean roll in, and felt the day begin to cool down into night. I was holding J and she was naked and warm. She kissed me deeply and as an alarm went off, she sat up and shot me. I lurched up and realized I was dreaming. However, the alarm was real, as the phone she gave me was ringing.

She was the only person who knew the phone number, so I answered anxious to hear her voice. Instead, a male answered my hello with, "Dr. Sanders?"

I almost said yes until I realized I was Robert Klingman and not Steve Sanders. I responded, "Sorry, wrong number." Nevertheless, before I could hang up I heard him say, "Dr. Sanders, I have a message from Jennifer Blade."

I paused a minute and said, "I don't think I know the name. Who is this?"

"Listen, Doc, I'm Special Agent Matt Dawson with the FBI and I know you're a friend of J. I have an agent outside your door and I'm on my way up to see you. Don't do anything stupid. I only want to talk."

I heard the phone cut off and sat staring at it for a long time. The FBI was coming to see me. "Shit," I said as I heard a knock. "This cannot be a happy surprise."

I put the chain on the door and opened it enough to see a man standing outside. He was in his mid-thirties, with short dark hair, dark suit, and dark tie. Only the FBI would dress that way in Florida.

"Let me see some ID," I said to the space in the door and he handed me the credentials that read Special Agent Matthew Dawson, Federal Bureau of Investigation, New York City, New York. In reality, asking for ID and looking at it carefully was a waste of time because it could be a fake and who the hell would know. By the looks of Special Agent Matthew Dawson, if I gave him back his ID and told him "no thanks, I gave at the office", I would find my door knocked down and my own body in serious trouble. I handed back his ID, closed the door, undid the chain, and opened to let him into the apartment. Along with Special Agent Matthew Dawson, another well-groomed man entered the apartment, but he had on a sports coat and light slacks. He was probably with the Miami FBI.

"Dr. Sanders, you're a hard person to find," said Special Agent Matthew Dawson.

"Gee, Matt," I replied with a smile. "I forgot all about the fact you were trying to find me. In fact, I don't think I ever even knew you were trying to find me, and that is why it was hard to find me, because I'm on vacation and didn't want to see anybody, especially somebody that I don't know."

I finally ran out of breath and stopped talking. When I'm nervous I rattle on, and that might have been a new record. "Now that you found me, what are we supposed to do? Is this a "Tag your IT" move, or are you simply passing through and wanted to say hi?"

I finally told myself to shut the fuck up before they arrested me for talking too much.

139

"Dr. Sanders, you've been a busy person and are in some real deep problems. We have strong evidence you were involved in a shootout today over in Everglade park. That little party left three men dead and a limo very torn apart. Would you like to tell me what happened out there?"

"Matt, I've been here enjoying the Florida sun and getting some siesta time. I really don't know what you're talking about."

He motioned for me to sit down and I obeyed. I saw the gun under his jacket, and even if he was a male and had all his clothes on, I still follow direction from those who have the gun.

"Dr. Sanders, we really don't have time for the games. We found your rental car, rather beat up and filled with your fingerprints. I know you will tell me it was stolen, but the prints on the keys match yours, so nobody drove it except you. You left it in Thruway Mall hoping someone would steal it, but nobody wanted it. We know you are friendly with Jennifer Blade, and we know you are under the alias of Robert Klingman. All in all, we know enough to take you into custody, but we can avoid that unpleasantness if you will simply tell me the truth."

He gave me one of those "fuck you" smiles and waited for a reply. Well, I am a terrible liar, and J told me these were her people so what the hell, truth time.

"Matthew, Special Agent Blade knows all that is going on and I'm sure she'll bring you up to date when she arrives." I said this with my best "fuck you back" smile.

He shook his head and staring directly at me replied, "There is no Special Agent Blade, Dr. Sanders. Jennifer Blade is a con woman who's been tight with the Columbian families for a couple

of years. We finally got enough on her to bring her in for
questioning and she agreed to help us if we cut her a deal. We did,
but she decided to do it her way. She killed off one of the top drug
leaders, stole a bunch of money from a dealer who is way up the
ladder of bad guys, and we think she was involved in the shootout
in Everglade Park. I think you need to tell me what's going on so
we can work together to try to keep you out of anymore trouble."

He smiled at me with a "fuck you and checkmate" look, while
I simply sat there and stared at him with the appearance of a man
who was dead meat. My thoughts were frantic and confused.
Dawson claimed J was not a Fed? No way was that true. She'd
called for backup in the mountains when we shot Carlos. However,
as I further thought about that day, I had to admit I never saw the
backup. She did arrange a new identity and gave me money, but I
didn't know if it was Fed work or her work. Carlos did say he
knew she sold Juan out, but he never said she was a federal agent.

Suddenly I had a thought, "If she is not an agent, what was the
story in the New York Post. It said she was the agent who died. I
know she wasn't killed, but I also know they wouldn't print that
unless someone could vouch for it."

"Doc, you really don't believe everything you read in the
papers do you?"

I had a growing feeling that I really did not like Matthew
Dawson. He shook his head as if I was a child doing something
stupid and said, "That was the cover we gave her after the shootout
with Carlos in the mountains. It was part of the deal she made and
it would have worked if she hadn't cut out on us. Now enough of

the bullshit, Dr. Sanders. Tell me what you and J were doing on that parking lot and how the hell three men ended up dead?"

I had a sinking feeling I'd fallen into a lie and now I was going to be put away for life with no chance of parole. This vacation really sucked.

"Anything you would like to say, Dr. Sanders"

I continued to stare at him and finally said, "Shit."

He pulled out a notepad and said, "You probably should amplify on that thought."

"Special Agent Dawson, I think I've gotten in over my head and now I'm going to drown. J told me she was undercover with FBI and Narcotics. She and I met in New York and came down here for some fun. This thing in the parking lot was supposed to be a time of getting information she could pass on to what she called her "office." We met with a guy named Junior, and things went okay until this black limo pulled into the lot and headed toward us. I pulled away and cut around behind the limo as it started to pour out gunfire. I think either J or Junior killed one shooter and I caught the other one on my front bumper as I went back for J. She told me to ditch the Chevy and head back here. That's what happened until you showed up and blew my world apart."

Special Agent Dawson made a few notes in his little book and put it in his coat pocket. He looked up to the other agent who, I realized, had not been introduced nor had he spoken. The agent shook his head "no" to Dawson and left through the front door. I had no idea what the "no" meant, but I truly hoped it wasn't a reply to "should Dr. Sanders live?"

Dawson stood and went to look out of the balcony doors. "Sanders, you have really gotten yourself into a mess," he said as he looked out toward the ocean. "This is what's going to happen, and you don't have a choice. You will pack your bag and be at the airport for the first flight you can find back to New York. You'll forget all this happened and go back to your safe life. If you ever decide to talk about this or to try to find J, I will be sure to open a file on you that will guarantee you a permanent practice in one of our worst prisons for life. Do you have any questions?" He turned and looked at me with a look that would turn cotton candy to stone.

I shook my head no, but thought again and said, "What if she calls me?"

"If she does, call me," he said as he handed me a business card. "But I doubt she'll live long enough to ever talk to you again."

Once again, I summarized the events of the day with a profound thought, "Shit."

CHAPTER 18

After my new friend Special Agent Matthew Dawson left, I
went to the bedroom and found it in a state of disarray. Obviously,
the other agent had been through my things while Special Agent
Dawson was ruining my life in the other room. I now understood
what the "no" signal was from the other agent. He was looking for
something and didn't find it. I went to the bed, lifted up the
mattress and pulled out J's briefcase. This could have been what he
was looking for, but that was only a guess on my part. I looked at it
for a minute and tried to open it. Unfortunately, I found that it had
a combination lock and I didn't have the combination. I threw it on
the bed and went to the kitchen to see if my friend Johnny Walker
was up for some relaxation.

Sitting on the balcony, I tried to sort out all I'd been handed
by Special Agent Dawson and the not-so-Special-Agent Jennifer

Blade, also known as J. I couldn't get my head around the thought that J was lying to me. If she was who Dawson claimed, why would she even want me around? I thought back on the shooting of Carlos and I really believed she wanted me out of there for my own good. She arranged for a doctor in Monticello, but he had never said he worked for the feds; he could have been a mob doctor for all I know. The people who shot at me certainly found me fast, so J could have sold me out. Nevertheless, she seemed genuinely upset that I'd been shot at and did arrange for me to leave town quickly. If she wanted me dead, why not let the drug guys finish the job?

I tried to remember our time with Junior and I vaguely remembered his reference to her white-collar friends. I assumed he was talking about her fellow drug agents, but hell he could be talking about a Chinese laundry for all I knew. The bottom line was—I simply didn't know anything. Nevertheless, whether I understood what was going on or whether I didn't, Agent Dawson had made it clear I was to get my ass back to New York pronto. I pulled up my laptop to check on flights out of Ft. Lauderdale and found a 7:00 am on Jet Blue.

Just for the hell of it, I checked my email and sure enough—another 13 from Laura. I deleted them all. I saw a different one that said, "Call me." I opened it and all it said was 732-665-3871 J. I've lived in New York long enough to know 732 was New Jersey. What the hell was J doing in New Jersey? It could be a cell phone number or maybe she decided to visit the Jersey Shore for some rest and relaxation. I knew the Feds were probably tapping the cell phone she'd given me, but I had no other choice.

I dialed the number and an operator promptly informed me that the number was no longer in service. I dialed again and got the same response. What was that all about? She leaves a number and disconnects it? That didn't make sense—but in the scheme of my rapidly deteriorating life, nothing made sense.

I stared at the numbers for a while and then had a crazy thought. Maybe the numbers were not a telephone after all; maybe they meant something else. Feeling somewhat as if I was in a James Bond movie, I went to the bedroom and grabbed the briefcase. The combination was a four-digit number. First, I tried 7326, and got nothing. Next, I tried 6653 and found the lock unchanged. Finally, I tried 3871 and, behold, the lock opened. I gloated for a few minutes about how smart I was and finally opened the case. Inside it, I found three stacks of $100 bills. A quick guess put the total at about $3000.00 a stack. If nothing else, the vacation was definitely paying for itself. There were several Manila envelopes in the case and a white envelope with my name on it. I opened it and read:

Steve,

If you are reading this, I'm in a place that I can't get to you. You will find another cell phone that is on a phone card rather than a service. Use it to call me at 705-884-3333. We can only talk for a few minutes, so please listen to me and do what I ask. You may need more money, so take the cash with you. Above all things, the envelopes inside have to stay with you at all times. I don't care how you do it, but do not let them out of your sight. Call me.

J

I know my new best friend Agent Matt had said that if J called me, I should let him know. However, he didn't say I should let him know if I called her. I thought about this long and hard, but decided I needed some answers from her before I left for New York. I took the cell phone from the brief case and dialed the number. It rang a few times and I heard, "Hey lover."

I knew the voice and, in spite of my confusion about her identity, I was really glad to hear her, "Hey J, I got a problem. Do you know Special Agent Matthew Dawson?"

"Is he there?"

"He was and gave me some insight I need to have explained. First question, who are you?"

There was a long pause and finally she said, "Was he alone?"

"No, he had some other agent with him, but I never got his name. But you didn't answer my question."

"The other agent—mid thirties, slick back hair, casual dress with a cleft chin?" she asked.

I thought for a minute and remembered the other guy did have a cleft chin like Kirk Douglas. "Yeah, that's him. Do you know him?"

"What did Dawson say?"

I was getting frustrated; she was asking all the questions and I was getting absolutely no answers. "He said that you were not with the Feds, you were with Juan, at least until you took him for a lot of money. I think they were looking for the briefcase because Cleft Chin went through my things in the bedroom, but didn't find it. Now how about answering my question?"

There was a pause and finally she said, "Steve, I know it is hard but you really have to trust me. I am who I said, but now I know Dawson is the leak that's giving me all the problems. The other guy is not a Federal Agent, he is one of Juan's men. I'll explain more later. What did Dawson tell you to do?"

Why is it whenever I get answers to questions I seem to know less than I did when I asked them. "He told me to get my ass back to New York and forget all this happened. I'm going to take a 7am Jet Blue and follow his instructions."

"Ok, stay with that plan for now. I'll call you on this phone."

Then the line went dead. My plight reminded me of the old Abbot and Costello routine about "Who's on first?" I not only had no idea who was on first, I couldn't even find the ballpark. If Dawson was working for Juan, that may be why he didn't introduce me to Cleft Chin; or maybe Dawson was an impolite Federal Agent. If Dawson was the leak, he would want J dead. If Dawson was the leak and he knew I'd talked to J about him, there was a good chance he also may want me dead. Now I had both Juan and Dawson writing my obituary. All I knew for sure was that the 7:00 am flight was definitely my priority. I wanted to get the hell out of all of this as fast as possible.

I looked around the apartment and tried to calm my thinking, a good trick at this point in my adventure. I was not a person who blindly followed other people; however, for some reason I'd allowed J to lead me around like a blind beggar. Granted, she was a gorgeous woman who obviously enjoyed being sexual, but I knew enough women back in New York who leaned the same direction and would be a hell of a lot safer than J.

148

I remembered our time back at the falls and how I felt I had known her before that day. It wasn't a sense of remembering a passing stranger; rather it was like seeing an old friend who I had forgotten. I've read some book on the aspect of connecting to a soul mate, but honestly never placed any credibility in the theory of our meeting people we knew in previous lives. While the concept still wasn't something I embraced, my feeling of knowing J wasn't something I could rationally explain.

One thing I clearly recognized was the voice of my ego screaming at me to get away before someone killed me. My ego didn't want to play J's game, no matter how much pleasure she provided. Nevertheless, a deeper feeling kept pushing to the surface and that one said, "Trust her." I didn't know why I should trust her, but much like the trout, I had to go with my instinct—so I would trust her, until I found a reason proving it to be a bad choice. I secretly hoped that reason would never appear.

I went to the closet and found a red suitcase that must have been J's. I threw all my new clothes in the case and stuffed the cash into my sweat socks. However, that left me with the manila envelopes. I decided I could slip them into the waistband inside my shorts and hope the airport security didn't do a strip search. It was now 11:00 pm on Monday and I was rapidly heading to the fourth day of my vacation. I couldn't wait to get back to work.

My partner Johnny Walker helped me fall asleep and I was dreaming about being in a circus where I was walking a tightrope. When I looked down, I saw J and Dawson looking up with their guns pointed at me. Looking past them, I saw my Mom hollering at me to get down from there before I killed myself. I awoke and promised myself I would do dream work on that one when things settled down. I realized the phone was ringing next to me and that was the reason I had woken up from my Mother's lecture. I answered, "Hello," unsure of what to expect.

"Hey baby, you sleeping?"

Damn that woman's voice did something to me every time I heard it, "I dozed off for a while, what's happening?"

"I have a red suitcase in the closet. Put all the envelopes in it when you go to the airport. Go in the airport and get in the longest check-in line you can find. Keep the suitcase next to you but only hold it when you move. A switch will take place while you're in line. Get a ticket and go to the flight, but do not check the suitcase, carry it on to the plane. When you're on board and in your seat, wait until they are about to close the door, then tell the flight attendant you had an emergency call and have to leave the flight. You'll have to clear your sudden departure with the gate attendant, but do it as quickly as possible. After that, go to the men's room and in a stall open the suitcase. Got it?"

"I guess that means I'm not going to New York."

"Honey," she said quietly. "This is almost over."

"What about Dawson?" I asked.

"I'm sure someone will follow you to the airport, but they will only wait until you're on the plane. What you need will be in the suitcase. Are you OK?"

"J, I am so not okay you wouldn't believe it. I remember you said don't trust anybody, especially the people you trust. I desperately want to trust you but the question keeps shouting in my mind, 'Why should I trust you?'."

She hesitated for a while and finally said, "Because I love you Steve." Then the line went dead.

I sat there for a long time and said nothing. "Because I love you Steve," kept going through my mind. I was supposed to trust her because she said she loved me? I was supposed to put my life on the line and go against Dawson's instruction because she said she loved me? That was absolutely the craziest thing I'd ever heard. Nevertheless, I was convinced that I was one of the craziest people I had ever met, so I decided I would do what she said. Besides, deep inside, beyond where my ego lived, I was sure I loved her too. In the back of my mind I heard my mother say, "Steven, get down from there before you kill yourself." "Ok, Mom, but I'm going to stay a while longer."

CHAPTER 19

I left the condo in a cab about 5:00 am. It was only a 15-minute trip to the airport, but I wanted to have plenty of time to get through all the complicated routine I was facing. It dawned on me that once I parted company with the suitcase, I would have nothing left to possibly help me with the Feds. Nevertheless, if J wasn't a Federal Agent and I was going against Dawson's orders, I was in so much trouble that a few envelopes of paper wouldn't help me much.

We arrived at Jet Blue and I was surprised to see how many people were in the airport at this hour. With my little red suitcase in tow, I moved toward the longest check in line I could find and planted myself. The woman in front of me was a typical New York business-person who was all uptight and stuffy. Behind me was a woman with two small children, neither of whom liked being up at this hour. I was glad I was going to get off the plane, because, with the way my luck had been going, I would be sitting next to them.

The line was slow and wound around as a snake. I moved my suitcase along and tried to see who was going to make the switch. The line moved and I reach for my bag and found it gone! I looked to my right and saw it sitting by my feet. I was sure I had it on my left, but now it was on my right. I guessed the switch had been made and I was impressed with how well it was done.

I finally got to the attendant, bought my ticket with my Robert Klingman identification and more of the taxpayer's money; or maybe it was Juan's money. Both ways, it was not my money and as that was the only fringe benifit I found on this trip, I had no problem spending it. I got my red suitcase and me through security and went to the boarding area. It was now 6:30 am and Jet Blue was preparing for a prompt departure by boarding rows 17 thru 30. My seat was in row 5 so I simply waited for them to call my row. I looked around to see if I could spot anyone watching me, but as an amateur, I'm no good at surveillance analysis.

I finally boarded, put away my suitcase and waited for the attendants to get everyone secure. They announced they were preparing for final departure and wanted everyone seated with their seat belt buckled and the seat in an upright position. That was my signal.

I got up, retrieved my suitcase, and moved toward the door. The flight attendant asked if he could help me and I explained my emergency. He gave me a great Jet Blue smile and signaled another attendant to walk me back to the gate. I handed in my ticket stub where they took my name off the roster and told me to go to the service desk to arrange for another flight. I headed straight to the bathroom and slid into a stall with my suitcase. I felt like it was Christmas and I was about to open my big present.

Inside I found a smaller green suitcase, which contained a pair of jeans, a windbreaker, knit shirt, and a pair of deck shoes. A quick check found they were all the right size, and I wondered if J was that good in guessing sizes or if all my specifications were on some national database. Inside was also a note that read:

Steve,

Change into these and leave the red suitcase behind. Be sure to leave it unzipped and open so we don't have a national security problem. Head directly to National Car Rental and pick up a luxury car from the lot. You don't need to go to the counter, use the Emerald Isle. When you pass the gate, they will need your driver's license and credit card. Use the Robert Klingman ID's I gave you. Leave the airport and head south on 95 to exit 29 and get off. There is a Ramada Inn there and you need to go in and ask if anyone left a package for Robert Klingman. Next ask them the fastest way to Sarasota, Fl. You are not going there, but that is the direction you requested if anyone should ask. The information you get at the Ramada will tell you how to find my location. I can't wait to see you and get this mess finished.

Love,

J

I had the distinct feeling I was on a scavenger hunt and had to go find my next clue. I first checked in my Robert Klingman wallet, found I did have a National Rental Car Emerald Club card, and was happy I didn't have to go to Hertz and answer questions about the Impala I treated so poorly. I slipped out of my clothes, into the new outfit, and stuffed all my other things into the new green suitcase. I left the old red one by the garbage can, unzipped and opened so everyone could see it didn't have a bomb. Fortunately, the bathroom was empty and no one was able to see my quick change.

Leaving the bathroom, I walked back to the main terminal and worked my way to the car rental locations. The lot was empty of people and I found a shiny white Lincoln sitting in the luxury section of the Emerald Isle. Handing my identification and Emerald Card to the gatekeeper, I was out of the terminal and on my way in a very short time. I tried to see if I was followed, but again, as an amateur, I sucked at these things.

The new car was a smooth ride and I hoped it would fare better than my last rental. Spying the Ramada Inn down the highway, I followed the exit to the main entrance. The Florida sun was already warming the morning air and the short trip from my car to the entrance demonstrated that air conditioning was not an option in Florida. A bright and cheery blonde beauty was at the reception desk and I asked her if my friend left a letter for Robert Klingman. She retrieved my letter from behind the counter and, as per instructions from J, I asked the best route to travel to Sarasota. I smiled as she showed me on the map, but I was only interested in the unopened letter I held in my hand. Thanking her for her time, I headed out of the door and spotted a Denny's close to the Ramada. Breakfast had been a cup of coffee and I decided I would take a break and read my mail there.

155

I settled into a booth, ordered coffee with pancakes and opened my mysterious mail.

Steve,

I located Juan and I think we will shut down both his operation and Mr. Matt Dawson at the same time. I have not reported Matt yet, as I want to get them both together. I am waiting for you at the Continental Downtown Bayside in Miami. Directions attached with this note. I am in suite 1812 and will not leave until you arrive, so hurry. I miss you and can't wait to see you.

Love,

J

This now totaled two notes signed "Love J," and I was happy to read that. I ate my pancakes on the fly and left for Miami before they even reached my stomach. Unfortunately, my quick stop placed me in early morning rush hour and I averaged about 15 mph all down 95 until I reached the Biscayne Blvd exit. It took another half hour to get to downtown Miami where I found the hotel overlooking the Bay area and the Miami Port. Several cruise ships were docked across the way and more big yachts than you could count. I gave my new Lincoln to the parking attendant, very happy that I spent almost two hours in the car and it was still in one piece.

The hotel lobby was typical Miami luxury with indoor palm trees and good-looking men and women everywhere. I got in the elevator and rode to the eighteenth floor, which was the same floor we were on in the Hollywood condo, so I guessed J had a thing for eighteen. Finding the room, I knocked on the door, which immediately opened to the most glorious sight I had seen since the last time I saw her. I stood looking for a minute until she grabbed my arm, pulled me in the room, and closed the door. She wrapped her arms around me and we kissed long and deep. The fact that once again she was stark naked was somewhat a distraction, but I forced my way back to reality and kissed her in return.

"Oh shit, am I glad to see you," she whispered in my ear as she continued to hold me tight.

"I'm thrilled to see you too," I said as I held her. "And I really love the new outfit you have on to greet me."

She laughed and held me close, "I wanted to give you a little reward for all you've been through, and I thought this would be a good beginning."

She led me through the suite as I left a trail of clothes all the way to the bed. The feeling of flesh on flesh took away all the bad thoughts I had about my vacation and somehow, my life still seemed worthwhile. We spent the next hour lost in the passion of each other and finally collapsed together in a satisfied and yet exhausted pile. Out of necessity, we both fell asleep and didn't wake until about two in the afternoon. It took a while to orient myself, as I hadn't spent much time looking at the suite when I entered. J was in the shower so I wandered out of the bedroom and grabbed a Coke from the refrigerator.

The suite, which was quite large and well-furnished, had a great view of the harbor with a balcony overlooking the American Airlines Arena and the boats in the bay, some of which deserved to be called ships given their size. J had a pair of binoculars by the window and I looked at these "ships" with great awe. I'm not a great judge, but I think the smallest was over 40' long. Some had boats on their decks and one had a helicopter. It was amazing how much money was in the world and how people spent it.

"When you stand naked in front of a window, people are supposed to look at you and not you be spying on them."

She came up to my side and put her arm around my waist, smelling tropical fresh and wearing my favorite outfit—nothing. Putting down the binoculars, I gave her a big hug. "I guess we're here for more than loving," I said as I held her close.

"I'm afraid you're right," she said as she let me go and sat down on the couch. "Let me bring you up to date. After our parking lot experience, I went to another place I knew to get some information. It seems Juan has put out strong feelers to try to locate me and added some dollars to help find information. I think Junior was set up, but I still can't be sure. Junior said Juan was in the harbor, but he died before he finished telling me where, so I spent some money and finally located him. I checked the office to see the whereabouts of Special Agent Dawson and they said he was on extended vacation for a month. I decided not to pursue him with my boss and figured Dawson would find us or we'd find him. Either way, I'm going to stop the leak permanently."

I moved to the couch and sat next to her, "What do you mean permanently?"

She looked at me for a minute and opened one of the envelopes I'd been carrying in my red suitcase. She spread them out on the table and pointed at the first sheet. It contained a series of numbers with the figure $1,500,000 next to them. I noticed that the sheet had many such numbers and more references with dollar signs. As she pointed to the numbers she said, "This is a financial transfer sheet to accounts in many different places. In the last month, I have drained off over $10,000,000 of Juan's money and placed it where he can't find it. He needs these sheets to recover his money."

"Dawson was right when he said you had taken money from Juan," I said as I stared blankly at the maze of numbers.

"I've heard several different interpretations of how much I took, but yes, he was right about the money being stolen." She pointed to the other sheets she had spread before me. "These represent all the accounts I pulled the funds from and it's a direct indication of how Juan works his money laundry. The money is nothing in comparison to the damage these sheets will do to Juan as they show all the places and names of his contacts, and when we hit them, we'll cripple the drug market in a major way. The problem Juan faces is that he can't tell anyone what I've done or they'll kill him because he let this information out. Therefore, he has to recover this and terminate me so his contacts, and his life, are safe."

I looked at her and felt the sinking feeling in my stomach that accompanies really bad news. "He's pulling out all the stops to find you, and you're calmly sitting here?"

She stood and walked to the window waving for me to join her. Taking the binoculars, she looked out over the boats below and handed the glasses to me. Pointing toward the boats she said, "See the fifth one back on the left with the red deck? That's where Juan is staying as we talk."

I looked at the boat with the binoculars and saw a beautiful yacht about 50' long with a bright red deck. I looked around for

159

bodyguards but saw no one there. "Are you sure he's there, I don't see any protection."

"Oh he's there; he doesn't want to draw attention to that fact." She replied as she left the window and returned to the couch. "I was on the boat often and it's secure with alarm systems. He also has his top protector with him somewhere on the boat—the cleft-chinned man you met at the condominium the other night. He was the other 'agent' who tossed your bedroom while Dawson gave you misinformation."

I remembered the cleft-chinned agent with the slick black hair and the casual clothes. From what J was saying, he was very different from a Federal Agent. "Juan and his friend are on the boat and you and I are sitting here. I doubt if he is going to come visit us—so what happens next?"

She reached over, kissed me, and said, "We are going to get dressed and go visit some friends of mine."

"Friends like Junior?" I asked her.

"These are more friendly friends, but similar in occupation. They are one of the names on that list you see before you and they are really pissed that Juan screwed up this thing."

"But you're the one who screwed it up, not Juan," I said with some amazement, "Why would they work with you and not with Juan?"

"Because they know I can make their names disappear from the list before it goes into hands of people who will cause them trouble. I do a favor for them; they do a favor for me."

I considered this for a minute and asked the obvious question, "What makes you think you can trust them?"

"I trust them because I have you."

That made no sense to me. If I were looking for a good safe plan, I wouldn't include me in it. She obviously saw my concern, laughed, and said, "You are Special Agent Robert Klingman. You'll provide them information about some things they want to know, and they'll provide me information I want. In addition, you'll let them listen to a segment of a taped conversation they will find very disconcerting. Your offer is to give them the tape when we take care of Juan. The tape goes to another agent on Friday. If we are alive and well on Friday, you'll get the tape and give it to them. If you and I are not alive, then the tape will go to the agent and life will become difficult for my friends. See baby, you are a very hot Special Agent who is protecting me with your tricks of the trade."

"Lover, you got the wrong man!" I said to her as I got up and started to pace the room. "I can't pretend to be an Agent and be cool about these things when I am going to be wetting my pants from the time I meet them. I'm sure you have a tape, and it is a good tape, but I have to convince them I'm a threat and even my secretary knows I'm not a threat, and she has known me for a long time. I'm not even a good threat to the trout, and they have no brains, how can I be a threat to these people? We are going to get killed and I love you too much to do that to you; and I love me too and won't do it to me."

She jumped up from the couch and placed her lips on mine. Then she pulled back and said, "Do you always talk so much when you're nervous?"

161

"I talk a lot when I am nervous, but I talk without a break when I'm terrified. I don't live like you and I'm way out of my league. Besides................"

She kissed me again and said, "Steve, be quiet for a minute. You're making me nervous now. I'll go over all the details with you so you are comfortable before we get to my friends. I'll do most of the talking; you just need to be calm and trust that the plan will work. You can't screw it up, and remember, I saw you under fire with both Carlos and during the attack in the parking lot. I know you can do this. I make a living knowing people—and you I know intimately. Now, Agent Robert Klingman, go take a shower, cool down, and I'll give you all the information you need to pull this off." She kissed me again, turned me around, and gave me a swift smack on my naked behind.

The shower was always a place for clear thinking. I really wanted to have the water wake me from this dream, but it only took off the grime, not the anxiety. Junior was no easy person to be with, but these people sounded as if they were higher up the food chain and I was way down the chain near the slugs and worms.

I had to calm myself, so I practiced what I told my clients. "It is not the people, places or events that cause us emotional problems; it is what we believe about the people, places, or events. This situation is not terrible, horrible, and awful; it is simply complicated. J is a professional and will know how to handle everything; I am simply a quiet partner." I repeated this about three times and got tired of talking to myself. Hell, this had all the earmarks of being terrible, horrible, and awful, but I was in this far; what the hell would one more problem represent. Them killing me

162

would be the worst that could happen, and then this mess would all be over. At least I wasn't married to Laura.

With that last thought, I took a deep breath, turned off the water and stepped into the shoes of Special Agent Robert Klingman. After a quick shave, I went into the bedroom and found J in a red dress that astounded me—there was not much material to the dress but what was there covered her body like a glove. She turned around, smiled at me, and said, "Like my new dress? I got it for you." As she turned, I saw that it was as low cut in front, as it was at the back, and both sides had a web design that showed a lot of flesh.

"If I'm going to die," I responded looking at her, "this will be the vision that will make it all easier."

I looked on the bed and saw a dress shirt, a pair of slacks, and a light tan blazer. Once again, the size was perfect. "How do you know my size so well?" I asked.

She came up, suggestively ran her hands over my body, and said, "Baby, I know every inch of you. Besides, I looked at your clothes when we first met and got the size. It's a force of habit to be able to describe someone with detail; therefore, clothes size is something I pay special attention to in my profession. Now get dressed and I'll fix a drink. We have to meet them at seven, so we have a few hours to go over things and have dinner. I know a great place on the water and we can head to the club from there."

She blew me a kiss and walked toward the living room as I watched the few inches of material on her body move in all the right ways. I put on the shirt and found it was not only my size, it was so light it felt like my own skin. The slacks had a perfect cut

and I had to admit I looked good too. With a man, it is better if the
clothes fit. With a woman, it is better if there is just not much there.
I chuckled as I thought how a sexist thought like that could
probably get me censured with the State Board of Psychology, but
decided I didn't care—I was Robert Klingman, Special Agent with
the FBI, and they couldn't take that away from me. Hell, they
never even gave it to me.

J invited my good friend Johnny Walker to cocktails, and I
knew I would need a lot of him to get through all this. We sat down
and she set a tape recorder on the table. "This is the segment we'll
play for them," she said. "The full tape is in my safe in the office.
Nobody knows it's there, but if anything happens, my boss will
find it. So our threat is true, just not all the details. The first voice is
Bingo Bob, who we will see tonight."

"Bingo Bob, you have to be kidding me!" I said in disbelief.
"I thought Louie Two Fingers or Lefty Bam Bam might be a better
name."

"Bingo Bob got his name because, as he says, you cross him
and "Bingo" you're dead."

She hit the play button and after a few seconds of silence a
voice said:

*"You fucken me. I told you 1,000 Russian PPS 43 and you tell
me I can now only have 250? I told you 4,000 Glock 39 and you
tell me I can now only have 500. Are you really liken to fuck with
me?"*

J stopped the recorder and said, "Bingo is an arms dealer for
the cartel. He keeps them supplied with tens of thousands of guns,
rifles, and other toys. He is talking to a Thompson Sandford, who

164

interestingly enough, works for Senator Mike Harris, the illustrious member of the Senate Arms Committee and Chairman of the Subcommittee on Readiness and Management Support. That committee has control over the stockpile of weaponry in the USA." She pushed the button again and the tape began:

"Bob, I know this is difficult, but my boss told me to tell you he will make good on the order and will add some interesting extras. It's harder because of all the National Security crap. But it will get done."

"Listen Mr. Asshole Thompson Sanford, tell your boss, the Senator Asshole Michael J Harris, that I need that order filled now and not next year. I tipped $4 mill into his slush fund and it was not for hookers. Either he puts up or I start leaking information he will not like."

J again stopped the tape and said, "By now I think you see this is bad for both Bingo and the Senator. The problem is that Bingo needs the Senator, and, in spite of his threat to Sanford, Bingo will do anything to protect his interest in the Senator. When he hears this, he will go ballistic, but he will also know that he has to deep six the tape. Your job will be to guarantee that the tape will be in his hands by Friday if we accomplish what we want with Juan. Bingo and the Senator are a good catch, but Juan is the big trout we really want. In about six months, the Senator will probably decide he needs to resign and all this will be for nothing. Of course, the Senator will resign because someone is going to play ta similar tape for him too. However, that won't happen until this is over. We'll give the tape to Bingo, and it's the only copy we have. As far

165

as I know, it doesn't exist anyplace else, or at least that's what my boss said." She smiled and waited for my reply.

"I will tell Bingo Bob," I said, "that as far as I know, and to the best of my resources, I have the only tape. How I got it I can't say, but I will suggest that he hire a good firm to check for bugs in his walls."

J threw her head back, laughed, then came over and sat on my lap. "I do declare Special Agent Klingman, you are one tough dude. It makes a woman hot listening to you."

"This is dress rehearsal baby." I said. "Let's hope I don't fuck up the real show."

She got up, rewound the tape, and handed it to me. "Put it in your pocket and hand him the recorder. You wont have to worry about carrying it after he hears it, I'm sure he will smash it against the wall. Don't let his toughness and rage get to you. He'll know he has only one deal and that is to work with us. He knows I'm fed and we could have pulled the plug on him and the senator if we wanted, but choose to give him a deal if he helps us out."

"How is he going to help us out?" I asked.

"By taking us to Juan," she replied sweetly.

"What? You're going to let him take us to Juan? Are you out of your mind? We won't live long enough to even say hello. Tell me you are kidding."

She sat back, closed her eyes, and finally said, "Bingo will call Juan and tell him I was there. He'll explain that I was trying to sell him a piece of Juan's bank accounts and Bingo will ask Juan how much I'm worth if he brings me to him. Bingo will take the price and tell Juan he'll call him when he has me and is ready to

166

drop me off. I'll go to the boat, sneak on, and wait for Bingo to call Juan and tell him he has me. Juan will send his boys out to get me and when they are gone, I'll pay him a surprise visit and then, my love, it will be over."

"Do you know how many things can go wrong with your plan?" I asked. "Do you really believe Juan will go for this and Bingo Bob will actually play along? Hell, he could let Juan kill you and his problems would be over."

"Don't forget the tape lover. Without the tape we would be dead before we left Bingo. He will assume we have a copy of the tape someplace and if he doesn't make a deal, or if something happens to us, he will be in hot water. He needs us alive. Trust me; it will work. Now come on, let's go eat and relax before we go meet Bingo."

"No, wait a minute," I said as I replayed our conversation in my head. You said you were going to be on the boat when Bingo called and you would take Juan down. What am I supposed to be doing?"

"I'll come up with something. Don't worry," she said as she turned toward the door. "You are my partner aren't you? Now come on, let's go eat."

"Somehow I feel like I am going to the Last Supper," I said. I looked at her in that dress and decided that the best thought was "You who are about to die, we salute you."

167

CHAPTER 20

Dinner was a beautiful memory, even if the rest of the night was not. We walked down the street to the Bay and, as J promised, sat by the waterside watching the day turn into evening. While she attracted many a look in her new dress, she was one of many women who sported more flesh than material. You really do have to love Miami and its ability to produce such healthy bodies; it must be the Florida oranges, or perhaps the abundance of plastic surgeons. What ever caused it, the results were spectacular.

We were among the few early diners when we arrived, which provided us a choice spot overlooking Biscayne Bay and all the money it represented. Avoiding the task that loomed before us, we shared about each other's lives and looked to all the world as a couple on their honeymoon rather than two people who may not live out the night. The restaurant also had my friend Johnny

168

Walker, but I decided he was not going to be much help to me if I let him have control.

After a quiet moment, she turned to me and asked, "What do you want to do when this is all over?"

"If I survive I've been giving serious thought to going into the priesthood and living in a monastery," I replied calmly. She looked at me for a minute, laughed and shook her head. She was having trouble following my insane humor, but that was okay—I was having a lot of trouble following her insane life. I smiled and said, "I guess I'll go back to New York and do what I do best. I don't think I'll fill out an application for the FBI, I want these days behind me."

Leaning back to look out over the Bay, she quietly asked, "What if you never had to work again, what would you do?" The light was dimming as the sun went down behind us and her dark hair radiated as a halo circling around her tan features. J was many things, but above all, she was a beautiful woman.

"If I never had to work again," I said after some thought, "I think I would fish all over the world. I would start in the Keys and follow the wind to wherever it would lead. What about you?"

"Fishing sounds good," she replied. "I guess I want to go someplace where I can be me. I feel like I play a thousand roles and never really know who I am. I've had it with the job and I'm leaving when this is over. I needed to be a cop and do what I could for my Dad, but it has taken too much of a toll to keep doing it. I've thought a lot about what you told me and I know I have to change or die. I couldn't stand working in an office; maybe I would tag along and be your fishing buddy."

She smiled when she said it, but I could read her insecurity as she spoke. We hadn't talked about the "love you" thing since we got back together and I guessed this was a good time to discuss the relationship. Hell, it was the only time to discuss the relationship, as we might be dead in the next few hours.

"J, I would love to have you as my fishing buddy. I would love to have you with me as anything you want. No, let me rethink that. I don't want you to be in this line of work anymore, but I'm not sure you can leave it all behind. I'm really a fairly simple person, with a comfortable life, and a desire to fish. You thrive on the adventure and the challenge of life and you need it to survive. I've known you less than five days and really do love you, but we are very different. I don't know if I would be enough for you."

She reached over, took my hand, and continued to look out over the Bay. "I'm a handful, no doubt about that. I love life and the fullness of all it brings. I've seen so much of the shadow side that I long to walk in the light and enjoy it for a while." She turned and looked at me. "When we were at the falls that day, I decided to walk away from the job and never go back. I connected to you in a way I've never felt for anyone in my life. When Carlos showed up, my biggest regret was I would die before I really lived with you. Obviously, my White Knight, you rescued me and gave me more time. Now I have you, I'll do anything to be with you and discover what a real life is all about. The other night on the beach, when you were talking about feeling connected to me, it was as if you had read my mind. My fear is you have seen me in some pretty bad light and that may have turned you off a deeper relationship. I won't beg or plead for another chance; it's not my nature and I

170

don't think you would like it that way. Nevertheless, I will ask that you at least give us a chance to see how it works. If it doesn't, at least we can say we had a hell of a time together."

I looked at her hand as I held it and thought about all the shit those hands had been through. Undercover with a drug king has to be a real dirty job and I knew J would not pull back from any situation she confronted. How much she had been through was beyond my understanding and frankly not for me to know. Nevertheless, I also felt the connection at the falls that day and was surprised how it caught me off guard. I enjoyed being unattached and was in no hurry to rush into a relationship. Nevertheless, I was part of J now and couldn't go back. She squeezed my hand and I looked up at her and said, "Tell you what—let's allow this relationship to take us where it will. I do love you and am willing to see if it works. I mean five fun-filled, death-defying days is a good proving ground, and we are still together. So who know what ten days can bring?"

She put both her hands around mine and held them tight. As she looked at me I saw tears in her eyes and I was completely overwhelmed. As a tear ran down her beautiful face, she closed her eyes and simply said. "Thanks for loving me. You have no idea how important that is to me."

We leaned together over the table, kissed lightly, and sat back. She let go of my hand, dabbed her eyes with the napkin and said, "Let's go finish this mess so we can get on with life."

"I guess there is no chance of getting on a plane and running away?" I asked hopefully.

"You know the answer to that, Steve. We have to finish this the right way, or we will be running for the rest of our lives."

We left the restaurant hand in hand to see Bingo Bob— another beautiful Miami couple. I prayed to the God of the Trout that I would live to fish another day.

We took a taxi to the Golden Arm, which was probably named after the movie, "The Man with the Golden Arm." I couldn't remember much of the movie, but I think it ended badly for Frank Sinatra.

"The Golden Arm," a fitting name for the headquarters of a bunch of drug pushers, had an atmosphere of the "Gentleman's Club Gaudy." Throughout the room, there were tables with cloth covers, several grand pianos with beautiful naked women dancing on them, and women waiting on the tables with almost nothing covering their trim bodies. We went to the bar, tended by a man who was at least 6'5" and weighing a solid 250 pounds. I looked around, saw a few others of his size, and decided that the customers would either behave or end up in the emergency room.

"Hey J, long time no see," the Man Mountain said as we sat down.

"Been real busy Dave," J said, "but I think of you every night before I go to sleep. I always say to myself, how can I make Dave like women?"

Dave smiled and said, "Honey, if I ever go straight, you will be the first person I call. What can I get you tonight?"

"I'll have the usual and my partner will have a Johnny Walker on the rocks. Do me a favor and buzz Bingo that I'm here."

172

Dave nodded yes and produced a diet coke for J and a double Johnny Red for me. We toasted our glasses and I sat back to look around the place. I noticed a lot of champagne carried around and I guessed it was what the girls ordered when they slipped into one of the booths with a customer. One girl was in a corner booth dancing naked on the table of five Asian men. They obviously were having a great time and she was pretending to be ecstatic about being able to dance for them. J looked at the table I was watching and said, "Soon the gates will close around the table and she'll really earn her money."

"Tough way to make a living," I replied as I watched about ten different girls in various states of undress.

"Tell me about it!" She said.

"Did you ever dance here?"

"Not here," she replied. "But I played the role at another club. See that redhead over by the white piano?"

I looked across the room and spotted the redhead who was slipping out of an evening dress to expose her completely naked body. She had great moves and drew a lot of attention.

"She's from my office," J said quietly. "She started about a year ago and I'm afraid she may have picked up a drug habit. It's a danger in the business and takes out a lot of good people."

I watched Special Agent Redhead and couldn't help thinking of the life she chose and the amount of education and training she had gone through to end up in a place like this. "Can't they pull her in if she is having trouble?"

"She has to admit that she's having trouble," J said. "And that can be a career buster. She's damned if she does and damned if she doesn't."

About that time another Man Mountain came up to J and nodded to her. She set down her coke and motioned for me to follow. I gave my friend Johnny Walker a big goodbye and hoped to hell I would live long enough to see him again. We followed Man Mountain across the main floor through a pair of huge mahogany doors. We found another party going on back there, but in this place, the couples left no room for imagination. Little rooms along the way had men and women in various sexual positions that went beyond description. With a distinct smell of pot in the air, I thought I might get high walking down the hall.

We went through another set of doors and it appeared we had entered a lawyer's office. A receptionist sat behind her desk and the waiting area was right out of Trump Designers. Man Mountain knocked on the door, opened it for us to enter, and escorted us into a room very different from Junior's ghetto. The carpet was so thick, you thought it was a cloud, and several leather wingback chairs surrounded a desk on which you could land an airplane in a windstorm.

The form behind the desk offset the beauty of the room. He stood to greet us and I felt the temperature around him was thirty degrees colder. He was dressed in a dark green suit and dark green shirt that fit him as if he'd been sewn into them. He came around the desk and swallowed J into his huge arms. Looking over his shoulder, he checked me out like a radar screen and I felt the hair on my neck stand at attention.

174

"How can anybody as beautiful as you get things this fucked up?" he said as he continued to hold her and look at me. I couldn't tell if he was talking to her or to me, but I didn't think he saw me as beautiful. Maybe I was the fuck up he was talking about. J finally extricated herself from his arms and said, "Some things are not as they appear, Bingo. This is my partner Special Agent Klingman."

I didn't attempt to shake his hand and he made no move to acknowledge I was present. Moving back behind his desk he sat and glared at both of us. "I don't need two Feds in my place and I don't want this to last long. I also don't need Juan's people busten in here and shooten things up so it scares the customers. Let's cut the shit and tell me what this is about."

J sat back, crossed her legs, and looked him straight in the eye, "You know we have Juan's account setups with your name and a few of your close associates on the third page. I'll be sure you and your friends don't show up on the third page when this list migrates to the higher people."

"And for all this love and kisses, what will it cost me?"

"I want you to set Juan up so I can take him down."

Bingo stared at her for a long time, leaned back, and laughed, "I was waiting for the punch line, but decided to laugh at your stupidity instead of your joke. No fucken way I'm setting Juan up. He's a prick, but he's a prick who makes me money, and money is God. I know you too well, J baby. What's the rest of the story."

She leaned forward and said, "My partner works with people in the Bureau who take great interest in gun trades. He came across

175

some information that we will guarantee goes no further. All I need is your help with Juan."

"And this important information is what?"

Leaning across his desk, I handed him the tape player, and calmly said, "All you need is in there." I had actually spoken and my voice didn't crack, I didn't drool, and I limited it to a few words. I was amazed at myself as I sat back but quickly found the atmosphere changed.

"You fucken asshole! You come in here and give me a tape that you illegally took of me and try to scare me. Well fuck you and your mother. I got more tapes than I need and this don't mean shit."

I looked at him and smiled. I think I saw Mel Gibson do that in a similar situation, and Mel looked very cool and in control. It was hard to smile when I was spending time trying not to let my bladder loose on his expensive chair. Neither J nor I spoke or moved as Bingo stood and glared at us. Finally, he pushed the play button and listened.

"You fucken me. I told you 1,000 Russian PPS 43 and you tell me I can now only have 250? I told you 4,000 Glock 39 and you tell me I can now only have 500. Are you really liken to fuck with me?"

"Bob, I know this is difficult, but my boss told me to tell you he will make good on the order and will add some interesting extras. It is just a little harder because of all the National Security crap. But it will get done."

\I watched as Bingo Bob slowly started to shake his head and roll his shoulders. I'd spent enough sessions with Laura that I could spot a volcano a mile away from land and this one was going to be a beauty. He picked up the tape recorder, wound up, and threw it against the wall where it shattered into many small pieces. He jumped from his seat and went straight toward J. She went to stand but he pushed her down in her chair so hard it flipped backward and she rolled to the floor. "You fucken whore! You bitch! You are dead meat!" He screamed at her so loud the room shook. I jumped to my feet and he turned, pulled a gun on me with amazing speed and screamed, "And you, you, you sniveling peace of shit! You are dead now."

He raised his gun and I saw the dark hole of the barrel face me. I braced for the shot when I heard J shout, "Bingo, you fucking asshole! Look what you did—you tore my new dress. You fucking piece of shit, can't you ever keep your temper under control? Now get someone in here and have them fix this or there will be hell to pay."

As Bingo and I looked at her, she grabbed the hem of her dress and pulled it over her head. Other than the heels she was wearing, she was stark naked. She threw it at him and said, "Call someone to fix it now. I paid $500 for it and you are going to fix it as new."

I saw the dress fly at him and he lowered the gun to catch it. He set the gun on the desk and looked at the dress. "You paid $500 for this, you got took. Where is it ripped? I don't see enough material on here to even rip." J walked over, grabbed the dress, and

177

turned it to the side where one of the small web straps appeared torn loose.

"There, asshole! See it now? Goddamn it, Bingo! call someone NOW!"

Bingo picked up his gun and I tensed, but he put it back in his waistband and sat down in his chair still holding the dress. He pushed a button on his desk and said, "Irene, get the fuck in here and bring a robe or something."

The three of us stood around that desk and we made quite a sight. Bingo was playing with the rip in the dress as if it was important. I was standing with my knees shaking and the shit-eating Mel Gibson smile still on my face. J was standing in her heels glaring at Bingo, and looking beautiful in her nothings. Finally, Irene rushed in and handed Bingo a robe. He handed her the dress and said, "Get this thing fixed now and bring it right back. I mean like now!"

Irene grabbed the dress and got out as quick as she was able. Bingo took the robe and came around to J. "You know, baby, with that body you could easily pull $3,000 to $5,000 a night. Give up the shit life you lead and come join my party. Now put this on. We got business to talk and you're distracting."

We all sat down and he looked at me, "Where did you get this?"

I sat back and said, "I'm not at liberty to say, but rest assured it is part of a longer tape and I have the original."

He glared at me some more and turned to J, "So talk."

J tied the robe and sat back. "The original is going to be delivered to another agent on Friday. If we're still alive, we pick it

178

up from him and bring it to you and the conversation goes wherever you put tapes you don't enjoy. If we're dead, you and the Senator are in for some serious investigation. You made the conversation so you know what else took place that night. I don't think you want it to go any further. Bingo, you know we could have let this go and taken your ship and the Senator's down the drain. But we want Juan bad enough that we'll let this thing slide."

Bingo sat back and finally said, "Ok. If I help you, how do I know this is the only copy?"

I leaned forward and said, "As far as I know, and to the best of my resources, I have the only tape. How I got it I can't say, but I do suggest that you hire a good firm to check for bugs in your walls."

I sat back and looked at him. As far as I could remember, that was what I was supposed to tell him. Nevertheless, we hadn't rehearsed any further than that, so I just gave my Mel Gibson smile a few more laps.

Bingo sat and looked at me for a long time. I mean, I think he sat and looked at me for over five years. Well, it was probably only thirty seconds, but it felt like five years. He looked at J and said, "And how am I supposed to set Juan up for you? He and I are not exactly golfing buddies."

J stood, walked over to Bingo and sat on the edge of his desk, "When we leave here you call Juan and tell him I was here and wanted to sell off some of his bank assets. You turned me down, but thought about how badly I'd treated Juan and decided to see how much Juan wanted me back. You come to a price agreement to deliver me alive and tell him you'll get me and he can come pick

179

me up. You'll call him when you have me, and he'll send the boys on a trip. You'll call me and let me know the deal is done. From that point on, you're clean."

Bingo thought for a minute and said, "Whatever price Juan agrees to, I won't get it because he'll be dead. I want $500,000 in addition to the tape."

J stood up, took off the robe, and dropped it on his desk, "Fuck you, Bingo! Be glad you didn't end up at the short end of a senate investigation. Now get my dress so I can go. If Juan doesn't give you the money, I'll make good on whatever he offers. However, I will know if he paid you at the pickup. If you lie to me, Bingo, you're dead."

She bent over and kissed him on his head and he grabbed her ass so hard that I could see white fingerprints when he let go. She walked back to her chair as Irene entered and handed J the dress. J checked it out, smiled at Irene, and slid it over her somewhat flush body.

Bingo finally said, "Ok, I'll do it. But if I find you have another copy of that tape and it shows up anywhere," he turned to me, "I will cut her up in small pieces and make you eat them raw before I blow your fucking brains out."

I stood and gave one more Mel Gibson smile, turned my back on him, and headed to the door. I stopped and looked back as J went around and gave him a big hug and kiss, then walked toward me.

He stood and watched her go. "I don't like the way you set yourself up, sweetheart. And it smells like something that could really go bad. But I'll do it; you just be careful."

180

The door closed behind us and on very shaky legs, I left my Mel Gibson smile behind. I really wanted to go into the corner and cry. However, that was not a good action for a special agent.

We walked back into the main area and straight for the front door. My friend Johnny Walker may have been at the bar, but I wanted to be as far away from this place as I could get. We exited into the fresh air and J finally stopped and threw her arms around me. I felt her breathing different and when I pulled back from her, I saw she was crying. She wiped the tears from her cheek and said, "I am so proud of you."

Holding her tight, those were musical words to my shattered soul. "That was an experience straight from hell," I sighed as we stood and embraced on the street. "But your dress routine was the star performance of the night. I know I saw a bullet coming out of that gun until you distracted him with your dress. You may be different in your approach to danger, but you are the greatest in my book."

She took my hand and we started to walk down the street. "Bingo always gets mad and explodes. Once he gets it out, he is usually okay, but he can do a lot of damage until he gets it all out. I knew I had to distract him and that was all I could come up with at the moment. The good thing about you men is your predictability; no matter what's going on, a naked woman will always cause you to be distracted."

I wanted to jump to the defense of my fellow males, but as I thought about it, I knew she was right and kept my mouth shut. "Well thank God it worked, or my last vision would have been of you complaining about a torn dress. That is not how I want to go

181

out of life. And Special Agent Jennifer Blade, what do we do now?"

"We go back to the hotel, have a drink, and keep an eye on Juan's boat. When it's time, I go over to the boat, wait for Bingo's call, then enter, and take care of Juan."

"You left me out again."

"Steve, this is not the place for you. Bingo and Junior were one thing, but this time the stakes are real high. I can't expose you to this."

I stopped and looked at her, "J, I will not let you go alone. I don't know how I can help, but I refuse to let you do this without me. I know I'm breaking the rules, but I also know I can't sit back and let you go in there alone. You have your reasons for not letting your FBI associates do this, and I won't argue with them. Nevertheless, please, no more talk about leaving me behind. Can we agree on this?"

She turned away from me and looked at the surrounding people and buildings. Finally, she turned back and said, "I do enjoy having you around. Only stipulation is you do it my way with no questions. Taking care of Juan is going to be tough, but I think I know how to do it, and you would be a big help." She reached up, kissed me, and said quietly, "My White Knight is a crazy man."

I flagged down a cab and we headed back to the Continental Bayside. "You often refer to 'taking care' of Juan," I said as we rode through the traffic on South Beach. "You also said we would deal with Dawson 'permanently.' Those words have some nasty connotations to them and I guess I'd like to know what you're thinking."

182

"What I want to do and what really may go down are often two different things," she said. "Dawson is a leak, but he is also a Fed, so all I want is to expose him and get him the hell away from the really good people I work with. A guy like that will get good people killed, but it's not my intention to kill him. Juan is a piece of shit and I really want to rid the world of him. However, in all honesty, killing would be too good for him. He has information and we need to tap into it and close things down around him. The account records will damage a lot of people if we act fast, but what's in Juan's head is really important. I'll try to protect his life because of what he knows, but if it comes down to a choice between him or us, he goes."

We got to the hotel and quietly went up to the room. This was not a casual conversation for a public elevator. People might get the wrong idea, or worse, they might get the right idea and start a panic.

We entered and I turned right to find my friend Johnny Walker and tell him about all the different places I found his cousins. J turned left and went into the bathroom. I heard the shower running as I took my friend Johnny out to the balcony to watch all that was going on below me. I looked over to Juan's boat and it was quiet and dark. I saw some light from the cabin area, but it was faint. As Johnny and I settled into a deeper relationship, I tried to imagine going on Juan's boat and quietly bringing him into custody.

I tried to stay positive in my approach to life, but after being with Bingo, I was now a great respecter of angry people with guns.

183

I could still see the rage in Bingo's eyes as he held the gun to my face. He was ready to shoot and didn't even know why.

I have clients with rage that causes them problems. Most of the time they have unconscious triggers that set them off and we have to help them become conscious of these set-off points. When they're conscious of the triggers, they have a better chance at control. However, Bingo wasn't looking for emotional triggers—he was looking to pull a trigger and take his rage out on me. When J hollered at him, he literally transformed before my eyes. Her becoming naked was a big help, but even before that I saw that the simple interruption was enough to pull him to a conscious level. I guess killing me would have done the same thing, but I was a lot happier with the way it actually turned out.

The lights in the living room went dark as J came out and sat next to me. She was in a towel looking beautiful, and while I was getting used to her popping up in different forms of semi naked, I definitely was not getting bored with it.

"Anything going on with Juan?" she asked as she picked up the binoculars and scanned the area.

"Not that I see," I said. "But I'm not real good at this secret-agent-type lookout."

She watched for a while and set down the glasses. She took my drink and had a sip of Johnny. "Ugh, how can you drink that stuff?" she said.

Now making fun of my friend Johnny Walker was a real relationship tester, but I decided that Johnny liked sitting around with J as much as I did, so I let it go.

184

"Are you going to take your clothes off, or am I going to sit here and play by myself?" She asked as she opened the towel and ran her hands over her breast and down her waist.

I believe in following instructions, especially when it comes to being naked with a beautiful woman. I stripped quickly and as I went to hold her, she handed me my drink, pushed me back in my seat, and said, "Let's be together like this for a while. Unencumbered with life, clothes, problems, and anything else the world brings to us."

I sipped my drink and felt the tropical breeze blow across my flesh. She reached over and took my hand as we watched the world go by our balcony while we simply enjoyed the peace of being together.

"You do realize I'm dead," she said quietly.

The statement so shook my peaceful reverie that I sat forward in my chair and looked at her. "Are you talking about dying tonight?" I asked.

She pushed me gently back, came, sat on my lap, and nestled into my arms. "No, I feel okay about tonight. I mean I'm declared dead in the papers in New York and I think officially in some government documents."

I remembered the article reporting on her and Carlos death. While I was aware it was an obvious deception, the story did have a real enough ring to it that I remembered being quite stunned.

"I think I may stay dead," she said.

"I really am not following you," I said to the top of her head. "And frankly, talking about being dead is not a prime topic in my repertoire tonight."

185

CATCH AND RELEASE
TWERELL

"I guess all I'm saying is I'm really ready to stop being who I am. Jennifer Blade had a 33-year run with this life, and accomplished a lot. Nevertheless, I don't want to be Jennifer Blade anymore. Maybe I stopped being Jennifer a long time ago when I started calling myself J. Reading my obituary in the paper, a part of me said, 'Well it's about time'."

She sat up, threw her legs around me and looked in my eyes. "If I decided to never come back would you go with me?"

"Honey," I said, "I'm having trouble following you. If you decided to 'never come back?' Where is it you are never coming back too—Miami, New York, Planet Earth? And once we figure that out, where is it you want to go?"

She sat and looked at me for a long time and answered, "I guess it's hypothetical. I feel what I want to say, but can't put it in words. I want to go away from everything I know and start again. It isn't a place I want to get away from, it's my life I want to leave. Nevertheless, I don't want to die permanently; I want to go and not be known. If I can do this, do you think you would go with me?"

I sat back and looked at her, which was not a good place to look if I wanted to think deeply, but I looked anyhow. I had a life in New York and it was good. However, often I felt the emptiness inside that I couldn't touch. That place inside was one of the reasons I loved to fish. In the mountain streams I seemed to feel my soul relax and I became one with myself. Could I leave my practice and my life all behind? Who would miss me? My patients would all find someone else in the practice to see and in a short time would not even remember me. My parents had both passed away and I had no brothers or sisters. I had several good friends in New

York, but in reality, we enjoyed partying, but not really sharing with each other. I listened to people's problems for a living; therefore, I had a tendency to be rather shallow with friendships. In reality, I could disappear into a new life and few would even know I was gone. Damn, that was depressing.

I looked in J's eyes and saw something in them I never saw before that moment. A child gives a look to you when they've asked you for something special and are waiting to see if you will do it. On my lap sat this gorgeous woman who was bright, clever, brave, and sexy as hell. However, before me also sat a little girl who'd asked if I would go with her in her adventure. In those green eyes, I saw the desperation, hope, fear, courage, and joy that would bring a balance to every obstacle the world may offer.

Reaching out, I took her face in my hands, and simply said, "Ok, I will go." Her eyes opened wide and I heard her take a short quick breath and quietly ask, "Are you sure? I mean this might spell the end of everything you ever knew. I'm not saying we're going to do it, but if we did, it would be a whole new journey with no past. Are you sure?"

Continuing to hold her face in my hands I said, "I am very sure."

J leaned against me and started to cry. Not a small tear cry, but great big sob cry. Her body shook as if being exorcized and I felt the warm tears running down my chest. I held her and rocked her as she cried and felt her begin to relax in my arms. At last, she stood and went inside. She returned with a bath towel and wiped off her face and my chest. Sitting on my lap once more she said, "I haven't cried like that since my Dad died. I've seen more shit than

I ever want to remember, but I've kept it all inside. I love you, Steve, and I have never ever felt I could trust anyone before. Your answer touched me so deeply that I think I let go of all the hurt and pain I had inside myself. I don't know what it all means, you're the shrink. But I do know I love you and my world will never be the same."

She turned to lean against me but quickly jumped to her feet and grabbed the binoculars. I stood next to her and asked, "What is it?"

"It is Ricky Sonna, the cleft chin man you met and guess who he's letting onto the boat?"

She handed me the glasses and I focused on the boat and spotted none other than Special Agent Matthew Dawson. He came on board and was warmly welcomed by Mr. Cleft Chin.

I handed the glasses back to J and looked over at her. I saw her as the woman in my life that would change everything. I saw her as the love I needed to be whole. We looked at each other and turned to go get dressed, with both of us knowing, this was the beginning of the end.

CHAPTER 21

In my wardrobe provisions, J purchased me a pair of black slacks and a black shirt. As usual, the size was perfect. She wore a similar outfit but also wore a light jacket that concealed her pistol. She pulled up the one pant leg and strapped an ankle holster and gun. In the jacket pocket, she added several clips of ammunition and a few plastic straps that would work for handcuffs. Overall, she was a walking SWAT team with a beautiful body. I refused a gun, as I honestly have a real aversion to weapons that kill. Carlos was the first person I'd ever aimed a loaded gun and the results of that action spoke for themselves.

We left the hotel and moved toward the road running by the boat slips, which was dark and fairly well concealed from the water. She motioned to stop behind a trash dumpster directly across from Juan's dock.

"Stay here for a minute," she whispered. "I'll be right back."

I watched her slip out of our hiding place and dart across the road toward Juan's boat. The boat was dark except for lights in the forward cabin area. I didn't see any guards on deck or on the dock, but several cars parked along the road indicated someone was on board. The boat behind Juan's was a sleek twin mast sailboat, but it was completely dark and looked deserted. The slip in front of his boat was empty, so I assumed the cars belonged to people on Juan's boat. One of them obviously belonged to Dawson, but I hadn't seen which one he was driving before we saw him board the boat.

Looking back at our hotel, I tried to figure out which balcony was our room, but couldn't remember if the hotel had a thirteenth floor or not, which would make a difference when you're trying to find the eighteenth floor. I have no idea why I was even trying to find our room, other than the fact it took my mind off where I was and what I was going to do.

I heard a noise and J ducked back in behind the dumpster. I hadn't seen her heading back and she scared the shit out of me when she suddenly appeared.

"There are no alarms on the ramp to the boat," she said. "From what I remember the only alarms are on the cabin doors, and they are only activated when everyone beds down. We're going to go up the ramp and head to the bow near the inflatable on the deck. It will provide a cover and we can see in the windows on the starboard side from there."

She pulled the gun from her waistband and looked with a smile. "This will be a piece of cake. All you have to do is follow me and do what I say. As soon as the guards leave, we should hear from Bingo. We'll give them time to clear away and then head to the main cabin. I'm hoping Ricky will go with the guards and that will leave only Juan and Dawson on board. If Ricky stays then it's plan B."

"What's plan B?" I asked.

"I have no idea," she replied.

"Swell," I said. "Now I feel a whole lot safer."

She leaned forward and kissed me, "I love you, baby. Let's go finish this and have some fun."

As she led me out from the dumpster, I was thoroughly convinced she was having fun already. I was not, but I don't think my vote counted for much right then. We ran across the road and moved quickly to the bottom of the boat ramp where she pointed for me to head up and she would follow.

The ramp moved slightly as I went up, but didn't seem to be enough to cause someone to notice movement. At the top of the ramp, I ducked low and moved toward the bow of the boat. I came to an open area and saw the inflatable raft tied down on the deck above me. J came up behind and signaled for me to wait. She went farther up the bow and climbed a small ladder to the raft. Pulling on a corner of the raft cover, she slipped it open and slid under. Following her trail, I joined her in the raft.

The space was big enough to hold six people, so we had plenty of room to stretch out under the cover. I couldn't see anything in the darkness, but I felt her slide by me and open the corner on the back of the raft. Sliding up next to her, I peered out over the edge and had a clear view of the main cabin. Sitting behind a small desk was a man I had not seen before. He was in his mid thirties with thick dark hair and a sun-darkened complexion. He was talking to someone in front of him, but we couldn't see because of the angle of our vision. I guessed this man behind the desk had to be the one who had made my vacation such an interesting trip. I nudged J and whispered, "That Juan?"

"Yes, but I don't know who else."

I watched Juan as he stood and walked to a bar area and fixed a drink. He continued to talk but we couldn't hear what he was saying. He was a well-built man and fit into the yachting mode. Watching him, you almost felt his arrogance and confidence. Similar to Bingo, he appeared to have a coldness about him that colored the air. How do people end up being such a personification of evil? I really don't believe we're born that way, I think it's something we acquire. Nevertheless, maybe I'm wrong and evil is a part of some of the gene pools. In either case, Juan was pure evil.

As we lay there in our rubber hideout, one of the people below our viewpoint stood and walked to the desk. It was Mr. Cleft Chin, who I now knew as Ricky. He answered a phone on the desk, listened for a minute, and handed it to Juan who sat on the edge of the desk and listened. He said something and handed it back to Ricky who listened some more and hung up the phone. Almost immediately, I heard J's phone vibrate and felt her move to answer it. She flicked it open and said, "Yes."

It was quiet in the raft and I could hear the other person speak, "It's done; you got about half an hour."

192

I could tell that the voice was Bingo. I don't think I will ever forget that voice.

She said thanks and closed the phone. Ricky pulled another phone from his pocket, said something, and put it back. Juan picked up a small briefcase and handed it to Ricky. He pointed at the briefcase and then pointed at the floor and said something before Ricky took the case and headed out of the cabin. Another figure stood and started to follow Ricky, but Juan motioned for him to sit and he went back to the seat he had vacated. In that quick exchange, we both saw the other person in the room was Dawson.

J nudged me and said, "Stay here," and left the raft. I heard voices near the ramp and footsteps heading off the boat. After a pause, I heard a car doors close, and the engine started. The sound of tires on gravel indicated the car had begun to move, but then I heard a heavy thud near the ramp. I looked out and tried to see what was happening, but couldn't see around the corner. The heavy thud was not a welcome sound, especially when you are hiding in a raft on a boat filled with angry people. The corner of the raft cover flipped back and I saw J standing by the opening.

"Come quick," she whispered and then turned and left the raft. I followed and found her on the deck below the raft. At her feet was a large form who was obviously unconscious. Looking closer, I saw it was my cleft-chinned friend, Mr. Ricky. He'd been secured at his hands and feet with the plastic ties J had brought with her and a piece of duct tape was on his mouth. I wondered where she found the duct tape, but decided at this point that wasn't important.

193

J leaned close and said, "He'll be out for a while, but we have to move quick. The outer door to the cabin is open; we'll go in there. I'll go first and you follow. I'll hold my right hand behind my back and you follow close, pretending you are Ricky and have me apprehended. I'll make a lot of noise as we enter the room, when I say 'now,' hit the floor and stay put."

None of this made sense to me, but I didn't have a good plan and obviously this was not a time for a committee meeting. I simply nodded yes and followed her to the cabin door. J stood and put her right hand behind her back. In her hand was her automatic, but she had her arm bent as if someone was holding it behind her. She looked over her shoulder, nodded, and then said loudly, "You fucker, you're breaking my arm!"

With that, she barged straight into the cabin with me following closely. As we entered, both men turned to see what the commotion was. That was when she hollered, "Now."

I dropped straight down to my knees and saw Dawson reach inside his jacket for his gun. I heard J's gun go off and watched Dawson fall back. She'd hit him in the gun hand and the bullet looked as if it had penetrated and continued into his chest. He hit the couch behind him and rolled to the floor.

J had already turned and aimed at Juan who was lifting a gun from the desk, starting to aim at her. J fired and Juan's gun went flying across the room as his hand turn bloody. Turning toward her, I saw a look of rage in his eyes as he took a step and reached for her. She fired one more shot and I saw him crumble to the ground, his face lined with agony as he clutched his groin. I suddenly

194

realized she had shot him directly between the legs and I felt the man's pain deep in my stomach.

Finally, I stood and looked at her as she stood over Juan with the gun still aimed at him, her face expressing all her hatred for the man cowering beneath her.

"J, you don't need him dead," I said quietly.

She took a deep breath and slowly lowered her gun. She reached for her cell phone, and never taking her eyes off Juan, opened it, hit a number, and said, "It's over."

Suddenly bright lights went on all around the boat and I could hear people running. I looked over to the window, but my eyes fell on Dawson who was now holding a gun and aiming at J.

I lunged at J and grabbed her as his gun went off. I felt an impact in my back followed by a sudden pain in my chest. I heard another shot go off near my face as J and I hit the wall together where I lost my balance and fell to the floor. My chest felt as if I was burning up and I was having trouble catching my breath. I looked up at J and saw blood all over her face and chest. She looked at me as she slowly began to slide down the wall, leaving a red streak behind her. I tried to move to her, but my breathing was too difficult. Looking at at me, she softly said, "Oh baby, I'm so sorry." I had the strange sensation of other people in the room and voices shouting. I saw someone bend over J and he, or she, had a jacket with big letters saying FBI. I gave up trying to catch my breath and surrendered to the darkness.

CHAPTER 22

I was in the water trying to fight my way to the surface. I saw the lights above me and kept kicking toward the top when suddenly a hand reached out and began to pull me. Looking over, I saw it was J and she was pulling me but I wasn't moving. She pointed down and I followed her direction toward my feet. One foot appeared caught in a door of what looked like a safe. She moved down toward the safe and began to turn the combination. Grabbing the handle, she looked up at me, smiled, and opened the door. The safe exploded as I watched it rip her apart. The blast forced me to the surface. The light was getting brighter and suddenly I was out of the water. Trying to move, I realized my hands were tied to something. The light around me began to focus revealing a ceiling light. Looking around, I became aware I was in a bed with a cast on my chest. When I tried to move, someone leaned over me and pushed me back.

"Dr. Sanders, try not to move," the person said. "You've been hurt and you're in a hospital. Relax and try not to move."

Now able to focus, I saw the voice came from a female dressed in a blue uniform. As I relaxed, I realized it was a nurse and I saw her nametag said Jean Bently, RN.

"Where is J?" I asked through a hoarse voice.

"I'll call the doctor and he will help you with all you need," Nurse Jean Bently said softly. "You lie quietly and rest."

I lay back in the bed, looked around the room, and saw it was a private room decorated in typical hospital nothingness. I suddenly remembered why I was in the hospital as I tried to sit up and a pain went through my chest like a lightning bolt. When it hit, I gasped and found the very act of breathing brought even more pain. I decided I was comfortable in my current position and it was not necessary to move. At least the pain helped clear my mind and I began to remember all that had happened before my lights went out. I remembered J sliding down the wall and a bunch of people all running around the room. Who the hell had come in the room? Obviously, they were people who took me to a hospital and didn't kill me; for that I was grateful.

What happened to J that caused all the blood? I think I took the bullet intended for her, but she still appeared hurt. Where the hell was Nurse Jean Bently when I needed her? The pain was really getting large by this point and I was having trouble focusing on my thoughts. I knew a buzzer existed somewhere, but as I looked around for it, the room began to spin and the lights went out.

I was aware I was floating and the feeling was great. I saw the houses below and people waving at me. I waved back and spreading my arms, started to make circles in the sky. Rising higher, I felt a tug on my foot and realized I was tied to the ground by a long rope. I tried to break loose, but the rope was tied too tight to undo it. I started to pull on the rope and as I descended, I gathered it in my hands. I saw the rope tied to some type of box sitting right on the edge of a cliff and I saw J standing next to it.

Waving to her, I pulled myself closer to the ground. She waved at me, pointed to the box, and stepped off the cliff. She was falling and I flew after her as fast as I could. I was about to reach her when the rope on my leg stopped me and I watched her continue to fall and disappear. I looked up, saw bright lights above me, and tried to fly toward them for help. A voice kept saying, "Dr. Sanders, wake up. Wake up, Dr. Sanders."

Opening my eyes, I found I was back in the hospital bed but this time two men were standing next to me. "Where is Nurse Jean?" I asked for some reason.

"She is off duty now; you've been sleeping for a while." The one male voice said. "I am Dr. Brauer and this is Agent Swanson from the FBI. How are you feeling?"

I tried to focus on the man with the voice and slowly he came into view. Dr. Brauer was one of those people you meet that make you feel better by seeing them. He had a great smile and a kindness that said he had won the bedside manner award many times. I smiled back at him and said, "I feel like shit."

"Well that's better than not feeling at all," he said with a smile. "You've been through some difficult times, but the good

198

news is that you will recover. Do you remember what happened before you came here?"

"I was on a boat and my friend Special Agent Dawson shot me. What happened to J?"

The other man, who I vaguely remember was called Agent Johnson or Swanson, moved into my view and said, "Do you feel up to answering a few questions Dr. Sanders?"

"Who are you?" I asked.

"I am Jack Swanson, Special Agent in charge of the Miami FBI operations. I was Jennifer Blade's supervisor in the Miami area. Do you remember what happened on the boat?"

I tried to clear my mind and finally replied, "J and I hid on the boat and went into Juan's cabin. All hell broke loose but J had it all under control until Dawson took one more shot. Where is J, is she okay?"

Dr. Bedside Manors said, "The bullet from Agent Dawson hit you in the back and punctured your lung. It was a fragment bullet designed to break into small pieces on impact, but it missed your rib in the back and only fragmented when it tried to exit your front rib cage. It hit your second true rib off the sternum and fragmented as it continued on into Jennifer."

I remembered the impact on my back and the feeling of fire in my chest. I remembered the blood all over J as she slid down the wall. "How bad was she hurt?" I asked.

Dr. Brauer took a breath and said, "The fragments caught her in the chest, heart, and neck. We tried to repair the damage, but it was too extensive. I am sorry, Dr. Sanders, she was too badly hurt to rescue."

"Wait a minute," I shouted as I tried to sit up. Immediately the pain rushed through my chest and I let out a scream. I remember the doctor trying to push me down as he reached out and release something into the tube in my arm. Suddenly the pain started to decrease. I began to feel lightheaded but I asked the only question that mattered, "Is J dead?"

As I started to fade out, I never heard a reply, but the look in both their faces answered my question.

I woke up sometime later and saw the sun was shining brightly through my window. Another blue uniform was near my bed as I asked, "What time is it?"

"Well, hello Dr. Sanders, it is 11:15. How are you feeling?"

I guess they have to ask that question in a hospital, but shit, if I felt good, I wouldn't be in the hospital. "What day is it?" I finally asked.

The blue uniform came next to the bed and I saw this one's name was Sally Mayfield. "It's Friday. Are you hungry for anything? We need to get you on solid food."

"Very thirsty," was all I could manage to say. She brought a glass of water with a straw and I was able to suck some into my mouth. My throat felt as if an army had been on maneuvers in it, but the water was great.

"Can I sit up higher?" I asked Nurse Mayfield.

She pressed a button and my bed began to rise higher until I easily saw around the room. "You rest like that for a while and we will get you on your feet and into a chair."

She turned and went out of the room. As I watched her go, I saw a uniform sitting outside my door. I was either being protected

200

or under arrest, I didn't know which. As I looked around the room, a thought finally worked its way into my consciousness, "J is dead."

I felt the pain well up in my body, but it wasn't from the surgery, it was in my soul. She can't be dead, that's not how this was all supposed to turn out. I suddenly had the picture in my head of her sliding down the wall and saying, "Baby, I am so sorry." She can't be dead; we had the thing finished until that asshole Dawson shot her. I guess he shot me, but it went through me and killed her. I had a desire to jump out of bed and find that asshole and strangle him, but the pain in my chest reminded me that was a futile thought. I lay there and slowly accepted the fact that things had not turned out right, and J was gone. I felt emptiness creep into my inner being. I was becoming a hollow man.

The door opened and Agent Swanson entered the room. He smiled and came to the bed. "I hear you're doing better sport."

"I guess I am. Nevertheless, I need to know what happened. What happened to Dawson?"

Swanson pulled up a chair and sat next to the bed. "Dawson is dead," he said as he settled into the chair. "Apparently Jennifer got a shot off after you were hit and it caught him in the head. He never regained consciousness. I wanted to bring him in earlier, but Jennifer didn't want to spook Juan. I guess she was right, but that's hard to swallow now. J was one of the best I have ever had the privilege to work with, Steve, and I know she was special to you. We had it set up for her to call us in once she was on Juan's boat, but she wanted to wrap it up herself I guess. Juan is in recovery and will never be quite the same again. His bladder had severe damage and he will probably pee with a bag for the rest of his life. He also will have no sex life, but where he is going—that won't matter much. We started moving on the list J put together and by the end of this weekend we'll have closed up billions of dollars of drug money and crippled a large part of the big cartel."

I listened to him, and knew J would be happy about Juan and the cartels. Nevertheless, that didn't bring much happiness now. "J would be happy with the results," I said, then I had another thought, "What about Bingo?"

"What about him?" Swanson replied.

"We made a deal with him," I said as I had a flashing memory of J and her dress.

"Bingo is not on the list, just as J told him," Swanson said as he stood up.

"And the tape she had?" I asked.

Swanson looked at me quizzically and finally said, "I'm not aware of any tape, it must have been a subterfuge she made up. I'm sure Bingo is happy that he's not in the shutdown so I wouldn't worry about him."

The answer didn't make sense, but I was too cloudy in my thinking to process it further. As he turned to go I asked, "Why the bodyguard at my door? Am I under arrest?"

"This whole sting is really touchy," he replied. "We're taking no chances until we know we have everything finished. Juan knows what you look like but not who you are and we're making sure you'll be clear by the time you leave the hospital. You need to recover and go back to the life you had. I know your loss is great, but you accomplished a lot in a short period of time and did a great service."

"Can I see J?" I asked.

"Doc, do yourself a big favor and remember her the way she was. She left instructions for cremation and for the remains to be sent back to her home. I know you want some closure to this, but you'll be better off if you keep the memory and not the reality. I'll check with you tomorrow and see how you're doing."

With that he left, and I was alone with my memory. The trouble was, my memories hurt a lot, and I could not make them feel better. I didn't want to go back to what I had been before and I didn't want to go forward either. I really wanted to crawl in a hole and die. The pain inside grew too big and the release only came in sobs I could not control. "Oh baby," I choked out through my tears. "I am so sorry."

***

It was Monday morning before I finally talked the doctors into letting me go. After a few meals and some walking around, I began to recover rapidly. The pain was still there, but it was minor and I was sick of hospital walls and beds. They brought the dark slacks I wore that night, but they cut off my shirt so they gave me a hospital scrub top to wear. The Fed's removed the chaperone outside my door the night before and I surmised I no longer needed protection.

I hit the street about noon when the reality I had no place to go suddenly struck me. In my pant pocket I still had the hotel room passkey and I wondered if anyone had checked us out. The keys for the Lincoln were in the hotel room so I decided to go see if they

203

had packed us up and moved us out or if we still had a room. I had to correct my thinking at that point and remind myself that there was no we, it was only me.

The cab dropped me off at the Continental Bayside and I looked across the road to see if Juan's boat was still there. It was, but it looked like a Miami squad car parked by the ramp. As I looked at the yacht, a flood of memories hit me hard and I thought I would pass out. Turning away, I headed into the lobby and went to the desk. A receptionist finished with another customer and pleasantly turned to me. I guess I looked rather strange with my hospital scrubs, cast on my chest, and an arm in a sling. She smiled and said, "May I help you sir?"

"Yes, my name is Robert Klingman and I was staying with Ms. Jennifer Blade in room 1812." I produced the key, which was actually a credit card with no room number on it. I wasn't sure how to proceed and simply plowed ahead.

"We had an accident and I was released from the hospital and wanted to see if we had any messages."

She checked her computer, went back to a file behind her and pulled out an envelope. She handed it to me along with the room card I had given her and said, "No telephone messages sir, only this note that was dropped off for you. I'm sorry to hear about your accident, I hope you both are okay. Is there anything else I may do for you?"

I shook my head no, thanked her, and headed toward the elevator. At least I still had a room, but I wasn't sure I was ready to go there and find more memories. I'd settled into numbness the last few days, but coming back here was difficult. Everyplace I looked,

I saw something of J and desperately wanted her to jump out and say "surprise." I chuckled as I thought of her jumping out in the lobby stark naked and yelling "surprise," but the reality of her not doing that ever again hit, and I went back to numb.

I got out on the eighteenth floor and used my key card to enter 1812. The room was orderly and clean, but again, why wouldn't it be. Nobody had been here since last Wednesday. I went to the balcony and once again looked out at Juan's boat remembering how we sat on the balcony and watched it that night. I felt a strong sense of contentment knowing that fucking Agent Matt Dawson was dead. I still considered finding his corpse and shooting him one more time, but that was not a good thought to keep if you were going to move through grief recovery.

Taking off the sling from my arm, I threw it on the table. I really didn't need it as all it did was relieve the pressure of my arm on the shoulder cast. It didn't hurt to breathe anymore and I took that as a good sign. Doctor Brauer told me the lung would heal itself, as would the rib cage. I'd have some deep scars on my chest, but in time, they would even become faint. In short, I was going to recover fully. I could have told him I would never recover no matter what he said, but he was a nice person and I didn't feel like giving him any problems. Swanson came to see me again before I left and assured me that I was a great American and what had taken place was important in the war on drugs. I almost told him to go fuck himself, but didn't really have the energy to be nasty.

Slipping off the hospital scrub, I found the note given to me at the front desk. I took it to the kitchen, located my dearest friend Johnny Walker, and brought them both to the balcony. The afternoon sun was working up a real heat and it felt good to be in the fresh air. I poured a glass of Johnny and opened the note. Inside were a small key and a note that said, "Room safe."

I asked Johnny if he knew what that was all about, but he didn't reply. I remembered a room safe in the closet, which a guest could use for valuables, but I hadn't put anything in it. Maybe J did, but why did she leave a note at the front desk and not tell me? Pulling myself up, I felt the pain in my chest from the strain. I probably should take a painkiller, but decided Johnny would do better. In the bedroom closet I found the safe and the key opened it immediately. Inside were a small package and another note. As I went to the bed and lay down to open them, I looked over to the mirror, saw my reflection, and decided I really did look like shit. I'd lost a few pounds in the hospital and the cast on my chest and shoulder made me look as some deformed bulimic. I saw J's dress folded up on the dresser and once again felt the pain inside that even Johnny couldn't take away.

The note was typed and said,

"Steve,

This is Bingo's tape. You have to take it to him as soon as possible. It's the original and I have a copy for future security. Make sure he listens to the tape and tell Bingo not to worry, I'll never use it unless he causes trouble. Remember your promise; I'm going to hold you to it. I love you always, J.

I looked at the note and read it about five more times. I guess Bingo was safe, as J had the copy and she took the knowledge of its location to her grave. She asked me to remember my promise. I'd promised to go with her on her new life adventure.

Unfortunately, where she went, I wasn't able to follow. At that moment, a big part of me wanted to literally go where she was. Dying had crossed my mind several times in the last few days, but I didn't have the courage to face it.

I picked up the tape and thought about throwing it away. Fuck Bingo and fuck this whole fucking situation. I picked it up to throw it across the room, stopped, sat it on the bed, and picked up the note to look at it again. It was typed. J and I had the conversation about starting a new life when we sat on the balcony. We went straight from the balcony to the boat; she didn't have time to type up a note.

I got up, went to the phone, and dialed the front desk. "This is room 1812," I said when they answered. "I picked up a note from the front desk a few minutes ago and I was wondering if anyone had a record of when it was delivered?" They put me on hold for a minute and came back.

"Yes, Mr. Klingman, that was put in your file yesterday at 3:00 pm."

I hung up the phone and sat back down on the bed. Yesterday at 3:00 p.m! How the hell could that be possible? I grabbed a phone book and began to look for the listing for the FBI office in Miami. While doing this, I remembered the vague look Swanson gave me when I asked about the tape. I didn't think he was covering something, I thought he really didn't know about the tape. If J wanted Bingo to have the tape, she could have arranged for the FBI to get it to him. However, she left it for me to deliver. Moreover, if the note came yesterday at 3:00 pm, who the hell delivered it?

I went back to the balcony to see if my friend Johnny Walker had any thoughts about this. The nagging voice in my head kept saying, "She is not dead." I wanted to listen to that voice with all my heart, but I couldn't face the possibility that the voice was wrong. My insides became all tight and I really thought I would throw up on the balcony.

Dr. Brauer was very clear on how J had died. I really trusted him, and he didn't seem to be covering anything. Getting up again, I went to the phonebook and found the number of the hospital. When they answered, I asked to speak to Dr. Brauer. After a moment, someone else answered and asked me to spell the last name. I fished around in my pocket, found the papers from my discharge, and located the attending physicians name. It said, Dr. David Wooster. Who the hell was David Wooster?

I spelled out B R A U E R, and after a minute they said they had no listing for that name. I asked for Dr. David Wooster and they put me through. Someone answered and when I asked for Dr. Wooster, they said he was on three-month sabbatical and would be back in a month.

I headed back to Johnny, because he was the only one making any sense. I sat down and said, "Johnny, here is the situation. I've been in the hospital for five days and spent a lot of time talking to a doctor who does not exist. The doctor who does exist is on a sabbatical and won't be back for a while. The woman I loved died five days ago, but dropped me a note yesterday. The only thing I know for sure is that I have a tape I'm supposed to give to Bingo. I don't want to see Bingo ever again. What are your thoughts, Johnny?"

He was his usual quiet self, but a voice in my head said, "Better go see Bingo." I took another sip of my drink and simply replied, "Fuck you, Johnny."

I apologized to Johnny, because he was about the only friend I had. Heading to the bedroom, I opened a drawer to find a shirt and realized none of them would fit over my cast. I went to the closet to find a jacket and discovered one of those Cuban shirts that was extra large. I didn't remember the shirt at all, and the fact it was extra large was something neither J nor I would have purchased. I put it on and it covered my cast perfectly. How in the hell did it get there?

"In my business I make it a practice to know people's sizes."

Remembering her saying that, once again, the nagging voice within me tried to come to the surface, "She is alive." I pushed it back, but found myself starting to hope it might be true. She had played the "I am dead" game with me once before, and I really didn't like going through it again. It was more real this time, as I had seen the blood and the look of pain in her eyes before I passed out from my own pain. Nevertheless, none of the new evidence made sense, especially the kind and smiling Dr. Brauer. Looking at my reflection in the mirror I said, "OK, J, if this is your game, I will play. I just pray that it has a better ending than the one I have been through so far."

CHAPTER 23

I decided to be extremely brave and drive myself to Bingo's. The Lincoln had about twenty different seat positions and I was finally able to get me, my cast, and the remainder of my body behind the wheel. Taking a taxi would have been a lot easier, but I was tired of following other people and wanted to be in charge of something.

Heading out to South Beach, I remembered walking these streets with J and her hot new dress. I vowed, whatever happened, I would never part with that dress. Not that I would wear it, I hadn't become that bad, but simply as a place of memory. I glanced at Juan's boat as I left the hotel and, traveling down the street, the reminder of that night occupied my mind completely. Bingo's place was only a few miles down the road, but the late afternoon traffic in South Beach was atrocious. I think the majority of people drove slowly to look at the beautiful people walking down the sidewalk. If you wanted to see flesh on parade, South Beach was the place to go.

The sign for Golden Arm finally appeared and I drove up to the valet parking. A young valet opened my door and I slowly extricated myself from the car. I gave him $20 and told him not to move the seat position. He looked at me and said "Si Senor," then promptly pulled the seat up and drove off to the lot. The only consolation I had was the fact I still was using somebody else's money.

Inside the club, it was business as usual with fewer dancers and patrons, but the ambience remained the same. I went to the bar and saw Dave was working the day shift this time. As he came up, he smiled and said, "Your J's friend, right?"

I nodded yes and he said, "Man, I can't tell you how that news bummed me out. I really liked her and didn't think anybody would ever get the drop on her. Were you two friends or did you work together."

"She and I were very close," was all I could reply.

"I'm really sorry," he said and stuck out his hand to shake mine. I had some trouble getting my arm extended past the shoulder cast and he saw me grimace in pain. "Were you with her when it happened?"

"We were together when it happened and I still have trouble believing it," I said as I pulled my arm back. I think I had aggravated the stitches with my drive over, because the wound was hurting more all the time.

"Did you take one too?" Dave asked as he pointed to the cast under my shirt.

"Unfortunately I did Dave, but I lived through mine. I think I need a Johnny Red on the rocks for the pain."

"You got it, boss," he said. "On the house."

Dave poured me a double and set it before me. I had a great desire to down it and get another, but the thought of Bingo was ever before me and I needed to be in control.

"What brings you here this afternoon?" Dave asked as he busied himself wiping down the bar. There were three bartenders working and not enough business to really keep them active.

"I need to see Bingo," I replied.

"I thought you might say that," Dave said as he leaned over the bar. "I'll let him know you're here, but I can assure you Bingo would have never hurt J."

I looked at Dave and tried to understand why he said that. "I'm not here to try to cause Bingo problems. I think he's capable of hurting anyone he wants, but in this case, I don't think he's responsible for her death."

"I know who J was and what she did," he said quietly. "And if you got taken down with her, I assume you're in the same business. The only reason I say this is that a lot of Bingo's friends and associates have been in and out of here the last few days, and something big is going on in their business. Bingo has really been on the edge, even more than usual. So just know he may not be in a real good mood when you see him."

"Dave," I said as I leaned closer to him, "I'm not in a real good mood either and Bingo is the last fucking person on earth I

212

want to see. However, J left me instructions to come see him and here I am. No offense, but I really could care less if Bingo is happy, sad, constipated, or pregnant. I only want to see him and get the fuck out of here."

"I read you, friend," Dave said. "I'll let him know you are waiting."

The pain was making me irritable, but not as much as watching everybody walk around thinking these fucking pricks were important people. They were an arrogant bunch of hoods making money off other's pain. I hated them all and hated what they stood for in so many different ways.

Taking a deep breath, I tried to regain my calm disposition, as anger was not an emotion I used often—and when I did, it never worked well. I looked over the floor and saw a few dancers doing their moves on the pianos. I thought about the redhead J mentioned, but didn't see her anyplace. I hoped she heard about J and decided to get out while she could. I finished the last of Johnny when Man Mountain appeared next to me. He looked at me and said, "Come with me."

Even though my glass was empty, I slowly took another swallow and got up to follow him. I made him wait for me, and I can't tell you how good that felt. We followed the same path back to Bingo's office, but the bodies and pot were missing from the back rooms. We once again entered the outer office where he knocked on the door and guided me into Bingo's office. It seemed years since I had been here, but in reality, it had been only five days. Bingo was on the phone and he totally ignored me. Instead of waiting for his permission, I made myself comfortable on a chair. Bingo finally finished his conversation and turned to look at me.

"You were supposed to be here Friday," he finally said.

"Gee Bingo, I'm really sorry about that, but J and I have been busy getting shot and killed, so fuck you."

"Yeah, I can't believe the kid bought it," he said, and leaned back and looked at me with a softer projection. "You're not a fed are you?"

"No, I'm not," I said staring back at him.

"I didn't think you were," he said as he continued to stare at me. "I guess you and J were an item. How the hell did you get into this mess?"

"It's a long story, but it doesn't have a good ending," I said.

"No, life gets complicated fast when you play in this game. J knew that and I can't believe somebody actually got to her. I hear she did Juan something good, which does make my heart happy. Nevertheless, one of her cop friends shot her and that really sucks. You look a little banged up. They get you too?"

"Yeah, I got in the way of a bullet, but I'll live."

His phone rang and he pushed a button and said, "No calls Irene." He looked at me and said, "Do you have any idea of the shit that's going on around here. I've had people all over my ass about the feds closing up their accounts and they're all real curious why I'm not affected by all this. But I told them I'm really careful. You and J did me good by getting me off the list, so I guess I owe you a thanks. But I did my part, so I guess we're even."

214

I laughed and said, "Yeah, Bingo, you did your part. You got paid by Juan and bypassed charges from the feds. J did her part and got killed. Nice even deal."

"Hey smart mouth," he said as he leaned toward me. "This is a business and that's all. She gave me a deal and I took it; not my fault if her own people fucked it up and shot her. Now give me what you owe me and get out before you get more pain."

I stood and leaned over the desk and said, "You know you are a real piece of shit. You think you are god because you can use a gun and push other people around. Well, let me tell you Bingo Bob, to me you're just another cheap hood who is responsible for J being dead. You want to shoot me, go ahead. In ten days I've been shot twice, killed two men, got screwed over by the FBI, and lost the woman I love. You don't scare me; you may be the answer to my prayers if you did kill me." I reached in my pocket and threw the tape on his desk. "Here asshole, pardon if there is blood on it; J may not have had time to it clean up before she died. I hope you enjoy the recording."

I turned toward the door when I heard him push his chair back and stand. "Wait a minute," he shouted after me. I stopped and turned to look at him and watched as he came around his desk and walked toward me. "You had dinner yet?"

"Is that some kind of code for a killing?" I asked.

"You watch too much TV," he said. "If you haven't eaten and want to join me, I can guarantee you the best steak you've ever eaten."

He actually smiled at me, and for some reason I said, "Okay."

215

He had the tape in his hand and placed it in his pocket as he opened the door. He shouted something unintelligible to Irene, but she nodded yes and got on the phone. "How do you like your steak cooked?" he asked.

"Medium rare," I replied, still somewhat baffled at this turn of events.

"Got that?" he shouted to Irene, who nodded yes as we exited the lobby. Bingo guided me down the porno hall and out into the main lounge. We crossed the room and I noticed the piano dancers all managed to smile as he walked by.

A door near the bar opened for us as we approached. Man Mountain was inside and he waited until we went by and then left the room and closed the door. The place we entered had a long table covered with a deep green tablecloth. About ten chairs were around the table, but only two places had been prepared. Bingo motioned me to sit and he took a chair at the setting across from me.

"You want a drink or wine?" he asked as the waiter stood at attention next to him. Thinking I had better keep some level of sanity about me, I said wine and Bingo mumbled something to the waiter who scurried out of the room.

"I couldn't figure you out when you came last time," Bingo said as he tore off a piece of bread and dipped it in a dish of oil next to him. "I was sure you weren't a fed, but couldn't figure out what you were doing with J. Your last little ranting in my office finally answered my question. You and J were in love. If J loved you, I have to love you too."

He stuffed the bread in his mouth, but I was the one who almost choked. All I could get out was, "Why?"

"I'm from Brooklyn and I knew J's dad when she was a kid. When he died, I kept an eye on her and made sure she had things she needed. Her mother was a special woman and in many ways I probably loved her as much as any woman I know. We had some fun, but she wouldn't go along with my lifestyle and the relationship never worked out. When she was murdered, J called me to help and I kind of watched over her from that point until she finished law school. When Jennifer went with the feds, she came to see me and told me what she was doing. She was just like her dad, thinking she could solve the world's problems and never get hurt as she did it. When she got into the shit down here, she begged me to get out before it really went to hell, but I was too deep into this to leave. There is no formal retirement plan in my business, only death."

I thought back on the conversation with J about her "uncle" who had taken care of her after her dad died. I put this together and now understood that Bingo Bob was that uncle. I remembered J saying her mom and this Uncle had been an item, but her mom had broken it off because of her uncle's line of work. This was an interesting piece of information, but my brain was on overload and couldn't process anything else.

The waiter came in followed by several others. He poured Bingo some of the wine and Bingo did a tasting routine that would put a Sommelier to shame. Apparently, the wine passed his test and we both received full glasses. While all this was happening, the other waiters presented a platter with a huge steak on it. The headwaiter took a butter knife, cut the steak in two pieces, and placed it on the plates set before us. They gave us some mashed potatoes and other beautifully cooked vegetables and then wove a design on the plate with a thick sauce. Bingo nodded and the entire crew exited and closed the door.

"I guarantee you ain't never had a steak like this," Bingo said as he took his fork and cut a piece off. "They boil this or something, and then grill it quick. If you can't cut it with a butter knife, they throw it out."

I took my fork and cut a piece as if it was cake. After hospital food, anything would taste good, but this was absolutely beyond description.

Bingo watched me like a proud father and when I reacted very positively to the steak, he literally laughed and clapped his hands. This was obviously a different side of Bingo than most people experienced. We sat quietly and enjoyed the meal until he set his fork down and said, "Ok, I understand you and J were in love and that's good in my book, but why were you working with her?"

"She and I met on a fishing trip," I said, "and things clicked. We were spending time getting to know each other when Carlos, who you know, showed up to get J to talk about her fall out with Juan. There was a scuffle and Carlos didn't make it. J tried to get me away, but apparently Carlos didn't come alone and his friend tried to kill me. J got me out of town to Hollywood. She wanted me to simply lay low while she straightened things out, but I refused to leave her side. I don't know why I was being headstrong, but it seemed the right thing at the moment. She met with Junior, but Juan and his boys showed up. Junior was shot by Juan's men, but I

218

hit one of them with my car as I was trying to help J. She shot the other one, but Juan got away, or I guess I should say, we got away from Juan. After that we came to see you and you know the story from there." As I went through all this, I was rather amazed at all the series of events that had taken place in ten days.

Bingo took a few more bites as he contemplated my story and said, "Who else knows all this?"

I thought for a minute and said, "I really don't know. Matt Dawson knew all the details, but he's dead. Juan may know my face, but I'm not sure what else he knows. I guess the guy who saw me kill Carlos would know me, but I don't really have a clue who he talked to and what information was shared. I guess Swanson from the FBI knows about this, but I've come to a point of not trusting him at all."

"You mean Swanson who runs Miami FBI?" Bingo asked. "What did he do to you to lose trust?"

I didn't know what to say to Bingo. If J was alive, did she want him to know that or was he one of the people who she was hiding from with her death story. If J was dead, everything was a mess, and I couldn't logically explain why I didn't trust Swanson. I decided to limit my information and simply said, "There was a strange interaction with the doctor in the hospital and it left me not trusting anyone."

"Rule of the game, Robert, never trust anyone, especially the ones you think you trust."

"J told me that," I replied, "and as far as Robert goes, my name is actually Steve. J changed my ID when I left New York."

219

Bingo smiled and shook his head, "You and J have a lot of little secrets don't you. Tell me more about Swanson and what you think he did to you."

I thought for a minute before I answered, "After I got out of the hospital, I wanted some more information. I called a Dr. Brauer who had been my personal physician in the hospital, but they informed me a Dr. Brauer didn't exist. On my discharge, the attending physician was listed as a Dr. Wooster, who the hospital informed me was out on a sabbatical. There was something strange about all that, but I haven't followed up on it yet."

Bingo looked at me for a while and let out a deep breath. "Was Brauer J's attending doctor too?"

"I guess he was, but I was pretty messed up in the head and didn't ask many questions while I was there."

He reached in his pocket, pulled out the package with the tape in it, and dumped it out on the table. Along with the tape was a short handwritten note. He read it and handed it to me. All the note said was, ***Bingo, Play this tape NOW.***

"Let's go back to my office," he said as he pushed away from the table. I stood to follow him, but was suddenly hit with a pain in my chest that took away my breath. I sat down, grabbed the arms of the chair, and tried to relax.

Bingo turned to look at me and returned to the table, "You okay? You look white as a sheet."

"I think I'm pushing my recovery too hard," I replied through clenched teeth. "The bullet fragmented leaving quite a sizeable hole, and a collapsed lung. I'm supposed to rest, but haven't done a very good job with that." Bingo handed me a glass of water and left the room. He returned quickly with a bottle and two glasses. He filled the glasses and handed one to me.

"I been shot more times than I remember," he said, "and a good shot of brandy always made me feel better. Not a doctor's first suggestion, but not many doctors have been shot either."

I leaned back and swallowed half the glass of brandy. As it slowly burned its way into my body, I really did start to feel better. Maybe it was the pain of the brandy going down my throat that took my mind off my chest, but either way, it worked. My breathing calmed down and the pain eased in my chest. I stood and found I was feeling good enough to walk, "That really did help. I can walk now so let's go to your office."

He walked close to me all the way back to the office and told me to stretch out on the couch, put my feet up, and relax. As I lay there, I tried to piece together the last two hours. I had come to see Bingo, a man I loathed, and now he was attending to my needs as my closest friend. I was sure he had several hidden agendas, but I was very happy that we were interacting well with each other instead of him threatening me and calling me names. Irene came in and handed Bingo a small tape recorder into which he inserted the cassette. He came and sat in the chair next to me and pushed the play button. I expected to hear more of the dialog between Bingo and the senator's go-between, but was shocked to hear J's voice:

"Bingo, before you listen further, make sure my partner is with you. He delivered the tape and you probably pissed him off. If he is not there, go find him and get him back. He's not my partner, Bingo; he is what you always told me to look for in life. So please, get him back and then listen to this."

Bingo pushed the button and said, "I guess she's talking about you. Now what could I ever do to piss you off?" He laughed and then pushed play again.

"I assume you are both there now, so I'll start again. Bingo, this man with you is Steve and he can explain how we met and anything else he wants. Steve, this is Bingo who is one of my dearest and closest friends. He is a pain in the ass a lot, but you learn to love him if you ignore his temper. If you two are listening to this, you both know things went wrong with Juan. What you don't know is that they did not go as wrong as you think. I'm once again falsely reported as being dead, but this time it will stay that way. Steve, I am so sorry to put you through all this, but it was the only way things could work out. I will make it up to you, I really will. And I will do it as long as you will have me."

I signaled for Bingo to stop the tape. I just heard from her own lips that she was not dead. The little voice in my head kept saying, "I told you so," but I was having trouble digesting the truth. Finally I looked at him and said, "She's not dead, Bingo."

He smiled at me, put his hand on my shoulder, and said, "I didn't think they could get rid of her that easy. I'm happy for you, Steve, but believe me, I feel like I got my daughter back."

He pushed the play button again.

"Bingo, you are a stubborn man, but you have to listen to me and try to do what I suggest. In all the mess with Juan, I kept coming across strange interactions concerning your Senator Harris. They didn't apply to Juan, but I kept a file active to store what I was finding. The Senator seemed to have too much control over the gun market on his end. Things that could not take place,

222

happened with no problem. The only way that could happen was if someone in the FBI was helping out. Two months ago I found out that he had a lot of help and it was my boss, Swanson. I compiled a dossier on all I could find and am now working with the United States Attorney General's office to pull the plug on both Harris and Swanson. Bingo, it is all going to go down, and you're in the middle of it. It is not just a gun-selling problem, it is now Homeland Security. A task force has been operating and it's headed by the CIA. That means all your contacts overseas are also going to be taken down. You know as well as I do that this will be a bigger mess than anything you can fix. Bingo, I need you to work with us so I can get you off the hook. I know that goes against everything you know and understand, but it is the only hope I have of getting you out free."

Now it was Bingo's turn to stop the tape. He sat back in his chair and simply said, "Fuck." I knew better than to interrupt his thoughts, as I'm sure they were many and not pleasant. After a while, he leaned forward and hit the play button again.

"What I am suggesting is this. We can do an 'in camera' testimony that will only be heard by the judge in the case and will be sealed. You won't have to appear in court, but your testimony will stand in evidence. After that, we will make you disappear so nobody will be able to find you. I'm sure you have stashed away funds to live on, but the club and the accounts with Harris will be turned over to the task force. Harris and Swanson will go down and they deserve it. A lot of others will also, but you don't have to. I can make it happen. You know I love you and wouldn't do anything to hurt you. I want you to put Steve under guard until he

*leaves town. I think he will be okay, but Juan's circle of friends
may not be as uninformed as I believe they are. You think about
this and let Steve know your decision. If you say okay to the deal,
you and Steve fly out to New York on Friday. If you say no to the
deal, Steve will fly out alone. I am sorry it all came down to this,
but as you taught me long ago, if you build an outhouse, expect
somebody to shit in it. I miss you both and hope we can all start a
new life together. Dr. Brauer works for the CIA and set up my
death. Swanson thinks I'm dead, and that is the way it will stay.
Only the CIA knows I am alive, and I trust that both of you will
protect that information. If you don't, I will probably die a third
time, and this one will not have an obituary. Please Bingo, for once
in your life listen to me the same way I have listened to you for
years. I love you both. Try to get along.*

The tape ended and we both sat there and looked at the
machine like it would suddenly go up in smoke. Bingo finally
stood up and pulled out his gun. I thought our happy relationship
was about to come to a halt, when suddenly he aimed at the
recorder and shot it three times. Two doors of his office flew open
and two man mountains came flying in with guns drawn. They saw
that Bingo had only shot the tape recorder and stopped in their
tracks waiting to see what would happen next. Bingo simply raised
his hands and waved them away. Holstering their guns, they each
went back to their assigned door and exited.

Needless to say, my heart was going quite fast. I reached for
the glasses and bottle of brandy Bingo brought with him from
dinner. I poured two glasses and handed him one. He looked at me
and I simply said, "I don't think it will help the tape recorder's

gunshot wound much, but it might help us." He shook his head, clinked his glass with mine, and we both emptied our portion.

He sat for a long time and said nothing. I filled both our glasses again, but he held his and didn't move. Finally he said, "Where are you staying?"

"At the Continental Bayside," I answered.

"Marty will go with you and help you get your stuff. He'll take you to a safe place while I sort things out. Our little woman has turned both of our lives upside down and seems to be the only one with any control. I guess I taught her well. I'll make sure you're at the airport on Friday and will book you a ticket to JFK. If I'm with you we will both see what she has in mind. If I'm not, forget you ever met me. I mean it, Steve, you're in places you can't handle. You find her and get the hell out of this with her and make a life in Bora Bora or someplace. If I had left when her mother begged me, life would have been a lot different. But what the hell, life is just a bunch of choices all tied together."

He stood and I followed his lead. He walked to the door and before he opened it said, "After you have forgotten you ever knew me, just try to remember how good that steak was."

He opened the door and barked instruction to the closest man mountain, who I guess was Marty, and then went in and shut his door. As I started out of the lobby, he opened his door again and shouted, "If I don't see you, remember to tell her that I still love her. And you get some rest so you live long enough to take care of her." He closed his door and we headed for the exit.

CHAPTER 24

Marty got the Lincoln and I didn't fight with him to drive. While the brandy helped a lot, my chest was really hurting and now my calf was hurting too. I was exhausted, thrilled, and very confused. J was alive and now plotting some other intrigue, but this time she was with the Attorney General and CIA. How does one woman get into such wacko situations? At least I got my questions answered about the good Dr. Brauer. How could somebody with such a nice personality work for the CIA. Moreover, Swanson was another piece of work. All his bullshit about my being such a great American, and here he was milking the public blind by selling our enemies our guns so they could shoot our soldiers.

In the world of fish, the young hatch by the hundreds because predators, including the fish that birthed them, would eat a vast majority of them. Somehow, man has not progressed all that far from his animal characteristics. Nevertheless, there were people like J who would lay their life on the line to try to hold some sense of goodness. So I guessed we were making some progress along the way to our final destination.

Marty and I arrived at the hotel and he told the valet to leave the car where it was and gave him a $100 dollars to ensure that would happen. I realized that tipping was a very lucrative business in the Miami area.

Packing was easy, as I only had my airport clothes and the new ones J had bought me. I packed my bottle of Johnny Walker and told him I had a lot to tell him later. As we exited, I started to go to the front desk and Marty grabbed my arm and guided me to the car. "Shouldn't we check out?" I asked him and he just smiled at me and got behind the wheel. I had to keep reminding myself that I was not living like normal people anymore. J had used some credit card, and in a few days, someone would notice we were gone and charge the card. It was a nice hotel, but I guess I wasn't too worried how they were going to get paid.

Marty headed north toward Lauderdale and we ended up at a private house someplace between Hollywood and Lauderdale. Marty unlocked the door and carried in my small green suitcase.

The house had a large living room that flowed back to a pool in the yard. A huge screen tent that kept out bugs but let in light covered the pool. Marty took me to the master bedroom that also had a door out to the pool.

"Who lives here Marty?" I asked him as he went around and turned on lights.

"Whoever needs to when they need to." he replied. "I'll be in the room next to you. Don't open any door going out unless it leads to the pool. Don't open any window as the AC works just fine. Everything's wired and a camera monitors the entire outside feeding the picture into my room. You're safe here so do what the boss said and get some rest. The kitchen is stocked and there is a full bar in the living room."

He stood at the door for a minute and I wondered if I was supposed to tip him. Finally he said, "If Bingo says to protect you, then that's what I'll do. You need anything, or get uptight about anything, I'll fix it. Just don't do anything stupid like try to leave. Bingo gave you his word you would be okay and Bingo's word is worth gold in the bank."

He then turned and left as I opened my suitcase and pulled out Johnny. I hurt like hell and needed a quick drink. I worked my way out of my Cuban shirt and dumped my slacks on the floor. I decided to just close my eyes for a second and that finally ended the tenth day of my vacation.

When I opened my eyes, the sun was shining brightly and a quick check of the clock showed it was 11:30 am. As far as I could remember I must have fallen asleep sometime around 10:00 pm the night before and I saw that Johnny was still sitting unopened on the table next to the bed. I got up, went into the bathroom, and found that I was stiff, but not in a lot of pain. I washed wherever I could without getting the cast wet and then shaved and headed back to the bedroom. I found my shorts and decided that was all I needed to wear for now.

228

Marty was sitting at the table in the kitchen working on a computer. He pointed to the coffee maker and I helped myself. He cleared a place at the table and I sat down and enjoyed the coffee. "The cook went shopping," he said. "There are some donuts in the refrigerator if you want, but the cook will fix lunch in about an hour. Make yourself at home and relax. You have no plans until tomorrow. I just booked you a flight out at 1:00 pm tomorrow that will get you into New York at 3:30 pm. I don't know what happens after that. The boss didn't tell me."

It sounded like, once again, others were orchestrating my life, so I decided to just go and sit by the pool for a while. The sun came through the screen tent and felt fantastic. I had dreamt about J last night, and we were somewhere with a lot of fog. I didn't remember the dream, but I was sure I didn't want to go live in London.

I decided to call my office and let them know what was going on with my life. I called Shirley, my receptionist, told her to cancel my appointments for the week, as I would be taking an extra week off. After that conversation, I really didn't feel like talking to anyone yet, so I went back to my suitcase and pulled out my laptop. The house had a Wi-Fi connection, so I pulled up my email account. I noticed that Laura had not sent me any emails for the last several days so I assumed she was once again pissed at me and probably taking it out on the bastard. There was one from a Silvia Romanski and I was going to delete it as spam until I noticed it said, "About Your Promise." I opened it and found the following.

"My dear sweet White Knight, how badly have I treated you. I hope by now you are safely tucked away under our friend's protection. I so want to hear your voice, but cannot take a chance.

229

This email account will be a dead-end, so you can't even reply to me. I will know when you arrive at JFK on Friday and will have someone meet you there. I had them remove your car from the lot, so have arranged a ride for you. You will use your own name for now and should tell your office that you will be in on Monday. The person picking you up will take you to our doctor so he can make sure your wounds are healing. I am well, a little sore, but no major damage. The bullet broke your rib and then tore a chunk out of my neck. I still don't know why I passed out, but I think I hit my head hard when we both fell against the wall. When I came to and saw you covered with blood, I thought you were dead and I wanted to die myself. The people I work with got me out before Swanson came in, and in the confusion, I was taken away before you left. Brauer is a good doctor, and knows how to play the cover up routine well; he has had a lot of practice. I am so happy that I am dead and I can really be a new person. I hope you forgive me and will still be part of the new adventure. I have so much more to tell you, but this is not the place to do it. Know that I love you and that I am truly sorry for all you have been through. I never should have taken you along on my adventure, no matter what you said. But in all honesty, I felt safe when you were with me. I love you."

It wasn't signed, but I didn't have to be a rocket scientist to figure out the sender. She was not only alive, but obviously she was well. I wanted so much to tell her I was still with her and still loved her, but all I could do was trust that somehow she knew that was true.

I sent off an email to Shirley at the office telling her I would be back in on Monday and that all was well. The fact that I had been shot twice and was now hiding out at a mob safe house was just trivia she didn't need to know.

The cook came and fixed a wonderful lunch, but Marty told me to stay in my room until he or she left. He didn't want anybody to know who was staying at the house. After lunch, I lounged around the pool and actually slept for a few hours. By about 5:00 pm I was really feeling pretty good again. Marty came out to the pool and said, "The boss wants to see you later. He is going to come here and is bringing dinner, so just snack if you get hungry before he comes."

I was really getting tired of being told what to do and when to do it, but I decided I could play the game a few more hours. I went in the pool up to my waist and did a few laps in the standing up position. I cleaned up after that and settled in with my friend Johnny and some great antipasta the cook had previously prepared.

Bingo showed up around 7:00 and went straight to the kitchen with several bags in his hands. "What are you drinking kid?" he asked as he unpacked the bags.

"Johnny Walker on the rocks. Can I get you something?"

As he unpacked, the aroma filled the air and I realized I was really hungry. "Yeah, fix me the same and make it big."

Bingo told Marty to leave for a couple of hours so we could be alone. Dinner was a cross section of Italian food that could have served an army of people. Bingo said a friend of his had a great restaurant and always fixed him special food. I set the table while Bingo served out the many dishes. He opened a bottle of wine and I noticed he didn't do all the tasting thing he had done before. I

231

guess the tasting is his public performance and drinking is his private.

"So did you get some rest?" he asked as we both attacked the spread before us.

"I had a great day doing nothing," I replied. "My body feels like a new man, and this food is the final touch of healing."

He smiled and said, "I got some great places to show you in New York. Makes this taste like leftovers."

I looked up at him and asked, "Are we both going to New York tomorrow?"

He leaned back in the chair and took a long drink of wine. "This has been a very busy day and not one I want to repeat. I thought the problem with Juan was a mess, but our girlfriend really fucked up my life with her little message last night. I'm sixty-three years old, Steve, and I've spent about fifty of those years doing the same thing. I started running numbers in Brooklyn and slowly worked my way up to where I am today. I got married once but that was a joke, and I never had any kids. Jennifer is about as close to family as I have, and that hasn't always been a real close relationship. I hated the drug crap and got into weapons because I had to bump off a guy who shafted me and he had a shitload of guns in a warehouse. It was easy money and I got to travel a lot making deals. The Columbians and other drug people made me wealthy beyond anything I could ever spend. But you know what?"

He paused and took a long drink of wine and then mopped up his plate with some bread. I wasn't sure if I was to reply, so I just sat and looked at him while he ate.

Finally, he leaned back again and said, "I have hated this business ever since I started working with the drug shits, but it was a one-way street with no exits. Your girlfriend has given me an exit and after a lot of thought last night, I decided to take it. The alternative is either going to jail or being dead, and I don't think either one has any appeal to me. So it looks like we go to New York together and hope to God J knows what the fuck she's talking about. I shredded more paper today than they have on New Year's Eve in Times Square. Nevertheless, I kept a lot of things that will bring down people I don't like. There are others I do like and somehow I can't find the papers that will incriminate them."

He laughed at his little joke and poured us some more wine. I started to clear the table and he waved me to stop. "Let the help do it or just let them throw the whole thing in the garbage," he said as he stood. "All this crap is behind me and I couldn't give a shit if it all burns down. Let's go sit around the pool; I always like it out there."

He grabbed the bottle of wine, I picked up Johnny, and the three of us went out to the pool. "You heard from her at all?" he asked as we stretched out on the lounges and enjoyed the beautiful Florida night.

"I got an email from her, but it was a dead end so I couldn't reply. Apparently, we'll be met at the airport and they'll know what to do. I have a doctor's appointment she arranged, but other than that, she didn't say much. It seems she wasn't hurt all that bad at the boat, she just had a lot of bleeding. They got her out and claimed her to be dead before Swanson knew what happened."

233

"Yeah," he sighed, "between Juan, Swanson, and the Senator, she doesn't have a snowball's chance in hell of living out her life. Being dead and making it seem real is the only hope she has. What about you? What are you giving up and why? Juan is a problem, but I really don't think there will be any more fallout on you. If they think J is dead, and Juan is fixed for life in prison, they'll just move on to bigger fish. I wouldn't suggest going to Columbia to live if I was you, but other than that, you probably could get out of this. So why dump everything and run off?"

"I am a psychologist by profession and before you ask me, the answer is yes, you are nuts." He laughed and raised his glass in a toast, which I returned, and then continued, "I guess I did an inventory and found my life without a real purpose. I like what I do, but it's a job. I'm really a loner at heart, so I have no family or close friends. The bottom line is I really am hooked on J and willing to let everything go to just be with her. So to answer your next question, yeah, I am nuts too."

We spent a few hours chatting and I got to know the Bingo that J cared for and was willing to protect. To Bingo, what he did was just business. He took all the dirt in stride and just worked hard to get the job done and make a buck. He'd lost many friends to the violence of the business, but that also was just part of the job description. I think Bingo was amazed that he was able to live as long as he did and now had a chance to get a few more years. I wondered if he was going to be happy in a life where he didn't have power and authority, but with the little I knew of Bingo, I believed he would always have authority in what he did. He alluded to the fact that he had put some cash away for a rainy day and I am sure that it could rain a long time before he ran out.

Around 11:00, he said it was time to go and live one last night in his own house. He would be back in the morning to get me and then take off for New York. As we went to the door he turned and looked at me and said, "I'm really glad I didn't shoot you that night. It would have really pissed J off and I don't think I could live with her mad at me. Like I said, she is the daughter I never had and who knows, maybe you two can make me a grandpa someday. Wouldn't that be the shits!" He reached out, gave me a hug, and then walked out the door.

He painted an interesting picture; Me, J, little me or little J, and grandpa Bingo all together around the family fire. A song came to my mind, "What a difference a day makes, 24 little hours." I wandered to my bed singing the song knowing the reality of the meaning of the words.

I awoke early the next morning and found Marty out cleaning the pool. Somehow, a guy who was 6'6" and a solid 280 looked a little out of place cleaning the pool. He spotted me, smiled, and then went back to his task. I found the coffee and went out to the pool and the warm sunshine. Marty finished his pool boy duties and walked over to my lounge.

"Boss said to be ready at 10:00 this morning and not to bring your suitcase. You got anything real important you can't put in your pockets, let me know and I'll take care of it."

He then went into the house without another word. I decided that Marty was a one-way conversationalist and frankly that was okay with me. I finished the coffee and decided I had to have a shower or I would die. Finding a plastic bag in the kitchen, I rigged a covering over the cast and finally had hot water running over my body. I stayed there for a long time and then got out, shaved, and pulled out my meager wardrobe.

I was down to my last boxers, but I was heading home so that was okay. The Cuban shirt, along with being wrinkled, showed some signs of last night's dinner. I wandered out to find Marty and asked him if he had an extra large shirt I could use. He came back with a nice summer button-down that fit perfectly over my enlarged body. At about 9:45 I heard a car drive up and Marty came to fetch me. I packed the remainder of the money J gave me in my pockets, and decided to keep my Robert Klingman identification pack for a little longer. I took my laptop and left everything else in the room.

Bingo was out at the car in the backseat and another Man Mountain was waiting by the car. He opened the door and I slid in beside Bingo.

"Morning, kid," he said. "Don't talk about anything we're doing until we're alone. Nobody has to know anything about anything this morning."

I nodded that I understood, but I did wish he would stop calling me kid. Somehow, thirty-eight years of life warranted a better title than kid. Nevertheless, I guess that was a minor problem in Bingo's life right now, so I let it go.

Man Mountain II climbed in the car and we drove out of the property and turned north. I'm not always great on directions, but I could have sworn the airport was south; however, having been told to keep quiet, I simply sat back and watched the scenery go by.

About half an hour later, we pulled into a airfield marked Palm Beach Airfield, Private Property. I looked over at Bingo, but he just watched the road ahead as the driver pulled up to a Learjet parked on the field. Bingo turned to me and said, "I hate commercial flights. This is much better."

Once again, I simply nodded and followed him out of the door and up the stairs on the plane. Man Mountain got in the car and drove away as we entered the aircraft. A beautiful dark-haired flight attendant greeted us at the cabin door.

"Hello, Mr. Somolianti, good to see you again."

Bingo smiled at her and patted her ass as he walked by. So, Bingo's last name was Somolianti. That was the first time I'd heard anyone call him by his name. I walked by the attendant, but did not pat her ass, as I was only a guest not a player.

"I'm Regina," she said. "Make yourself comfortable and I'll fix you a drink. Mr. Somolianti is having a Mimosa, would you like something?"

I said I would have the same, went into the cabin, and sat in a seat in front of Bingo. The inside of the plane was simple but elegant. There were about twelve seats that could either turn to face each other or face toward the front of the plane. Regina attached a small table to the floor and as she bent over, Bingo reached out and grabbed her breast. "The new ones feel just like the old ones, just bigger," he said.

"Doc did a great job. Want to see?" She asked.

"Maybe later, sweetheart. Just to make sure I got my moneys worth," Bingo said and then looked at me as Regina wandered back to the kitchen. "Hey, I got to check out my investments don't I?

Those tits cost me ten grand and it better be a good job or I'll make her take them back."

He laughed and looked out the window. He was being Bingo as usual, but I felt his tension as the cabin door closed and the engines started up. He knew how to run his life and others were used to doing what he said. Now he was going to pull it all apart and head for an unknown world, but somehow, I knew Bingo would survive without any major trauma. Regina brought our drinks and said we should buckle up as the pilot was preparing for takeoff.

I flew in a Lear once before and it was a great experience. Commercial jets take a while to get off the ground and attain altitude, but the Lear was a completely different experience. When the captain hit the runway, we took off like a rocket and were high above the ground before I heard the landing gear retract. Regina came back and I noticed she replaced her blouse with a bib apron. The interesting thing about it was she didn't have anything under the apron but a pair of short shorts. The apron covered her breast, but enough hung out to show that the Doctor had done a good job for her.

Bingo looked up and said, "We'll start with two omelets, bacon, and some coffee. For desert I'll have you." He looked at me and said, "You want anything else?"

I cleared my throat and said, "Sounds good to me but, no offence to Regina, I'll skip desert."

Bingo shook his head and said, "You have to forgive him, he's in love. Beside, his girlfriend would probably shoot him if she found out."

238

Regina left us with a smile and a nice picture of her bare back and tight shorts. "She used to dance at the club," Bingo said as his eyes followed her. "But I decided she would be better in the Mile High Club."

I leaned back, took a sip of the Mimosa, and asked, "What happened to the plans J set up for us? She has people waiting at JFK."

"Never play your full hand until you know what the other people are holding," he said. "I got a lot riding on this and I need to be sure I keep control. When we don't show at Lauderdale, she'll probably call me on my airplane phone. Then we'll work out a plan I like. I trust her a lot, but even that has limits. Don't look at me so high and mighty, like I just crapped on your woman. She's kept you spinning like a top for a week, and part of you doesn't trust everything going on either."

I hated to admit it, but he was right. J was like mercury on your fingers. About the time you thought you had hold of her, she was off into something else. I would say 80 percent trusted her completely, but there was still a 20 percent I just couldn't get rid of, no matter how hard I tried.

Regina brought our breakfast and the omelet was perfect. I guess she cooked it herself, as there was no one else on the plane but the pilot and copilot. She obviously was prepared to be a good hostess, no matter what the request may be. We sat and finished coffee as Bingo talked about some of his early days in New York and the adventures of what he called "the good old days." They didn't sound so good to me, but I guess you had to be there to appreciate all that went on when he was younger. He told me that

J's dad and mom went to school with him, but he dropped out early to pursue other interests. They stayed in touch though, and that was how he remained part of J's life after her dad's death. He always sounded different when he spoke of J's mom, and I think when she died a part of him died too. J was obviously a very special part of his life and not many people occupied that space. As we talked, Regina came with a satellite phone and said that some woman wanted to talk to him. He smiled at me and pushed the speaker button so we both could hear.

"Hey J, how did you know I would be here?" he asked as he sat back in his chair and smiled.

"You piece of shit, why can't you just do what I ask and not make everything so hard," said the voice on the phone, who was obviously a very pissed-off J. It was so good to hear her voice live again I almost picked up the phone and started to talk to her. However, Bingo was beaming with smiles as he heard her holler at him. He did love to be in control.

"Now J baby, just calm down. I have you on speaker and Steve is here. If he knows what you're really like then he may want to turn around and go back to Miami."

"Steve, are you there?" she hollered over the phone. "Oh baby, are you there?"

"Hey J, I'm here. I can't tell you how good it is to hear your voice and know you're really alive."

"Oh Steve, I'm really sorry, but it will all work out, ok? Is Bingo being a shit or are you ok?"

"Bingo is the perfect host and I am actually enjoying the time we're spending together," I replied.

"Bingo, what is this all about?" she asked as her voice changed back to her pissed-off tone. "Are you coming to New York or not?"

"Is this phone secure, J?" he asked as he leaned closer to the speaker.

"It is top of the line in security, but you never know anymore."

"Ok, so let's cut this short. Face to face at a shot and a beer. Capice?"

"I understand, but you both better be there Bingo. I love you but if you let Steve get hurt, I will never forgive you. Capice?"

Bingo laughed and said, "Don't worry little one, I will bring him to you. Now cut this call baby, before someone listens."

"Bye Steve, don't let him take you any place but to me. I love you."

Then the line went dead. I looked at him and said, "A shot and a beer?"

Bingo laughed and stretched out his legs. "When she was a kid, about eight to ten years, I would pick her up on Saturdays and she would tag alone with me as I visited people. We would go to the local restaurants and things, nothing dangerous. Her favorite place was Joey's Bar, where the two of us would sit at the bar and order a shot and a beer. She'd get ginger ale and a shot of coke, and we would sit and drink together. She knew all the guys and they loved her. So, shot and a beer means we are going to meet at Joey's Bar. We'll meet her there and go over the details so I understand the game plan. Now get some rest while I go help Regina in the kitchen."

241

He winked at me, patted my knee, and headed toward the rear of the plane. I turned my chair around to give some sense of privacy to them. Somehow, watching Bingo have fun with Regina was not my idea of a turn-on. I pulled the seat back down, stretched, and looked out of the window. I thought about meeting J in a few hours, and that brought me a little morning nap.

Sometime later I awoke as Bingo was tapping me on the shoulder, "Time to buckle up, we're landing."

Through the window I saw the New York skyline in the distance. It was a bright, clear day in New York, and I was finally coming home. I looked over to Bingo as he settled in his seat and pulled the buckle around him. He looked at me and said, "The investment in Regina was worth the money. That surgeon did a great job."

For a minute, I was confused but then remembered Bingo's reference to Regina's breast job, and told him I was happy he had spent his money wisely. We banked and it was obvious we were heading into La Guardia Airport for landing. It always amazed me how much air traffic there was over this city. We have JFK, LaGuardia, and Newark airport all around the city, plus Mac Arthur out on Long Island. When you were away from the city lights, it was always amazing to watch the number of airplanes in the sky at night. I was always hoping the air traffic controllers were not playing poker or falling asleep on the job.

Regina came by and told us we were on final approach. She was back into her normal clothes and looked none the worse for wear. I wondered what she was going to do when Bingo suddenly disappeared, but decided she had many talents and would find employment easily. The Lear moved down fast and landing was as quick as takeoff. We taxied away from the main terminal and finally stopped somewhere near the old terminal, west of the main traffic. Bingo pulled down a briefcase from the overhead and motioned for me to follow him.

It was cool outside, but pretty normal for early May. I thought about my fishing trip that had started thirteen days ago, and how cold it had been in the mountains. Summer still lay before us, but I had no idea what was going to happen in the hours ahead, much less in the months that lay before me. We walked over to a limo parked nearby as the driver exited and opened the door for us. This was another Man Mountain and I began to wonder if Bingo ran a body-building camp where he trained these guys.

"So here we go, kid. The dice have been tossed," Bingo said as he opened the briefcase. He pulled out a short barrel gun and stuck it in his waistband. I guess I looked somewhat surprised at his action because he said, "What is the motto that J and I have trained you to remember?"

I said, "Trust no one especially those who you think you trust. Do you really think J would do something against you?"

"I am 99 percent sure I can trust her, but beyond that I am just wise. You know, I could really set you up in a thriving practice if I just sent you my friends. I think they are all wack jobs and need serious help. Then we could start with all J's friends, both with the law and on the other side, and you would make a fortune."

In thirteen very long days, I had almost forgotten what I did for a living. In three days, I would return to the office and continue my life like everything was normal. I began to wonder if I was able to pull that off, considering all I had been through in the last few weeks. The key was to just get through today and let tomorrow take care of itself.

We left La Guardia and drove to the Brooklyn-Queens Expressway, which, given the amount of traffic we hit, was an oxymoron in itself. The driver finally got off and began to wind through back roads that became more confusing as he went. Brooklyn and Queens are one huge conglomeration of streets, drives, avenues, and roads that all have the same name. You can be on 23rd street heading toward 23rd avenue and no place near 23rd Drive, which is two miles away. I always used a cab out here, and even then, I got lost.

We pulled into a section of Brooklyn I never saw before—not that I had seen a lot of it. The neighborhood was a step above rundown, but it was only a small step. Bingo told the driver to pull over as he got out of the car and told me to follow. He gave some instructions to the driver who promptly pulled away from the curb and drove down the street.

"No bodyguards in New York, Bingo?" I asked as we started walking.

"I don't want anybody else around when we meet, so I sent them all away. There was another car behind us with my guys, but they were told to follow the limo and that I would call them. If this goes bad, I don't want them involved. If it goes good, I don't think J will want them involved. So the short of it—no bodyguards."

We turned a corner and I saw a bar across the street that said "Joey's." Bingo looked around and then walked toward the bar with me in tow. We entered and I was lost in darkness. I don't think there were more than four or five lights on inside, and those were mostly over the bar. The place was empty except for an elderly man behind the bar. He turned as we entered, then came around and embraced Bingo who returned the gesture with deep enthusiasm. Neither spoke, but the elderly man finally stepped back, took Bingo's face in his hands and held it. A father might make the same gesture to a son who he hadn't seen for a long time. Then Bingo leaned forward and gave the old man a kiss on each cheek and said, "She here?"

"Just like old times," the old man said and simply nodded his head toward the back of the building.

Bingo patted the old man on the back and simply said, "Lock up the place and come back in two hours. I can let myself out."

With what seemed genuine sadness, the old man nodded and headed for the door. I heard him leave and the door lock behind him. "Hold this and stay here," Bingo said as he handed me the briefcase. "If things go wrong, head for the door and run like hell. If they go good, then give me back the case." I nodded as he pulled the gun from his belt and walked to a door in the rear. He stood for a minute, then quickly opened the door and stepped inside. I lost him in the light coming from the open door, then the door closed and I was back in the darkness of the bar.

I stood there with this briefcase and the distinct feeling of a child waiting to see the principal. Finally, the door opened and a figure emerged that was definitely not Bingo. The light cast an eerie mystical glow as she stepped toward me. She was dressed in a very conservative black pantsuit and her hair was auburn, but I would have known her even if she had on clown's makeup and a

245

big bow tie. We walked toward each other as I set the briefcase on the table and opened my arms. As she fell into my embrace, all the emotion of the last days welled up in me and I just held her tight so I wouldn't lose her again.

When you love someone and they die, it is hard. When they come back from the dead and are again with you, it is overwhelming. The game of catch and release was good in fishing, but not so easy in real life. I have to admit, tears ran down my face and we both just stood there and cried in each other's arms. I finally kissed her and felt the flood of life come back into my body. She stepped back a little, looked into my eyes, and said, "I was so afraid I screwed up our relationship with all my craziness. I've had so much anxiety this last hour I thought I would pass out. But it's gone now, and I feel whole again."

I held her tight as she moved back into my arms. I finally said, "I can't lose you anymore. The pain is just more than I could ever go through again. Is this over now? Are we really through with all the crap?"

I heard someone clear his throat and saw Bingo standing next to us with the briefcase in his hand. "I thought I told you to hold on to this," he said gruffly. I turned to say something derogative to him, but he smiled, set down the briefcase and threw his arms around both of us. "You got a good man here, little girl, but you keep pulling shit like you have been, and you might blow the whole thing. I made the mistake of not doing the right thing once; don't you do the same thing. Let's get this over with so you can get out of all this."

246

J kissed him on the cheek and we all pulled back from our group hug, which, considering the size of my chest cast was a large hug. We moved toward the back room where J and Bingo went in first. When I entered, I was surprised to see two other men in the room. I guess I didn't know what was going to happen when we met J, but somehow I just assumed it would be the three of us. J closed the door and took me by the arm.

"Steve, this is Jim Crowley, Special Investigator from the US Attorney General's Office," she said as she motioned toward a man in his mid-fifties who had the look of an accountant more than a special investigator. But then, I wasn't sure what a special investigator was supposed to look like; it just sounded like an important job.

She turned toward a man who looked like he was made out of rock. He was an African-American who was about 6'3 and 200 lbs. of pure muscle. "And this is Gerald Brocklen from the Central Intelligence Agency. These are two of the members of the investigative team set up by Homeland Security for this case." I shook Gerald's hand and immediately felt at ease by his firm handshake and great smile.

"J has spoken well of you, Steve," Brocklen said. "If you're half the man she said you are, then I think we better run you for president. The only drawback is you pick crazy friends to hang out with and have fun."

"Are you saying I'm crazy?" Bingo asked from behind me. "The only thing crazy about me was I let you go when you worked for me. The broads were nuts about this guy, but he never gave

247

them a tumble. I thought he was gay or something, but then I found out he was undercover and happily married."

I guess I looked puzzled about how Gerald and Bingo had previously worked together, so Gerald brought me up to speed by saying, "I was working on some illegal arms sales in France and needed a inside track. J introduced me to Bingo and he agreed to let me work in the club when some of the buyers came in from Paris to meet with him. I was only at the club a month, but it was enough to ruin my morals for a lifetime."

"Hey, I didn't tell you to look at all the girls," Bingo said. "That was your doing. I know you were just praying for them when you kept laying your hands on their ass." Bingo laughed at his joke, and I could tell his humor was a cover for his being uptight. "So let's get this party on the road," he said as he placed the briefcase on the table.

We all took chairs at the table and I waited for something to happen. I'm sure many poker games were played around this table, but the stakes today were really high. Crowley opened by looking at Bingo and saying, "The US Attorney General has authorized us to provide you protection and amnesty if you provide us with testimony and material evidence that will aid in the indictment of Senator Harris, Special Agent Swanson, and other parties that may be involved in the illegal sale and marketing of firearms. As a violation of the Patriots Act, we can take your testimony "in camera" and have it stand as evidence before a judge and then sealed for a hundred years. As such, we enter your testimony in the court record as a material witness under protection and there is no disclosure of your name. Further, your testimony will not be open to cross-examination, so you will not be called upon to identify yourself to any other party other than the people who directly work for this case."

Crowley sounded like he had been reading from a textbook. I decided he was the button-downed accountant-lawyer type who made sure everything was legal and correct. We need people like Crowley, but I really wouldn't like to hang around with them for very long.

Gerald opened a file and slid it over to Bingo. "The CIA has identified these people as potential foreign agents for those who traffic in weapons. We can tie about half of them to weapons sales in the Middle East countries. We need information that will assist us in finding who the top-level buyers and sellers are getting money from so we can infiltrate their ranks and shut down the money flow. In return, we will provide you with any identification and background you need to establish yourself in any foreign or domestic location. We will work with witness protection to make sure your life is secure. Nevertheless, you're a big boy, Bingo, and you know if you make waves, somebody will find you. As such, your life will no longer entail organized crime or any type of illegal merchandising."

Bingo took the CIA folder, looked at the pictures and information in it. He thumbed through each page, pulled out two, and gave the folder back to Gerald. "The people in the folder—I can give you all you need to know. These two—I can't seem to remember much if anything about them."

Gerald took the two that Bingo held in his hand and laughed, "Yeah, when you have dinner with people at least once a week, it is hard to remember who they are. Okay, I'll let these two go, but if they keep doing what they're doing, I'll shut them down without you. You can't talk to them or warn them anymore, so let's hope they get smart when they find you gone."

Bingo turned to Crowley and said, "Harris and his band of happy pricks are all covered by the information in here. You'll find a few other names and information that will excite your heart and mind. Swanson is not a contact I used, and was surprised to find he was Harris' connection with the feds. I thought it was somebody else, and that's the folder on top of the pile."

Crowley opened the briefcase, pulled out the top file, and openly appeared in shock when he looked at it. "Helmsly Jackson?" he said in disbelief. I didn't know the name, but from the reaction of the others around the table, he was someone important. J looked at me and said "Helmsly Jackson is the Chief of Staff for the Vice President."

"Of the United States?" I asked in disbelief.

"Same one," said Bingo. "I've been with him on some private outings, and he has been in on some of the overseas sessions we had with the people Gerald mentioned. Never saw him make a deal or really do anything that said he was making a buck off of this, but he wasn't there for his health, so I leave it up to you guys to figure it out."

He then turned back to Crowley and waved a thumb at me, "What about Steve? What is he gonna get? I think twenty-five to life for murder is fitting."

Crowley looked at Bingo and said, "All we want is a signed statement from Dr. Sanders that he will under no circumstances disclose the nature of these negotiations unless instructed by the Office of the US Attorney General. I am not aware of criminal charges against him."

"Jesus, Crowley," Bingo said. "You need some work on your hemorrhoids. I was kidding, and in all honesty, if he stays with J that will be enough punishment for any person alive. Ok, what now?"

J leaned forward and said, "We all sign some papers then Bingo, Gerald, Jim, and I will go out the back door and work on the case. Steve will go out the front door and there will be a car that will take him to the doctor he was supposed to see two hours ago. We will bring this all to a head, clean it up, and go on with our lives."

"You know, if I didn't love this girl like my daughter," said Bingo, "I would ask her to marry me. I love the way she talks. Bring on the papers and let's get this shit over."

They handed me a prepared statement, which simply said, "Shut up about everything." I signed it and gave it to Crowley. Bingo had a lot more paper, so as he worked away, J took my arm and we went back into the bar. She went behind the bar and grabbed a bottle of Johnny Red along with a bottle of tequila. She put two glasses on the bar, filled one with each bottle, then came around and sat next to me.

"Here is to the future, my love," she said as we touched glasses and drank down. "Now comes the hard part again. After I leave here, it will be deep disappearance time. Out of necessity, we will not be together or in communication for some time."

I looked at her with surprise and said, "You're kidding me. We just got together and you're going again? I thought this was over."

"It is baby, it is. Nevertheless, it has to be done right or things can really get fucked up. I need time to set myself a new identity and to help Bingo get set up in his new life. The charges will be filed and all hell will break loose. I need to make sure I don't get caught up in it."

"Then let me stay with you," I said. "I've been with you through a lot, so why not finish it together."

"It is out of my hands, lover. Juan was my case and I called the shots, but this is way above even my pay grade. Nobody who isn't involved is going to get close to this. But it won't take long and it will be over soon."

"How long?" I asked.

"I don't know, but I promise you I will find you no matter where you are. We have a deal I will not back out of or break in any way. I love you and will be with you, I promise."

I looked at her and knew that she was right. I couldn't help her and my presence was no longer needed. I had to go back to my life and wait for whatever came down the path. I reached into my pocket, pulled out a clump of material and handed it to her. She took it and unrolled it until it revealed a much-wrinkled dress.

"My dress from Miami—how did you remember to take it?" she said as she held it up and smiled.

"I figured I would keep it as a memory, but now I want a promise. When we meet again, wear the dress. Then we can start over where we left off."

252

She set the dress on the bar, reached over and held me. Our lips met and in that moment, we sealed the promise for our future. We walked hand in hand to the door and as she kissed me once more she said, "I will find you, Steve; no matter what, I will find you."

I exited the bar and found a driver and car waiting for me. As we pulled away I looked back, but J was gone. My only thought was, "I hope so baby, I hope so."

CHAPTER 25

J walked back into Joey's, locked the door and headed toward the rear room. Seeing the red dress on the bar, she stopped, picked it up, and carefully folded it into a small neat package. She smiled as she held it remembering the time with Bingo when she improvised in order to cool him off so he wouldn't shoot Steve. So much had happened since that night, but in the midst of all the trouble, Steve remembered to keep the dress and she hoped she'd be able to keep her promise of wearing it once more. She sighed as she put the dress in her pocket and headed toward the back room, knowing that so much could go wrong in this mess, it might all work out different than she wanted. "I will try Steve," she whispered as she entered the room, "I will really try."

Bingo looked up from all the papers before him and said, "Is he gone?"

"Yes, he's gone. So let's get this finished so we can get out of here too. I still don't like being in this neighborhood with all the eyes that can see us and send out information we don't want sent."

Bingo leaned back and looked at J as she sat next to him, "What the hell are you going to do about Steve? Your lifestyle doesn't exactly fit into his way of thinking or acting."

"I don't know, Bingo. I just want to get you wrapped up and set this case into its final phase. I plan to leave all this behind and move on with life, but sometimes it's hard to walk away, especially with some of the people I have managed to piss off."

Bingo stared at her for a minute and then turned to Brocklen, "I need to talk to J alone for a few minutes, and then we can finish the paper work. I'm not running away, so just stay back here while she and I have a chat out front."

Brocklen laughed and said, "Bingo, you never stop giving orders, even when you're not in charge. Go talk to J, but keep it short. We need to get out of here as soon as possible."

Bingo and J went out to the bar where he picked up the bottle of Johnny Walker still sitting there. "You want anything?" he asked her as he got some ice and fixed himself a drink.

"Just tell me what was so important that we had to come out here to talk," she said as she sat on the barstool.

Bingo took a sip of his drink, came around the bar, and leaned close to J, "You're not telling everybody everything are you?"

"You wouldn't ask me that question unless you had something else in mind. So why don't you just tell me what you think, and then we can talk."

255

Bingo laughed and said, "Oh Jennifer, I raised you right. You have learned to survive by keeping an attitude, but my beautiful FBI agent, you are trying to pull one over on Juan and the FBI. I want you to tell me what you've done and how you're going to do it. I'm not going to stop you, I just want to be sure you don't get caught."

J looked long and hard at Bingo considering how to handle this conversation. She trusted no one, yet Bingo had always been there for her and he did owe her at this point. She took his drink out of his hand and took a small sip, "Ugh, I still don't know how you and Steve can drink that. Ok, Bingo, I worked out some things for my benefit, and I don't think anyone will ever be able to find out what I did. I moved fifteen million of Juan's funds into deeply buried accounts. I gave ten million to my people so they could work the case, but I kept five million for myself. It's buried so deep and in so many places, it will never be found."

"If it is so well hidden, then how did I find out about it?"

"Why don't you tell me—then we will both know," J said as she looked Bingo in the eye.

He took a drink and then put his hand on hers, "I didn't know exactly, but I've looked over the figures you gave the feds, and I noticed a few large accounts missing. In the chaos that those accounts will cause in the next few weeks, nobody is going to know something is missing. But baby, someday someone is going to put two and two together and then you will be in the spotlight. The feds won't figure it out, but Juan's friends might and will not take kindly to having their money stolen. They will try to find it—

no matter if you are dead or alive. So you better have a plan J, or you'll be running the rest of your life."

J opened her purse, pulled out a small notebook, opened a page, and handed it to Bingo. He read it for a minute, and then smiled broadly, "This is good, Jennifer, really good."

"I thought you would approve, especially since it will make you even more prosperous when you're dead than if you ever were alive."

Bingo handed the paper back to J and once again took her hand, "You know what the icing on this cake is? After all these years and all the people we've lived with, it still comes down to trusting each other as family. I'm leaving a whole life behind, but I am never going to lose you Jennifer, and knowing that makes all this worthwhile. Let's go sign Crowley's papers, and then we can make our own plans.

Within an hour, they finished all the forms, bundled Bingo into the back of the car in the alley, and headed toward a safe-house. The plan was for Bingo to lay low for a few days, give testimony, and then arrange for his cover story to be played out for the public. Bingo changed the game-plan as he insisted on going back to his own house in New York so people wouldn't be suspicious if he disappeared too soon. The compromise was the safe-house for one night to get the testimony on tape, and then he would have a week to put his affairs in order before they removed him. The night before Bingo was supposed to enter into protective custody, he disappeared.

Brocklen found out about it the next morning and tried to contact J to see what she knew, but discovered that she also disappeared. While he was concerned about their not following the game-plan, Brocklen had what he needed. If Bingo wanted to take chances with his life that was his problem. J was legally dead and he couldn't really put out a missing person report, so Brocklen decided to just let them do their thing and if they showed up, great; if not, that was not his concern.

J and Bingo met at La Guardia Airport and boarded Bingo's jet. They landed a few hours later in Canada where they took a commercial jet for the Cayman Islands. Once there, they whisked through security and into a private helicopter taking them to their final destination.

"I haven't seen any signs of people following us," J said as she collapsed on the couch in their private suite.

Bingo stretched out next to her and said, "No, for now we're clear—but that will probably close quick when we start moving numbers. The accounts people will be here soon. You got everything ready?"

J opened her briefcase and pulled out a file that held all the account information on the five million she moved away from Juan. Handing it to Bingo, she watched as he opened his briefcase and pulled out a file. Smiling, he set the two files on the table and said, "So here are the financial remains of our misspent lives. Twelve million between us, and we are going to give it all away. This is either brilliant, or we will spend the remainder of our years kicking ourselves."

He went to the bar, poured two snifters of brandy, and handed one to J, "Here is to the Dr. Steve Sanders Trust Fund. May he always think of us fondly as he spends our money."

J lifted her glass and added, "And may we live long enough to enjoy being with him as he spends it." She went to the window and looked out over the beautiful beach below, wondering what it would be like to live without people following her. "Brocklen will be pissed that we ducked out, but I can get us back on track with him once we are back in the states. As we agreed, we will not notify Steve of this trust until I'm with him or I am dead. If I'm dead and you're alive, then you will have to deal with him by yourself, but I don't think that will be a problem."

"No," Bingo said. "He can be stubborn, but I really got to like Steve while we were together, and we can work out whatever needs to be done. However, bottom line Jennifer, you have to stay alive. We will mix the funds together, deposit, and redeposit them so many times in the next month that it is almost impossible to trace where they came from or who owned them. Nevertheless, Juan's people still have ways, so we will have to be diligent, but not worried. Life is too short to sit around and be worried. Steve comes into all this as a complete outsider, and no one will be able to connect the dots on his involvement, especially since he didn't know about the money in the first place. Overall, I think it is a good plan."

The phone rang, and as Bingo answered it, J turned and looked out at the beach one more time. "Okay Steve, that part is done and now comes the hard part," she whispered. "We are one step closer to happily ever after."

CHAPTER 26

Laura sat before me all aglow and happy. She was fresh from her lawyers and the divorce proceedings were going well. She filed as the ultimate victim and the bastard gave into her. I'm sure he would have given in to anything to get away from her, but I never met him directly, so that was only a well-educated guess. Sometimes the victims of the world seem to win, but in reality, it is just postponing the inevitable place of dealing with self-responsibility. I had been dealing with my own self-responsibility and it was not an easy thing to do. J and I parted with the promise she would find me and that was five months ago. I never directly saw or heard from her again. I couldn't believe how real all those moments were in my memory. Mostly, I still felt her eyes pierce into mine as she promised to find me. I believed her then, and I desperately wanted to believe her today. I couldn't accept as true that a woman I barely knew got so deep into me, yet she did.

I saw the doctor the day after I left J, who told me the cast would come off in two weeks and I would be as good as new. That was a long two weeks in my life, but I lived through it and finally took a shower without a plastic bag. The scar got better, and a combination of gym plus tanning salon made my chest look almost like new. For a month, I lived believing I would hear from her any day, but after that, it was simply a decision to get on with life. I said I never heard from her directly because indirectly there was a lot of evidence of her activity.

About three weeks after we parted, the New York Times posted a story about the FBI arresting Sen. James Harris, Republican South Dakota, for violation of Homeland Security. The story told of his suspected activities regarding sales and distribution of American arms to foreign countries. Over the next few days, amid strong denials from the Senator, the case against him grew. There was a separate story in one issue about a crackdown in Miami that dealt with the head of the Miami FBI office. While the stories didn't tie together at first, within a few weeks, it all came down and the Senator was forced to resign. The convictions spread to several of his staff and at last, his connection to Swanson in Miami came to the surface.

The fallout overseas didn't make much news in the US, but I was able to pick up bits and pieces of some of the activities the CIA was behind. I remembered a few of the names from the meeting in Brooklyn and did see them in some of the International News section of the Times. Mostly it was that they had died in a gun battle or car accident. Whether Gerald Brocklen and the CIA were directly involved in these premature deaths, I had no way of telling, but these were no coincidences in my opinion. Overall, it seemed the plans to round up the clan and bring them down had gone well.

The New York Times became my surrogate connection to J, as I scoured it each day to see if anything new would develop that might give me a clue about her activities. About two months after we parted, I was glancing through the obituaries and saw one that stopped me in my tracks.

Somolianti, Robert

Somehow, that whole thing just didn't fit Bingo, but it was his legal name. The obituary said he had died of natural causes and would be laid to rest in Pine Lawn Cemetery on July 26th, with the funeral being held on July 25th at the Cremore Funeral Home in Brooklyn. The usual information of "Loving Brother of Lydia, and Etc.", filled a few lines, but the entire obituary was very brief. A man like Bingo knew many people, and the obit didn't adequately reflect his circle of influence.

I didn't mourn at his passing, as I assumed it was a setup and besides, I was numbed out with two fake deaths, and couldn't really muster up much for another. Maybe Bingo did die, and the obit was real, but even if he did, he went out doing things his way. I looked at the date of the funeral and thought about attending, but then thought about who might be there and decided I didn't need to be part of the crowd. I hadn't had any contact from anyone since I left J and decided I liked that level of anonymity very much.

"So I am very happy that I have finally been able to get rid of the bastard and have a new life."

My mind had wandered during Laura's soliloquy and I realized she was finally finished with her, "I am the Victim of the Year," speech and it was my turn to speak.

"Well, things turned out well for you, Laura. I'm happy you're doing better," I said without real conviction.

"Yes, doctor. I feel so much better and I know my only problem was being with Oscar."

So the bastard had a name—Oscar. I thought for a minute and decided he would always be Bastard to me. No offence to Oscar, but somehow Bastard and Laura just seemed like a connection.

She smiled at me and continued, "So I'm afraid this will be our last session, as I am healed and will not need any therapy."

She smiled and waited for me to reply. I knew what she wanted, but like it or not, she was not going to get it. Her prize would be for me to beg her to stay in therapy and tell her how much I wanted to continue seeing her. Instead I said, "Laura that works out great as this is my last day in the practice. I mentioned that to you before, but you had a lot on your mind and may have missed it."

Bullshit, I thought to myself, I sent her three letters, told her twice, and Shirley told her after every appointment for the last month. Laura knew, but she didn't want to admit I could leave her.

"You are leaving the practice? What do you mean? What happens if I need you? How can you do this to me?"

I watched her begin to grow in her level of anxiety and fear, and knew we were in for one more storm before we parted. There was no thought about anyone else but Laura and she was now going to let me have it for not doing what she wanted.

"Laura, I'm leaving the practice and going to take some time off before I settle elsewhere. I've asked Dr. Harmon to be prepared to help you if you need it, and I am sure he will be more than happy to meet with you."

"You son of a bitch! How can you sit there, smile at me, and tell me you are walking away from me in my time of need. I will sue you and take you before the bar for malpractice."

It was the bar thing again. I didn't know why she thought I was a lawyer, but it was her own fantasy world. Hard to believe she was ready to leave me five minutes ago, but now I was deserting her in her time of need. It really had to be hell to live a life in a roller coaster. I leaned forward and said, "Laura, I am sorry you feel that way, but Shirley will give you Dr Harmon's number as you leave. Feel free to call him if you have any problems."

"Fuck you and fuck your Dr. Harmon. I don't need men to tell me what to do with my life. You are all just scum who bleed us to death and then dump us. Fuck you!"

On that gentle note, Laura stormed out of my office for the last time. I'd saved her for my last client, so in case I thought about changing my mind, her presence would assure me that leaving the practice was a good decision.

I packed up the few papers I was taking and took one more look around the office. Ten years of practice in this office had been good to me, but it just didn't cut it anymore. I'd saved enough money to live for a while, and sold my interest to my partners for a guaranteed income for a year. I guess not having pressure was a good part of why I had no idea where to go next. I sold my apartment, put my things in storage last weekend, and then spent the week in a local hotel until I was finished with work today.

As I walked out to the reception, Shirley got up and gave me a big hug. "I hope you find what you're missing," she said as she pulled away with tears in her eyes. "You used to be a happy man, but something changed in the last few months. Maybe you need to see a therapist."

I laughed and handed her my keys to the office. "I don't believe in all this psychology stuff. I think it's all make-believe. Give me a bottle of Johnny Red and I will be fine."

We both laughed and as I walked out the door she said, "If it is a woman, Steve, I hope she is worth it."

I didn't reply, but inside I said, "I think she is, but I just can't find her."

The early September sun was still warm and fresh, and New York was in one of its better moods. I pulled the car out of the garage and drove up the West Side Highway to the Holland Tunnel. I'd been up to the river a few times in the last months, but summer is not good for trout fishing as the water is too warm for them to be active. We had had a few nights of cool weather, so I decided to spend the weekend up at my favorite spot and hope something was feeding in the river.

I looked in the Times and on the internet for any sign of information about Juan, but nothing appeared. Bingo was probably right. Juan was out of the picture and his people had moved on to bigger things. I stopped looking over my shoulder every five minutes some time ago, and it was all becoming a distant memory.

In the fast world that Bingo and J came from, history was not important; it was only today that was worth living. I felt like the trout out of the water waiting to see if he this was "catch and release" or if he was going to become dinner. Not much he could do about it but wait it out and hope he didn't die before a decision was made. Over the last four months, I had confidence that J would show up any minute, but in the last few weeks, with the end of the practice and moving from New York, I began to waiver and doubt.

We'd spent a total of six full days together and three partial days with minimum contact. That was not a good foundation to build a long-term relationship. The intensity of those days gave us some false perspective of our connection, and she could have come to a more rational decision that pursuing this was not what she wanted for the future. Hell, she could be an undercover agent in Australia by now and I would never know it. As much as she wanted to get out of her lifestyle, it was in her blood, and it may have proven harder to leave than she thought. When Bingo was telling me about his trips with her to Joey's Bar, and her meeting all his friends, I had an insight to her childhood. She was on the side of the law now, but she was still one of the boys in the hood. I knew if I never saw her again, I would never regret the time we spent together.

Friday night traffic heading into the mountains was bad, but it was lighter after the Labor Day holiday than during the summer months. I cut up through Bear Mountain, worked my way over to route 17, and headed into the Catskill Region. I reached the parking spot about an hour later and pulled my gear from the car. The lot was empty, which was a sign that fishing season was over.

CATCH AND RELEASE
TWERELL

The sun was already setting as I reached my favorite spot and set up camp. Heading down to the river, I saw it was running fast from the rain this week, but it wasn't muddy. That spoke well for fishing tomorrow. I took off my shoes and walked out a little from the shore to see how cold the water would be, and found it was probably about ten degrees cooler than three weeks ago. "I will see you guys tomorrow," I said to the trout, "So get a good night's sleep."

Sitting around the fire eating my gourmet hotdogs, I was suddenly overwhelmed with the feeling of uncertainty. I had no job, no home, and no plans; just a lot of time to do nothing. I was a good enough therapist to know that these thoughts were early signs of depression, and I was going to have to start to set up some plans for the future if I was going to stay healthy. However, for tonight, a sleeping bag and an environment filled with the sounds of the woods was all I really needed. All was not well in my soul, but it was getting better.

The sun broke across the river about 5:00 am as I fixed some instant coffee, a couple of sandwiches, and moved to the river. There was a morning chill in the air, but the September sun promised that the day would be beautiful and warm. I fixed my rod and attached a sinking leader for fishing on the bottom with nymphs. The big fish just sat in the deep water and waited for the food to drop on them, as the summer waters had plenty of trout delicacies. I pulled on a pair of well-worn sneakers and walked out into the stream. The water was cool and my bare legs definitely felt the chill, but it didn't take long to get used to as I wandered out into the small riffles of the stream. I fished for about two hours and had a few small strikes but nothing major. I walked the stream to the bend that was all too familiar.

Rounding the bend, I saw the empty river before me. I felt my heart sink as I once again falsely hoped I would see her there in her army shirt and baseball cap. However, nothing was moving on the river except an early morning hatch of small larva. I headed to the bank and went up to the campsite J occupied on that fateful day over five months ago. It appeared no one had used it since we were there, but I couldn't see any signs of my last visit. I looked at the tree where Carlos tied and threatened J, but there were no signs of the struggle or of where he died. I pulled a sandwich out of my side pack and had breakfast with my memories. After about an hour of doing nothing, I headed back to the river in search of something living instead of thinking about someone dying.

I noticed a deep pool near the next bend in the river and set my line above it allowing it to drift. As I retrieved the line, it suddenly went stiff and I felt the life run through my body. I set the hook and began to retrieve it slowly. The trout realized it was not just a normal feeding time and took off toward the other side of the river. The line began to spin out of the reel, and I tightened the drag to keep the tension between me and the fish. I followed him down the river, bringing him a little closer every minute. I saw him heading for the rocks and I pulled a little harder to keep his head toward me. With that he went straight up out of the water and landed with a huge splash. He was magnificent and appeared to be a good-size rainbow. I pulled him again and he began to run once more, but I could tell he was tiring.

At last, I could see him in the water and I watched as he darted back and forth trying to escape the inevitable. Finally, he was near my feet and I reached down, grabbed his lip, and pulled him up. He was a good 20" long and glistened in the late-morning sun. My heart was probably beating as fast as his as we stood in the middle of the stream and looked at each other. I wanted to hug him, but decided that was a dumb thing to do, so I just removed the hook and set him in the water opting for a catch and release instead of a catch and kill. I moved him around a little to get the water flowing over his gills and then let him go. He hesitated for a minute, and then darted into the shadows. At that moment, life was good for both of us.

"Catch anything?"

I felt my footing slip and almost went into the river. I turned and saw the most unusual sight any fly fisherman has ever seen. Standing on the shore was this woman in one of the most gorgeous dresses I had seen in a long time. It looked good in Miami; it looked even better in the woods. All I could stammer was, "Jesus, you scared the shit out of me."

"Now we are even. Seems you did that to me the last time we were here."

She stood on the bank of the river and smiled as I remembered those many months ago. She was in the shadows, but lit up everything around. Her hair was shorter and lighter than the last time I saw her, but everything else seemed the same. "My God, J, where the hell have you been? It's been five months without a word."

269

"You can stand in the river and bitch about things you can't change or you can come and kiss me—your choice."

I was so dumbstruck I couldn't move. The river flowed by my feet and my life flowed by my eyes. Five months of hoping and now she was here.

"Okay," she said standing. "I'll just come to you." With that she entered the river and walked toward me. The dress didn't work well for wading, so she pulled it off and threw it on the shore. I always take care of my fly rod like my own life, but as she came close, I dropped it in the river and took her in my arms. I felt the warmth of her arms around me and the firmness of her back in my arms. I held her tight and felt a release of my inner being. I lifted her out of the water, spun around, and then kissed her. When she pulled back, I saw she was crying and laughing at the same time. "Oh my God, I have dreamed about seeing you again," she said. "I don't know what you did to me, but I have missed you more than you will ever know. I stayed alive for this day and now it's here." With that, she kissed me and we dissolved into each other in the midst of the river.

I'm sure a trout watched our coming together and relaxed knowing that today he would not have to match wits with a dumb angler. Today he would be able to simply sit in the river and do his natural feeding without worry or care. Today I also knew that if you wander far enough and long enough, you find what you're looking for in just the place you want. The river was like that. It was a place that my soul finally became free.

The End

CATCH AND RELEASE
TWERELL

Signal 30 by J.T.Twerell

If you enjoyed J.T. Twerell's book, Catch and Release, you will want to read his award winning novel, Signal 30.

Signal 30 is Winner of the Readers View Readers Choice Award for 2011.

Writers Digest declares, "Undoubtedly, *Signal 30* is a must read for fans of the "cop novel" as well as for general mystery and suspense aficionados."

Signal 30, the police designation for a crime scene with extreme or imminent danger, is a riveting mystery about the intricacies of a major crime investigation. The terror builds as the investigators follow the unknown path of an insane bomber who continues to move one step ahead of their search, forcing them to face the reality of living in a time of terrorism.

In a quiet suburb of New Jersey, a 12 year old girl returns from Christmas vacation and finds an unopened gift at her front door. In the excitement and exuberance of a young child, she opens it. The early evening is shattered as the gift explodes and begins a tangled search for the person who would send this destructive present. Unexpectedly, other devises show up at a shopping mall in New Jersey, the Holland Tunnel in New York, and the home of the Mayor in a nearby town.

Detective Shane Murphy, a 40 year old senior officer with Special Case Investigations, is thrown into the maze of confusion as he attempts to sort out the facts before the perpetrator strikes again. While his personal life crumbles around him, as his wife informs him of her decision to pursue a divorce, Murphy finds assistance with the arrival of Stacy Landou, a 38 year old Special Agent with Alcohol, Tobacco and Firearms. Their relationship grows slowly, professionally, yet passionately as they try to solve a crime out of control.

Dr. J. T.Twerell is a practicing Psychotherapist in Manhattan, NY. His works are a cross-section of fiction and non fiction including his award winning novel Signal 30.

For more information on Signal 30 and other books by J.T.Twerell go to
www.JTTwerell.com.

CATCH AND RELEASE
TWERELL

**For your enjoyment,here is Chapter 1
of Signal 30.**

CHAPTER 1

The wipers pushed back the light covering of snow, producing streaks filled with rainbows of countless Christmas lights. Remembering this kind of clean snow from his childhood, Donald glanced in the mirror to watch the vibrant house lights mesmerize his daughter. She was the image of her mother, with long blond hair and blue eyes that lit up with every smile. While only 12 years old, she was already getting boys' attention, and that made Donald somewhat sad. Trish was growing up, but she was still his little girl.

"It's beautiful, isn't it sugar?" he asked his daughter as she continued to absorb the magic of the snow-filled Christmas tint.

"Oh Daddy, it's my favorite time of the year. Can we keep the lights up so we can see them in the summer?"

"Somehow they just don't look as good in the summer honey," he said as he turned the car into the driveway. "But we'll leave them up until after New Year's and then see how long we want to keep them".

Turning off the engine, Donald leaned back in the seat and exhaled a deep sigh of relief. "Six hours and thirty two minutes in ice and snow; never again."

A sleepy voice next to him said, "I know. Next year your brother and his family come to us for Christmas. You say that every year after that long drive back, and every year we pack up and go to your brother's."

Turning to look at his wife's sleepy smile, he laughed to himself. She was right, but maybe next year he'd win the toss and his brother would come to New Jersey. "Humor me," he said as he reached out and lightly squeezed the back of her neck. "It's six o'clock at night and after such a long drive, I need sympathy and love

He heard the rustle in the back of the car as his daughter opened the door and put her tongue out to catch the falling snow flakes. "Can I go to Cindy's and see what she got for Christmas?"

"Take your backpack upstairs and put your pillow on your bed, Trish," her mother replied. "Then call and see if she's home, but you have to be back by 8:00."

"Ok, will do!" Trish hollered out as she made a mad dash for the front door. Donald hit the remote to unlock the doors of the house as Trish charged through on a run. "Someday she'll remember we lock doors when we leave the house."

Clearing the stairs two at a time, Trish took a flying leap into her room and onto her bed. "I'm home you wonderful room," she shouted to the familiar surroundings as she grabbed the phone next to her bed and called her friend Cindy. Reaching for her pillow, she realized she'd left it in the car, and knew she had to retrieve it before her mom discovered the mistake. Dashing out of her room, she almost collided with her dad dragging the suitcase and box of Christmas gifts up the stairs. She ducked under his arms, bounded down the stairs, and ran into the backseat of the car. Her mom was entering the house with another box of Christmas gifts and Trish decided to wait until mom was upstairs before she took her pillow to her room.

The snow was coming down harder and the windows were starting to cover with thickening flakes as she sat and watched her neighborhood turn into a winter wonderland. Christmas had been fun, but she was glad to be home as it was the first day after Christmas and she still had ten more days of vacation before going back to school. Sitting, watching her front door, she spied something colorful to the left of the landing. Exiting the car with her pillow in hand, she closed the door and wandered toward the colorful area. To her amazement and joy, she saw the bright arrangement was an unopened Christmas present someone must have dropped off while she was gone.

Trish grabbed the gift and looked for a card or note to indicate who it was for, or at least who'd left it there. Looking at the beautiful green paper and colorful red ribbon, Trish tucked the pillow under her arm and entered the house with the gift tightly grasped in her hands. "Mom, Dad, someone left a Christmas present by the door."

Her mother shouted down from upstairs, "Put it in the kitchen, Trish." Looking at her husband she quietly asked, "Are you expecting anything?"

"I'm expecting to put away these suitcases and take a nap for a few hours. I'm expecting that the thought of more Christmas will make me nauseous. I'm expecting that I'll be very hard to get along with until I wake up in a few hours." He set the suitcase on the bed and placed the box of gifts on the floor.

Softly his wife purred, "I love it when you talk nasty, makes me hot all over."

He turned to look at her and smiled. "But I will be awake in a few hours, so hold that thought." Though he was exhausted, he still admired the woman who laughingly teased him with a quick lift of her skirt. He never got tired of looking at her well-toned body and disarming beauty. He was a very fortunate man.

Trish carried the package into the kitchen and set it on the counter. She wondered why it didn't have her mom's or dad's name on it, and thought it might be a surprise from one of her friends. Deciding it was after Christmas, and it wouldn't hurt to take a quick peak, she tore open the paper and found a box inside. It didn't look like an adult present, so it just might be something for her. But then again it might not, so she decided to let it go and head to her room. Going to the refrigerator, she pulled out a cold 7up and took a drink. Looking once more at the box, she decided to peek inside just in case it was from one of her crazy friends. Sheila would do something like that. Leave a box all wrapped up and put a note inside that said, "Fooled you."

She set the 7up on the counter and opened the cover. Lifting the lid, she heard it make a strange hissing sound. "Daddy!" she screamed up the stairs.

*****

Donald threw himself on the bed and breathed a sigh of relief. Five minutes in the prone position and he would get under the covers. He took consolation in knowing that at least they'd be home for the New Year holiday. His wife suggested a vacation in Vale, Colorado, but he'd convinced her home was a better idea. In addition to his hating skiing, the thought of flying and fighting with commuters at the airport was more than he could handle.

His wife stretched out next to him, "I wish you would let me drive on these excursions, that trip's too long for one person."

He laughed as he reached out and took her hand, "That's a good idea. Next time you fall asleep one hour into the trip, I'll wake you and let you drive."

"I would if you asked me too," she replied in mock anger, "but you always say you make a lousy passenger, so I figure why torture us both."

From downstairs, he heard Trish call out, "Daddy!" and immediately heard what he would later describe as a noise that sounded similar to a gunshot under a pillow. Leaping from bed, he rushed to the stairs and hollered out, "Trish, what was that noise?" The only reply he received was a huge cloud rapidly rising up the stairs. As he flew down the staircase, he smelled the smoke and a terror flooded his body. It was only a preview of all he would discover.

CATCH AND RELEASE
TWERELL

www.ingramcontent.com/pod-product-compliance
Lightning Source LLC
Chambersburg PA
CBHW061552170626
46811CB00001B/173